The Document Matters

Praise for
THROUGH THE DARK

"Daily's *Through the Dark* is part love story, part ghost story, and a stirring exploration of one man's reckoning with his past when he embarks on an unfulfilled road trip unlike any other. With a colorful cast of characters along the way, we see how each of these bit players ultimately lead Matt to his inevitable destination. *Through the Dark* is a winding journey of a marriage and ultimately a life, with all its complex twists and turns. I was hooked by the end of the opening scene."

—Kali White, author of
The Monsters We Make

"Daily takes on love and loss through a haunting blend of realism and romanticism. His characters are well-drawn, and his themes are delivered with insight and atmosphere. *Through the Dark* is a painfully poignant novel that explores the power of relationships and the promise of letting go. "

—James Wade, MPIBA and
Spur Award-winning author
of *Beasts of the Earth*

"In his newest novel, Brandon Daily winds his taught authorial metronome for a narrative journey with an inescapable pace. Varying tempos pull readers along— willingly, if not cautiously— as they traverse a darkly satisfying tale of love and loss."

— Keith Hoerner, founding
editor, *The Dribble Drabble*
Review

"A beautifully spare literary telling, Brandon Daily's *Through the Dark* maps an evocative journey navigated by a grieving widower, his wife's ghost, and memories—an odyssey of self-discovery exploring humanity's need to be part of something greater than ourselves"

—Robert Gwaltney,
award winning author
of *The Cicada Tree*

THROUGH THE DARK

Kristen,

Wishing you the best in absolutely everything!

by

BRANDON DAILY

ABC Group Documentation //
878 Mallory Drive
Marietta, GA 30062

The characters and events in this book are fictitious. Any similarity to real persons, living or dead, is coincidental and not intended by the author.

Cover design by Eric Adrian Lee

Interior design by Jack Webster

ISBN: 1-957034-18-1
ISBN-13: 978-1-957034-18-8

For Amanda

PART 1:
LIFE

Chapter 1

The moon shines brightly above Matt as he digs into the wet ground of the cemetery. The sounds of crickets surround him, and he stops what he is doing for a minute. He lets the shovel drop to his feet and he closes his eyes, listening intently to the sounds of the insects. They make him think of his childhood, the places where he grew up. When he was a young boy, he would lie awake at night and listen to the palmetto bugs just outside his window, the crickets and others out there also, their screeching calls becoming a lullaby that would carry him off to sleep. His dreams would be filled with these sounds, their symphony playing in the background of his imagination.

When he was six, Matt woke early in the morning and tiptoed through his parents' small house and opened the front door quietly. He sat on the small porch swing his father had built the year before. It was fashioned out of a felled tree the two of them found in the woods; Matt always remembered the countless nights he spent in the shed out back, watching his father smooth the dark wood with different blades and paper. On the last night before the project's completion, his father sat Matt on his lap and helped the boy carve his initials into the dark frame.

That night, Matt's six-year-old body rocked the swing steadily, the hinges protesting the movement in groans. The boy looked at the blue-black of the sky, tracing with his eyes the darker outlines of the surrounding woods. The trees created a jagged horizon. He could not tell what hour it was, though he knew as he looked out to the western sky that he was witnessing a time of day he had never known before.

He propped his feet up so that his knees rested together, and then he laid his chin in the small crevice created between his knees. Matt listened to the howls of wolves or coyotes off in the darker places of the world, the hum of the bugs constant behind every other sound. If he closed his eyes, he would forget the sounds of the world he knew and instead think that what he heard in that moment was, in fact, silence and that there was no other sound but this. But the boy's eyes stayed open so as to watch the coming of the day through the woods. A gentle, cool breeze coasted through the yard and made the boy wrap his arms tightly around his body, his hands feeling the warmth of the pajama fabric. He kept a watch on the trees out there in the woods and saw them come to life before him. Each breath of air that passed by awoke a new grouping of trees in the distance—a wave of movement that spread from one end of the horizon to the other. He followed their movements, believing that the dancing, dark bodies of the trees were meant only for him. Their heavy arms all draped in leaf and vine swayed back and forth in greeting, their insect voices sang out in high staccato. He had never felt so alive as he did in that moment. A moment he would never share with anyone.

Matt has not thought of these memories of his youth in years, and his mind shifts quickly to his mother, though he can no longer recall her face or the sound of her voice. It is only her smell, the lavender scent of her perfume, that he can still remember.

When he opens his eyes now, Matt is brought back to the reality before him. He finds himself once again standing within the earth, a pile of moist, black dirt to his left. He bends down and picks up the shovel from where it had fallen earlier and begins to dig again. He has only been digging for an hour, but his arms and legs are heavy and tired, his hands beginning to blister. He wipes the sweat from his forehead with a muddy hand and continues to dig; his breath is shallow and full of phlegm.

The shovel sinks into the ground easily. A sucking sound, then a scrape, followed by the sick plop of wet earth on wet earth. The movement and sound, repeating again and again. The rain from earlier has made the ground soft, and Matt feels the earth sinking slowly beneath his weight. *If I were to stand here forever, will the earth swallow me whole?*

He digs by moonlight. Around him, the world seems void of anyone or anything else. The small cemetery is vacant, the lights have long been cut off in the adjoining church, and the streets, turned a golden hue from the streetlamps, are stagnant and without life. His truck is a few yards off in front of where he stands, its back to him, the tailgate dropped down. Matt moves his eyes quickly from the truck to the ground before him. Below him. As he does so, he tries to avoid her eyes, though he knows she is still standing there to his left, waiting silently next to the pile of grass and mud and dirt. She is still watching him.

It has been just over a month since she first appeared to him in the kitchen, though he has yet to speak to her, to look at her longer than a second before turning away in fear or embarrassment. *What are you?* he wants to ask but cannot. She is waiting for something, though he can only guess at what it might be.

The minutes pass quickly. His breath comes in short gasps as he works; his hands are cramped, and his shoulders burn with the movement. After another half hour, the shovel hits something solid. Far off in the distance, a bird flaps its wings and cries out. It is the first sound he's heard since arriving at the cemetery. When he hears the heavy sound of contact, Matt drops the shovel and looks over to his left, his eyes skimming briefly over the headstone that reads "Elizabeth Blaire 1984-2012." He glances briefly at the figure of his dead wife who still stands there looking at him quietly. She is dressed in jeans and her favorite T-shirt—a blue fabric with the image of a sun breaking over dark clouds aglow with lightning. He can still remember when he bought her that shirt—it was at a concert he'd taken her to a year after they were married. Since he first saw her ghost, or whatever she was now, she has worn this same outfit. When he looks at the shirt, he smiles sadly at the memory it brings and then he quickly looks away.

Matt tosses the shovel out of the deep hole that he now stands in and kneels down, palming the wet earth off the wooden box and throwing it in handfuls to the pile that now stands nearly as tall as Liz.

He climbs out of the hole and walks past his dead wife, over to the truck. From the bed, he takes one end of a heavy metal chain and brings it over to the hole and eases himself in again. He attaches the clasp of the chain to one of the handles at the head of the narrow box and then he climbs back out and walks to the truck, the chain guiding him. He attaches the other end of the chain to the trailer hitch.

When he turns the engine of the truck, he quickly makes sure the lights are switched off. Then he pauses. His eyes search over the surroundings of the place for anyone who might have woken from the sound of the engine. After several seconds of waiting, he eases the truck forward, his head stuck through the open side window, looking behind him to the newly re-dug grave. The tip of the wooden box shows just over the hole, and he stops the truck, unhooks the chain from the hitch, and runs back to the grave. Inside, the casket stands on end, its cover now resting snuggly against the muddy side.

Matt grabs the shovel once more with his blistered and burning hands and begins to fill in the open space behind the standing box with mud from the pile. Liz moves away from him slowly, though Matt does not notice. Instead, his eyes are focused on the job before him. Sweat drips into his eyes and runs the length of his nose, and he brushes the drops away with the back of his hand.

After nearly a half hour of this, Matt stops and climbs out of the hole. He looks down at what he has now created: a level incline that slopes in diagonal from the far tip of the grave down to the bottom of the standing casket. He looks over to Liz. She seems to nod slightly, though Matt is not sure if this is only his imagination. A cloud passes over the moon, and she is thrown into a dark shadow. He takes a deep breath, realizing just how close he is to finishing and then runs back to the truck.

The truck moves forward again and then slowly turns, being guided around the other headstones of the cemetery. Eventually, the truck comes to a stop. Matt backs it up so that the bed now faces the open grave where the earth slopes down toward the bottom of the casket.

After he reattaches the chain to the hitch, Matt climbs into the truck and pulls forward again. The tires move over the wet ground, and Matt apologizes silently to the bodies buried beneath. The chain grows taut and then, as Matt continues moving the truck forward, his heavy and muddy shoe pressing lightly down on the pedal, the casket tilts back and falls heavily onto the earthen slope. The box makes its slow climb up and out of the grave.

Matt stops the truck and then puts it in reverse, backing up nearly to the casket that now lays on its back in the open air.

Standing over the box, he bends down and lifts it so that the casket is standing on its end once again. The wooden box is heavier than he imagines it to be, and he braces its weight on his shoulder. Not far away, a bird lifts off in flight, shaking the branches of one of the trees that guard the small cemetery. The bird coasts back and forth overhead, flapping its wings gently in the night before it flies off and disappears into the dark.

He remembers the day of the funeral, realizing that he had stood in this same place a year ago. Like earlier today, it had rained that morning, and the smell of rain was heavy in the air during the service. The few people who had come stood because the chairs were covered in rainwater. Matt only stayed to hear the first prayer from the minister before leaving the group that huddled around the casket. He had walked off, making his way down the street with no direction and no sense of thought, and he continued walking until his legs were tired and his feet were blistered and raw. Eventually, he made his way to a small park on the outer region of the town and sat on a bench under the cover of a tree. He stayed there through the night, dozing off every now and then and feeling the moon's glow brushing over him. After several hours, more rain began to fall, and he woke completely. The tree above did little to shelter him from the rain, and he stretched his hand out, feeling the steady drops on his cold skin. In the distance, the sky lit up with lightning, and the sound of thunder came shortly after. Matt had thought then that if you were able to see inside a person's mind, then this storm would be what you'd find inside his.

Matt shakes this memory away and then walks the casket, one shuffled step forward at a time, toward the truck, where he then tilts the wooden box over the tailgate and pushes it into the bed. He secures it tightly with straps and then shuts the gate behind it.

When he gets into the truck again, he looks at the clock and sees that it is only 3:30. His arms are heavy, and his feet and hands are cramped and blistered. He is covered in sweat and dirt and mud; if he were to look at himself in a mirror right now, he would see that he no longer resembles a human but has instead been changed into an entirely new creature, some new species that he has never heard of.

Before pulling the truck out of the small cemetery, he pokes his head through the window and looks around. All that is left is a partially filled hole in the ground and a small pile of dirt next to it. The windows are still dark in the church, and the streets remain empty. Liz's ghost sits in the seat next to him, while her body is held safely in the bed of the truck. The moon still shines brightly above.

Chapter 2

They had this conversation in the dark, just before they said goodbye to each other. The sand engulfed their toes and heels that night, the grains smooth under the arches of their bare feet:

"I don't believe in the past," she said to him. Her voice had grown deeper, more serious somehow. "There's no point in trying to bring it up, to talk about or think about it. I always hear that we need to learn from the past, but that's just bullshit."

"What do you believe in, then?" he asked.

"The present. Not the future, but the now. You live once, and then you have to accept the fact that you've blown your chances at life or at experiencing different things."

"I guess." Matt sighed loudly. "I guess trying to cram too much into life just scares me."

She was silent for a while. Then she said: "We only become what we're afraid of."

He nodded his head. "What are you afraid of?"

"Nothing," she answered. She looked away quickly so as not to see his face, not to show her lie.

He pulls the truck slowly into the driveway, and gets out, looking up and down the street. With quick steps, Matt moves into the garage and grabs several heavy blankets and some bungee cords he had laid out earlier. He covers the box in the bed of the truck with the blankets, leaving extra fabric to hang off the sides in hopes of disguising the casket from passersby. The other blankets he tosses onto the back seat. The bungees are stretched tight and hold the blankets onto the casket.

Matt nods in approval at the disguise and goes into the house. The silence follows him as he walks to the back bedroom, shedding his body of the damp, heavy clothes as he moves, letting them stay wherever they fall. He'll deal with them later: throw them in a trash bag and set it on fire in the backyard or take the bag with him. He hasn't decided yet.

He wants to clean himself quickly and then leave. There isn't time for anything else, he thinks, as he steps into the shower and starts the water. The police are bound to come knocking on his door in a few hours. Someone will find Liz's grave and report the theft to the police; he'll be the first person they'll want to talk to about it all.

Matt pushes these worries from his mind, concentrating on the water as it falls off his fingertips, his nose, balling his arm and leg hair together in small clumps.

The water from the shower is cold. He'd drawn the curtain closed behind him, but, as he scrubs the darkness from his body, the mud and dirt and wet of the earth from his skin, he knows she is on the other side of the curtain waiting for him. He looks down at his feet, watching the brown water circle the drain before disappearing. Some small pieces of earthen debris stay in the tub and slow the draining of the water.

He closes his eyes tightly, wondering if he is doing the right thing, wondering if he is insane. He wants to think he isn't, but he is still confused and worried. Coughing, he bends over slightly, placing his hands on his knees. Bile moves up his throat, and he cups water into his mouth and spits, the clear liquid turned a dirty color. A pain in his stomach has now begun, and he takes deep breaths to try and alleviate it. When that doesn't work, he reaches down and turns the knob on the wall all the way to the right. The water feels like ice, but he forces himself completely underneath it in hopes of numbing his body, numbing his life. He breathes loudly as the freezing water covers him.

Stepping out of the shower, he dries off with a towel and sees her. He stops short, having forgotten for a moment that Liz is there standing alone in the darkness of the bathroom.

Still drying his cold skin with the wet towel, Matt walks past her quietly, making his way into the bedroom, where he takes a pair of jeans and a shirt from the dresser and puts them on. He tries not to look at the bed as he dresses.

He has not slept in the bed since she died, has not disturbed it or set anything on its sheets. It's become a shrine of sorts. The bedspread is still pulled tight, the way Liz always kept it—he used to watch her with a smile as she smoothed away the loose spaces and folds in the fabric. The pillows remain where they landed last, where Liz had absently thrown them in a hurry at the head of the bed. He was already at work at the hospital that day.

Near the foot of the bed, their clothes still rest in a clump from where she had left them after taking the laundry from the drier. The clothes have since become set in place, sedimentary as stone. A fossil now of her absence.

Since her death, whenever he walks by the bed and glances over briefly to the laundry waiting there, he imagines Liz folding the clothes. He thinks of a day long ago when he walked into the room and helped her; he can still remember her rolled-eyed protests at the way he folded her shirts and the towels, the fabric becoming deformed in his attempts. It was a game he liked to play with her, doing all he could to push her until she snapped at him, and then he would smile at her for it.

On that day, he remembers, she smiled back and undid each of his folds, refolding each towel and shirt in her own specific way. But that day was long ago now, and these visions remain his imaginings of a time that has passed and won't be again.

Matt glances briefly at Liz, still standing in the bathroom doorway. He nods at her and then moves out into the hallway, careful not to disturb the rose petals on the carpet of the bedroom and hall, though the petals have now all but dried into scabs and shells of what they had been a year ago.

Years before, they laid on their backs with the cool sand of the California beach under their bodies. Above them, the sky bled from late afternoon to night, the colors marking the progression—pale blue to a red ochre, a deep orange cutting through the night colors that seemed to burn awhile before the sky eventually slipped into full darkness.

Matt watched her next to him, followed her eyes as they shifted back and forth across the night above them, as if she were seeing a beautiful painting in a gallery for both the first and last time. He noticed the twist of her neck, the tiny creases that formed around her mouth when she smiled. The sound of her breath.

On that beach, as they watched the transformation of day to night, he told her of his life—first, his name, and then he explained that he was only visiting the west coast beaches with his brother, Travis, to celebrate the latter's graduation from college.

Matt had grown up in a small coal mining town in the eastern mountains, a town called Corvin Valley—a place she had never heard of, and that did not surprise him. His mother had been killed in a drunk driving accident years ago—though to call it an "accident" always seemed a misnomer to him. The driver had blown right through a red light and ran her over as she carried groceries home from the market, he said. Matt's father was in prison, serving a fifty-year sentence, though Matt didn't say what for and she didn't ask. All Matt said about his father was that he hadn't spoken to the man in nearly eight years and that he doubted he ever would. Travis remained Matt's only connection to their father, and even that seemed too much of a relationship; when Travis would call Matt, the former would always tell of his recent visits to their father in prison, and Matt would listen in silence, unable to hang up or tell his brother to stop.

Matt had gone to college in the northeast. He told Liz that he hated calling it New England: "That part of the country is the farthest thing from *new*. The cities, the land, it's all the oldest parts of America," he'd said.

After graduation, he moved to Omaha. He was a medical student at Creighton, just finished with his third year in the program. When Liz asked why Creighton? Why Omaha? he said simply, "Because they're paying my way through it, and Omaha isn't Corvin Valley." He smiled and looked away and then said, "It's the smart move." He seemed to speak to the ocean then, saying the words quietly as if he were still trying to convince himself of the decision. When she asked if he always played life safe and smart, he laughed and then shied away briefly. Her eyes were large, a beautiful shape; a green hint inside them seemed to shine brighter in the late afternoon sun. The night was almost on them by then. He thought in that moment that he loved her, and he didn't know what to say.

After several seconds of staring blankly at Liz, Matt answered, saying that he wasn't one to jump out of airplanes and that the most spontaneous thing he'd ever done was to walk up to her earlier that day and say hello. "It's something I'll never forget or regret," he told her.

Matt had always fallen back on his own judgments, yet he always felt himself inferior to the world around him and those people in it; he constantly sought new ways to prove his worth.

When he succeeded at something, and this was often, Matt would step back after the fact and analyze his actions, the results, deconstructing it to its core, scrutinizing the success. There was no such thing as perfection for Matt, only examples of how to better himself for the future.

To say he was his own biggest critic would be an understatement; he was constantly pushed onward by some unsaid thing. Though he knew it was the absence of his father, he would never admit it aloud. He would always remember that morning when he watched as his father drove away from the house; it was a month after his mother died. Matt watched the car through the open blinds of the front window and followed the car with his eyes as it disappeared around the curve in the street. He hadn't realized it then, but that was the last time he would see his father.

Later that afternoon, the flashing blue and white lights of a police car shined on the white walls of the house, blinding the two boys as they stepped out into the falling sunlight.

Travis and Matt were taken away from the house, told by one of the officers to each pack a bag of clothes, keepsakes, photos, whatever they needed to bring with them. The officer then drove the boys to their grandmother's in Barrett, the next town over. They would never see the inside of their house again; what few possessions inside were sold to cover the expenses of their father's trial. That night forever haunted Matt; he and Travis never spoke of it directly, though they could each see it in the other's eyes, the sadness that hid beneath the smiles and laughs. The pain that was always there.

While Matt was open with her, freely telling her his whole life story, Liz was not. The only thing she gave up was her name, and when he asked questions, she seemed to find different ways of changing the direction of the conversation. She mentioned the weather, pointed out a family down the beach, laughed at a seagull stealing dinner from a couple who napped quietly on towels a few feet away, smiled at a cloud that looked like a zebra. But Liz continued asking Matt more about himself, and he continued to answer her, hoping that his openness might persuade her to talk more about herself. *Everyone has their story*, he had thought, *Tell me yours*.

But his words and memories only seemed to make her quieter.

She felt comfortable in his voice, lost in the movement of the beach beneath her weight, the shifting sands. She never wanted to leave. Speaking seemed a duty, but listening to his world, inserting herself within it was the only luxury she had ever known.

Liz's hands moved carelessly over the sand, her fingers raking and swirling the microscopic pieces of rock and earth with no set pattern; her cupped palms dug craters in the beach that she filled back in seconds later. After a while, she moved her head over toward him, turned her face and met Matt's eyes; she smiled and let a low giggle of embarrassment sound from her throat as she turned to face away from his direction. Then she turned back to him and smiled.

"What'd you think when you first saw me?" she asked.

"Honestly?"

She nodded.

"I thought I'd seen you before. Like déjà vu or something. I saw you sitting there all alone, looking out at the water. I watched you for a while, the breeze blowing your hair around your face."

"What'd you think?"

"That you looked beautiful."

Her smile widened.

Matt turned his face to look up at the sky. Then very quietly he added: "And I thought you looked sad." Beneath him, his body had carved out his form in the sand and he felt himself settle snuggly in the outline. He glanced at her, afraid at what he had said.

A shallow breath escaped her lips and she turned the other way from Matt. The tide steadily crept up the beach before slinking back down to rejoin the ocean. Tears began to well in her eyes, and she sat up and brushed the tears away with her palms. Looking out at the water, she slowly tucked her feet under her like she was back in kindergarten waiting for show-and-tell to begin. "The ocean's nothing more than the tears of lost lovers," she had once heard. She wondered if her tears would ever fill the ocean.

Matt sat up quickly, though she did not turn to look at him; her eyes remained forward, watching the ocean; it seemed as if she were waiting for the water to give her a sign, some answer to it all.

Even in the darkening light, he could see her clearly. He noticed the light brown freckles on her neck, a faded scar on her jaw, just under her chin. He wondered how she had gotten that scar, if she would ever tell him. Her once straight brown hair was now curled and knotted from the beach air, and it fell loose and ragged on her shoulders, the bangs blowing into her eyes. She kept brushing the hair away from her face.

She swallowed what tears might have been hiding under the surface, and then she smiled. There was some strength in her that he did not understand, and it only added to his fascination of this strange girl.

"I can see why they used to think the world was flat." She stretched her hand out before her, tracing the horizon line with her fingers. He looked out to where she pointed. "How we could sail right off and fall into oblivion."

Out there, the last remnants of color were fading quickly from the sky.

Matt nodded.

Behind them, a group of teenagers were building a bonfire, stacking wood high on top of other pieces. One of the teenagers—a boy in a white tank and green shorts—was pouring lighter fluid over the logs as two other boys his age kept adding more wood to the collection. The kids had long hair that had been bleached, either by the sun or dye. After the last log was put in place, the boy in the green shorts lit a cigarette with a lighter. He took two long drags and then threw it into the pit. The fluid lit quickly, and before long, the bonfire was raging high into the night sky—a pyre erected and lit in honor of some long-forgotten god. The sacrifice simply awaiting.

Even from a distance of twenty or thirty yards, Matt and Liz could feel the heat from the fire behind them, and they turned to see the throngs of teens coming from out the darkness of the beach.

Liz watched quietly as the flames grew higher. Matt moved his hand slowly up and set it gently on her shoulder. His heart beat fast in his chest as he felt her skin for the first time. Bumps ran the length of his arms in the warm summer night.

Liz looked down at his hand on her shoulder and slowly moved her body away so that his hand fell onto the sand.

Matt nodded and then looked away quickly. His chest felt heavy. "I'm sorry," he whispered.

"Don't be," she said. Liz reached her hand down and covered Matt's, her fingers interlocking with his. He squeezed gently and then relaxed his hand. "I just don't want this to be something more than it is."

"Then what is it?"

"Two strangers on a beach."

He smiled sadly and then nodded. The last bits of color in the sky, red and blood orange, had been erased by deep blues and blacks. Slowly, deliberate in his movements, Matt dusted sand from his legs and arms.

"I just think if we start getting into the big, obvious questions like 'Where are you from?' 'What do you do?' 'What did you want to be when you were little?' 'What's your family like?' then it just becomes something it's not. And it won't ever be that. You know?"

Matt looked away and then back at her. He stood, feeling the cramping in his legs as he did so. He hadn't realized how long he'd been laying on the beach until he got to his feet.

Liz also stood. She looked at her feet, noticing how, in the flickering light from the fire, they had become lost in the sand of the beach. She was transforming into something, returning to the earth. "I'm sorry, Matt. My life is just . . ." She paused. Her hands moved frantically in front of her as if they would help her find the word she was looking for. She finally gave up and said, "My life's just wrong." She shrugged her shoulders, feeling as if she were about to cry, and then she clenched both her fists tightly, pushing the pain and sadness to some deeper place within her, a place she could find later.

She continued: "You tell me about your life and how good it is, even the bad parts. But I don't have that. I don't have any of that. Mine, it's all just bad parts."

"There's always some good."

She took a deep breath. "No," she whispered. "Not for me."

Liz drew her lips tightly across her face. Tears fell from her eyes again, but Matt couldn't see them in the shadows. She looked back out to the ocean. It was dark now and she could only see the white foam of the rolling waves near the shore, and she could only hear the steady beating of those waves upon the beach. It sounded like applause, though she did not know for whom or what they were applauding.

"Can you stay with me here? Just a little longer?"

He nodded.

They moved a few steps closer to the bonfire and sat again on the sand, once more facing the rolling waves.

They were quiet for a while. Finally, Matt broke the silence. "Let me ask one thing. Just answer me this—you don't have to say anything else."

She nodded. "Okay."

"What is it that you want most in the world?"

She looked over at him, her eyes turned up in thought, and then she looked out to the hidden water they could only hear. She answered, speaking softly: "I look out there and I think how I'd love to just fall into the water and float. Float away, float on forever until you can't see me anymore, or know that I was even there. Become part of the water, you know? Become part of something bigger than me, or you, or anything else. I think that's what I really want some day."

They left each other that night at the beach. The flames from the bonfire had all but fallen to a scattering of ash and a glow of embers inside the dark pit when they walked up to the parking lot. Matt offered to walk her home or to her hotel or wherever she was staying, but Liz only smiled and said that she was fine, that she wanted to be alone and think. She couldn't tell him that her car was her hotel, that it had been her home for most her life—the only thing that was hers. She watched him as he walked away. Her bare toes sought out the cool parts of the sand and she smiled at the feeling.

Midway to his car, Matt stopped and turned for one last look at Liz, but he couldn't see her in the darkness of the night. She had simply become lost in the sand and the wind and the water.

Chapter 3

Patricia Dravinsky was born in Omaha. It was the only place she had ever known; she'd never traveled outside of Nebraska. Though an only child, she never seemed to hold the feeling of entitlement that only children seem to carry with them.

Both her parents were doctors, her father an orthopedic surgeon and her mother a dermatologist. Patricia's life had been designed for her early on by her parents: Valedictorian in high school, then on to University of Nebraska for pre-med, and Creighton for medical school—both her parents' alma maters. She went along with these plans without complaint, knowing that the path had been set for her long before her birth and that to deviate from it would be a disaster in her relationship with her parents. A disaster she doubted could ever be set right again.

Growing up, she always felt herself the perpetual outsider, a loner even to herself; her own wants and desires came second to the people around her. For the most part, she was fine with this, happy to be a shadow against the walls of other people. And so, Patricia retreated away from the world, holding fast to her parents, making them her friends, her sole confidants. Though she never was asked, had she been invited to a sleepover with other girls in her grade school class, she would have told them no, lying about some previous plans her family had, some pressing issue that kept her from having fun with others her same age. Had she ever been asked, she would have said all this with a roll of the eyes, a dramatic huff in her voice, these things done only for show because she had learned them on TV—this is how a sincere person acts when turning down an invitation, so she believed.

She had short blonde hair that she always kept pinned back, away from her face. And, whether attending a formal dinner, sitting in a lecture hall, or drinking with classmates at the college bar, Patricia always wore white. She also, up until med school, had never dated; instead, she focused her thoughts and desires only on her study and her family. Though she had a happy childhood, so to speak, she always felt as if there was something important missing from her world. Throughout high school and college, she was constantly teased, called "Patty the Prude," "The White Virgin Queen," and dozens of other nicknames and insults that she often found herself remembering. She never showed it to the outside world, but Patricia would go home and cry until she fell asleep. When she woke from these tear-induced naps, she would always make her way to a mirror and stare at herself, trying to see her body and face from the outside. To see herself as others did. She would lean in close to the glass, searching for something different about her, something wrong.

It wasn't until her first year of college that she decided to go by the name Trisha; with that name change, she felt as if she had been liberated from her old self, yet she still looked at her reflection in mirrors when she passed them, always looking for something else, something missing. She knew she wanted more.

So, when Matt Blaire asked her to dinner during her second year of med school at Creighton, she nearly shouted her answer of yes before he finished the question. As their academic lives progressed, so did their relationship, and though they genuinely cared for one another, they each felt as if there were pieces missing, things or thoughts they didn't have or no longer had, feelings lost from time and complacency. Both of them would secretly admit it to themselves, though never to each other. Over the years, what they had simply became stale. Matt found himself saying "I love you" out of necessity; he had forgotten what the words actually meant, the importance those three syllables had, the feeling it once gave him to tell her this. Likewise, Trisha would kiss Matt every time she saw him, but the kisses grew quicker until they were just brief pecks on the lips. In the beginning, their kisses had been full of passion and tenderness; not so anymore.

Yet Matt and Trisha stayed in whatever relationship it was they had, and neither complained to the other about anything. Neither whispered their personal worries. Instead, they both believed that ignorance might actually be bliss, that they might forget their personal troubles or that, even better, their issues might magically be fixed one day.

As an unsaid test, when Matt went off to California with his brother, he left his cell phone in his apartment in Nebraska. The hope was that the week apart, with no communication, would strengthen their affection, make them revert back to how they were when they first met.

But after Matt returned, they found themselves in the same place they had been before he left. The week hadn't changed them; if anything, it had only made things worse, more awkward now. For Trisha, this awkwardness came from Matt's new quiet standoffishness. He now whispered answers to questions and agreed completely with whatever Trisha suggested, even when she knew he preferred otherwise. For Matt, this new solidarity in himself came from the memory of the quiet and strange woman from the beach. This woman he knew nothing about except for her name. And he would whisper this name quietly in his mind, over and over. "Liz."

Matt saw Liz's face at different places throughout the city. When he and Trisha had sex, he would close his eyes and imagine Liz underneath him instead. Matt could not understand his fascination with the mystery woman from the beach—Liz was not as pretty as Trisha and Trisha had a personality that he knew and, for the most part, liked. Liz was a stranger to him, one who intentionally pulled herself away at the beach, refusing to answer any questions he asked. But there remained something about Liz, or at least his memory of her. When he was alone in his apartment and he found himself lying awake in the middle of the night, watching the slow turning of the overhead fan blades, Matt would call into question his memory of the woman. He would seek some imperfection in her, some tell that she was not what he imagined or what he wanted. He told himself on those nights that what he remembered, what he found himself wanting, was simply an exaggeration. He could never convince himself of this, though, and nearly all of those nights thinking of Liz ended with Matt reaching hurriedly for the tissue box that sat on the desk next to the bed. On those nights, he would come with the image of her tanned body above him, her brown hair falling on his face, her scent covering his skin, her mouth on his.

Trisha showed up unannounced at Matt's apartment one evening. It was two and a half months after he returned from California. He'd been expecting this, though he had hoped he was wrong. She sat down on the old couch, the cushions sagging downward, which only forced her body closer to Matt, who sat quietly next to her. After several seconds of looking at her hands, wondering what to say, how to begin, Trisha moved farther down the couch away from Matt and turned her body to face him. Her hands worked over each other as she spoke. She had few words to say, the pain and hurt on her face speaking more loudly than any sound she could utter. She finished by saying quietly to Matt, "I love you still. But it's just not there anymore. I wish it was." And finally, after some quiet seconds between them, she added, "I'm sorry."

She walked out of the apartment, the door closing silently shut behind her. Matt had remained quiet the whole time. He knew she was right, but that didn't make any of it hurt less. He had listened to her, watched her face, eyes and lips, beautiful still, her hands scraping over each other—her nails were purple, he always remembers that.

Years later, on the road trip west with his dead wife, Matt will still think of that moment and feel sorry for how he acted, what he hadn't said to her. Regrets are stored in file drawers in our minds; it is best not to disturb them, not to reopen old files. It's too easy to become lost so deeply in the past that you cannot find your way back, and if you do, you will be forever changed. Forever alone with your actions and decisions, thinking only of how things could have been.

During the days after the break from Trisha, Matt found himself having trouble concentrating in class, during rounds, at lunch and dinner. He knew he needed to focus on school; he was in the final year, but he found himself constantly thinking of Liz—there was something magical about her. This woman who had vanished back into whatever place of the universe from which she had emerged. Skin from sand and blood of ocean.

And so, when he walked out of the hospital five months after the trip and saw Liz standing twenty yards away, a small bag at her feet, Matt merely dismissed her as another hallucinated specter of her. This woman, whose face was Liz's, who nervously shifted her weight from leg to leg and quickly lifted her hand in a wave of greeting, this woman could not be Liz. It was just a cruel trick his mind was playing on itself, a show put on by the universe to confuse the already empty feeling in his heart.

On that day when he saw her outside the hospital, Matt turned and started walking away from her, trying to distance himself from the past. As he walked away, though, he did not realize she was running to catch up with him.

The past has a strange way of staying around.

Chapter 4

The last thing Matt takes from the house before locking the door and getting into the truck is the map. It had been hanging on the wall above the table by a thumb tack, put there by Liz a year and a half earlier. Next to the map is the calendar, untouched since Liz's death. In a highlighted yellow, the date is still circled on the map, though the color has faded some and the circled date is almost a year past.

Inside the truck, Matt turns the overhead lights on and looks down at the map. A country pasted together in shades of green and brown, purple, a salmon color, all surrounded by the blue of the oceans connected by the dozen blue lines of rivers. Lakes are dropped at random points on the land portions of the cartoon, and he thinks of how simple everything seems on the thin map. This land, this place. Cutting through the map in a gentle down-sloped line of highlighter ink is his guide. He will follow this directive given to him months earlier by Liz. This pale-yellow line is now his world, his bible to live by. And he studies this path with his eyes and then again with his finger, tracing along as he follows the line from right to left—starting in Nebraska and ending in California. He reads this blotchy line one last time with his mouth silently echoing the names of cities and towns that the trip will pass through. Looking in at Matt from outside, you might believe Matt to be praying, his mouth whispering secret words. And maybe this is so; maybe this loose sheet within Matt's grip is his salvation. The figure seated next to Matt—the woman who watches him so intently, who wishes with all her power to be able to reach over and touch the skin of his hand and whisper some word of assurance—this figure can only watch her husband and smile because she knows.

Though if you were looking inside the truck, you would not see her. Liz would not exist to you. Only to him.

"I know our anniversary is still five months away, but is this a trip we're gonna take every year?" she asked. She knew what Matt would say but wanted to hear him tell her. She always needed extra assurances.

They had spent their anniversary in California for the last two years, both times visiting the same beach where they met; they reenacted that moment, finding a strange joy in the repetition.

Matt stopped what he was doing—taking hot dishes out of the dishwasher and putting them in the open cupboards—and looked over at her. Liz sat at the table, a high-top made of wood—on it were the remains of their lunches and a vase of fresh flowers he had surprised her with after work the previous day. She gave him a playful smile.

"That's the plan," he said. "Unless you want to do something different." Matt walked over and stood behind her. Wrapping his arms loosely around her middle, feeling the softness of her skin under her shirt, he bent low and kissed her on the side of her face, the tender flesh beside her closed eye. This was a good day and they both knew it; they each tried to hold on to these small moments, to memories of days like this, when they were both together at home, both relaxed, both happy.

Liz brought her arm up and moved her fingers gently through his hair. She shook her head. "No," she said softly and turned so that they now faced each other. "That beach is where all my happiness is; it's where I found you."

Matt smiled. "Then the west it is." He brushed his cheek across her shoulder blade. The stubble of face hair tickled her sensitive skin and she jokingly pulled away from him. Near her ear he whispered, "Forever and always, Liz. That's how long I'll love you."

She was quiet, as if she needed to take the words in and store them somewhere deep in her mind before answering. "I know," she said finally. Though they had been married now for just over two and a half years, she still felt a giddy excitement in her chest. "Butterflies," she called it. This feeling still felt as strong now as it did that day on the beach. She only wished she had told him of the feeling that night under the dark sky years before when they had the fire at their backs and the sea at their feet.

Matt began to walk back to the dishwasher when she said his name. Her voice shook slightly, and he turned, his face growing serious.

"Instead of flying, I thought maybe this year we could drive it." A nervous expression had come across her face, as if she feared the question she asked or the answer she thought she would be given.

Matt's face lifted, and he smiled. "Yeah?"

"Might be fun seeing the country together. And I thought maybe the extra time together might help us figure some things out, you know? Get us a little better with each other. I don't know." She shied away from him and looked out the window that was next to where she sat.

Things had been rough. Matt's hours at the hospital had changed so that his shift now ran through most nights. When he was home, he was asleep or a zombie, shuffling his feet sleepily through the house, making his way from the bed to the couch to the kitchen and then back to the couch. Liz felt alone, and whenever she mentioned this, Matt would say tiredly that if she was so alone she could get a job and actually do something rather than sit by herself at the house doing nothing. These words hurt her, and she would turn away from him, brushing the tears away. Finally, she stopped complaining about being alone.

As Matt made his way back to where Liz sat at the table, he thought over what she had said. He smiled. "I think that'll be perfect." Liz turned to face him; her eyes were red. "We still have a couple months for me to work it out at the hospital," he said. "I can't see there being a problem with me getting a few more days off."

Liz smiled. From her pocket, she pulled out a tightly folded map. The route was already highlighted, and Matt looked at it closely over her shoulder. The meandering yellow line stretched from the middle of the map all the way to the western coast. The highlighter, he noticed, had leaked past the coast and ended somewhere in the blue of the ocean.

Liz stood and walked away from Matt and into the kitchen; next to the refrigerator was a cork bulletin board—photographs of the two, invitations to parties and a wedding as well as important dates scribbled on lined paper that cluttered the brown space of the board—and she took down one of the unused thumb tacks. She walked back to the high table, back to where Matt stood, and tacked the open map onto the wall just above the flowers on the tabletop. She left the room quickly and then came back after a few seconds with a calendar he had given her for Christmas the year before; it had stayed in its cellophane wrapping on the floor of their room since January. Liz tore the plastic off and flipped through the pages until she found the right one. From the table, she took the highlighter and circled a date five months in the future—

their anniversary. Then she thumb-tacked the calendar on the wall next to the map.

Liz looked at the wall, its two new decorations seeming out of place, and smiled. She turned and wrapped her arms around his thin body. "That way we'll see it every morning and night and remember." Liz felt Matt's arms surround her shoulders; she felt the pull of her body to his, and she sank her face into the loose folds of his shirt. His smell was his own, and she loved him for it. If someone had told her years before that she would one day feel this way, she would have called that person a liar and walked away.

Liz grew up in North Michigan.

She had never had a real place to call home, at least not until she met Matt. "Home" was something made up, a place created by others, a fairytale told to children. When she was a girl, the word conjured up fantastic notions in her mind, but none of them were true. It was not a real place, it couldn't be. The home she had seen in television shows and movies—the sense of belonging and comfort that home seemed to possess in stories and books—it was all simply that: fiction. Fake. And in her world, there was no family. That was as much a phantom thing as home. For her, these simply didn't exist, and they never would.

She hadn't known her father, hadn't been told his name, even. No photographs existed of him, at least none that she ever knew of. When she asked about him, her mother always changed the subject abruptly, and Liz eventually realized this; by the time she was ten, Liz quit asking her mother questions, accepting the unsaid as true, the quiet as answer.

For the most part, Liz's two older sisters ignored her. Instead of including the young girl in any of their games, they would keep to themselves, lowering their voices to giggled whispers when Lizzy entered the room. When she begged them for answers about who she was and where she came from, they would tell her random facts about who their father was—how he acted, the color of his eyes, the way he laughed and the words he used—but these answers changed in each telling; finally, Liz stopped believing their stories. She instead began to study her sisters' faces, watching the way they talked, the long gliding steps they each took when they walked. Liz searched for some kind of connection to their father in them, some showing of who he was. Like an anthropologist, she hoped to learn a stranger from two other strangers.

Liz explored the small world around her alone. In high school, she told herself she would someday make a difference in the world; she hoped that by telling herself this over and over she would eventually be able to convince herself of these stories, that it would all one day come true. Though she had friends in school, she never felt comfortable with any of them. With each passing year, she would make up another fictional aspect about her life and tell her friends, hoping these untruths would gain her more affection. She hated herself for doing this, though it helped her through those early years. Instead of confronting the reality of her life, she figured it better to escape it completely, at least when she wasn't home. And with each new story she told, each new part of herself she invented, Liz grew further and further away from who she really was, instead moving toward some created person she liked better: a girl who lived a life she only dreamed of.

Her childhood house backed up to the small lake, and her earliest memory was of this place. In the early mornings and late afternoons of spring and summer there would be fishermen in small boats, their lines dragging across the water's top. But in the winter, the lake froze over. The ice was always crusted over with snow, shavings from skaters that braved the surface. High schoolers would go out there on dares from friends—stand in the middle of the lake with a hatchet, raise it up to eye level and let it drop from your hand so that it stuck in the ice: hear the cracking beneath you, try not to run.

She was five, and it was February when Liz went outside that morning, dressed in a thin sweatshirt and jeans, boots on her feet. She brought the hood of her sweatshirt over her head to cover her tingling ears. The sun was just higher than the trees from where she stood, and she walked out back and made her way to the middle of the frozen lake. She slipped two or three times on the ice but each time she caught herself before she fell. When she reached the center of the lake, she brought the arm of her sweatshirt over her hand and scraped the snow and ice flecks away with it. Then she sat on the glossy ground.

It felt cold at first, but the longer she sat, the warmer her body became. Below her, she could see the large fish of the lake swimming in the cold water. They moved quickly, passing under her in darting movements. From above, the water looked black. She wondered how the fish breathed and she thought briefly of breaking the ice to give them air; at one point, she hit the flat of her hand against the surface and called to them through the ice, but she eventually stopped and then laid back on the frozen lake, eventually closing her eyes from the climbing sun.

When she woke, she was shivering, her lips and cheeks had turned blue, and she felt a burning in her fingers and toes. She could only open her eyes a little, and when she did so, she saw her mother's face, blurry through the cold and tears. She was being carried inside by her mother. It was the safest she had ever felt—the first and last time she remembered being held by her mother. But the moment passed quickly, and her mother never spoke of the incident at the lake again. Throughout Liz's youth, her mother never changed her ways, and Liz remained alone, still separate from everyone.

As she got older, Liz would escape her family in the afternoons. Her mother would be away from the house and her sisters in their shared room. Liz would lay out in the lawn and watch the clouds gather, outlining their various animal forms with her finger, one eye closed tightly. When a storm passed through, she would dig her fingers into the moist ground and look up and watch the darkened afternoon erupt in light, and it was as if she were in the clouds themselves, lost in their soft, pillowy folds. She became the lightning and thunder, the sky and earth the same, in these moments.

Often, strange men and women would enter their house. These people disappeared quickly behind the closed doors of her mother's bedroom; sometimes they would stay in the room for minutes, other times for hours.

Liz once found a box of needles under her mother's bed; she was seven years old then. Her mother was away at one of the odd jobs she kept at the time—waiting tables and serving drinks down at The Filling Stop or scrubbing faucets and vacuuming carpets at the high school. Liz had wanted to see what in her mother's room attracted so many different people so much of the time. When she found the box, she looked carefully at the needles, studying their shape, recognizing the glass and metallic things only from shows on TV. Liz smiled and quietly shut the box, pushing it back under the bed. She came away from the discovery with the belief that her mother was a doctor helping sick people who came to her for help. It was not until years later that Liz understood the box and what it meant in its entirety.

Yet it was not until after she walked in on her mother in the room—the woman passed out on her bed, the rubber tubing still knotted tightly around her arm, the spent needle dropped to the carpet—that Liz decided to leave her family, leave this notion of "home" behind. There were no goodbyes. Simply a note she placed on her mother's pillow. The writing was cramped and small, written by a shaky hand. Tears stained the bottom of the paper, though these tears had not come out of sadness but rather pain and worry and fear. Only six words: "Dad was smart. I'm leaving too."

She was seventeen then. Liz took to the roads, supporting herself in whatever place she passed through, working wherever she was given a job. She never stayed longer than seven months in one place, though. One day she would be there at a restaurant, serving dinner to a family, and the next day she would be gone, sometimes without collecting her final paycheck. She was a wanderer, a lost soul searching for some answer, some hint that balance in the world existed. Liz would not find this for another six years. And she found it in the strangest of places: on a beach in California where she sat alone with the tide creeping toward her.

But she found it.

Chapter 5

The sun begins its rise over the black prairielands of Nebraska. To the left and right of the interstate are fields of corn, tall and bunched together; out past the corn are other fields. In this light, you cannot tell one stalk of corn from the entire crop, and so it is with the rest of the world. To the north is a solitary train; it moves quickly, though from a distance it is hard to tell. It looks as if it does not move at all, as if it is waiting for something, signaling some person far away with its puffs of white and gray-black smoke—Morse code that cannot be deciphered. This train moves over farmlands rich with black soil, the seeds from centuries past buried somewhere beneath. The engine of the train pulls along twenty or so cars, all filled with different parts of the earth—crops, land, dirt and rust and mineral. The stories of other times and of different people exist in the soil of this place, and it is said that if you place your ear against the earth, you can hear these stories spoken to you from within. There are no people in this land at this hour, except for the workers on the train, and they do not count themselves part of the world's making, though they are.

Matt sees the first hints of the day's beginning in the rearview mirror, watches the land come to life in color behind him. A new day now. Today. Those people in the east have already been presented with the day; they've seen what is to be—they are witnessing the future. But for Matt, he can only know what has been and what is. He sees this in the mirror, wishes he could look into the sun's light and see those things to come. But before him still is a dark road, and he must continue to drive into the night before he will be shown the morning.

Matt studies the darkness of the road ahead. The black of it etched only by the stretching white and yellow, the colors of this place all around him—there is no separation of road and sky and world; the yellow and white marks of the road that move out into the horizon make him think of the map and its highlighted route. He travels this route now, and there is no turning back from it and where it ends.

Part of him wants to look over at the passenger seat and see Liz sitting there, but he can't bring himself to turn his head, so he instead focuses more intently on the road.

After another fifteen minutes, the sun's reflection in the mirror glares brightly at him, and he pulls over onto the open shoulder of the interstate. With hands shaking, Matt opens the door and steps out onto the road. His legs feel weak under him, his feet cramped inside the tennis shoes he wears. Shoulders hang low, blistered and red hands shoved inside his pockets. The air is cold here, and this surprises him since it had been such a warm night earlier. Looking in either direction of the interstate and seeing nothing else besides himself on the road, he walks toward the rear of the truck and stops. Surrounding him are fields turned gold in the sunlight. It looks as if the crops are illuminated from within, the soil charged by some power. When he looks over to the cab of the truck, he sees her sitting peacefully there. She does not notice him. Instead, she is looking only at the sun behind him, watching its steady climb upward.

She had always loved two times of the day: sunrise and sunset. He knows this. Always at these times, she would carry her camera around her neck. She would constantly look out the open windows at the colors and shadows, and he would smile at this.

It had been his gift to Liz their first Christmas together. She opened the box and lifted the camera out. It was the second time he had seen her cry, and, like the first, he knew that these were tears of joy, tears that could wash away all the other tears she had shed in her life.

December twenty-sixth, she woke him early, shaking him from whatever dreams he was having. Through the window, Matt could see that it was still dark outside. He dressed himself quickly, unaware of what was going on, and was greeted by her at the front door of the apartment. She stood there quietly, looking like a small mouse while she moved her weight from leg to leg. Draped around her neck was the new camera; in one hand she held a blanket, which she offered to him, and in the other hand she held a mug of hot chocolate for them to share.

Without saying a word, Liz opened the door and led him outside into the frosty morning. The grass was frozen in night-dew that crunched under their steps. The lamps shined brightly on the slick, wet streets, and Matt felt as if he had stepped living into his dreams. There was a surreal quality to it all—the hanging fog and smell of it all. Somewhere far away was a fire warming a house, and he could smell the smoke as it lingered throughout the air, carried to him by the wind. Matt wrapped the blanket tightly around himself, offering it first to Liz, who only shook her head no. They walked to the edge of the apartment complex and sat on one of the benches that were scattered throughout the place. They sipped from the mug, burning their tongues and cheeks with the hot liquid, laughing at one another and the faces they each made. Chattering teeth, shaking lips. Smiles. Their breath was visible in the low lighting, coming from their mouth and nostrils in clouds of steam that disappeared before either had time to notice.

The sun rose slowly that morning, and Matt watched Liz stand quickly and point the camera at the rising star in the east. The Missouri River was just beyond the trees in the distance there. She turned the camera quickly at different angles, aggressively twisting the lens in focus and refocus, the sound of the shutter snapping closed, all of it creating images of distorted color, shaky blobs of light, radiant and at the same time repulsive, each one unique in a beautiful way. He watched her do all of this knowing he had found someone truly special.

He didn't mean to say it, hadn't realized he was whispering aloud the words until after they'd already been released into the cold, frosted air. But it was different than he expected: the silence was not shattered but somehow calmed by the words. For the first time since the sun peaked above the eastern horizon, Liz stopped taking pictures. She lowered the camera from her eye, and her face serious. She walked the few steps back to where he was and sat next to him.

"I love you, too," she said.

It was the first time they had said those words. They might have thought them silently in their minds, weighing the magnitude of what those words really meant, they may have analyzed the various pros and cons to loving each other and wondering in what ways, if any, the mention of love might change each other and themselves. But they had never said them out loud. Until that morning.

Matt could only shake his head, a smile forming on his face, a quiet laughter beginning. "It's crazy, though. Right? We only just met."

"Yeah," she said. "But does that really matter?"

He shrugged his shoulders.

"Then ask yourself this: how long will you love me? The way you feel now."

He looked at the sun briefly, turning away after a second and blinking his eyes from the brightness. She had disappeared in the spots he now saw, and he reached out and gently placed his hand on her jacketed arm. "Forever and always." The spots began to leave his vision, the world materializing before him. Her face was looking back at his, her lips drawn tight, turned a hue of light blue in the cold. "I will love you forever and always," he whispered.

When he pulls the truck back onto the interstate, Matt can see clearly the road before him. The headlights have turned off automatically, and he knows that this is right—he knows his path is set for him, he doesn't need any extra help finding it. The west is only a direction on a map, a point on a compass, though it is where he is headed, and he hopes there are answers for him there.

Hope. He wishes for it in the silence of the truck with his foot pressing down on the pedal, his right arm set unmoving on the middle console that separates himself from the strange phantom of his love. He still does not look over at where she sits beside him. He is too afraid. If he had looked, though, Matt would have seen her pale, lucent left hand resting on top of his right hand. She cannot feel his skin, but she senses its presence. She can only feel the air. But he does not look over at her and does not see this.

The west is calling too loudly.

Chapter 6

In the beginning, they would lay awake each night and ask each other questions. Their voices came quietly from the darkness painted on the wall. They talked of the day and their interests and beliefs. They whispered their hopes and dreams, both waking and not. They learned one another in these conversations, finding new pasts each night.

During these nights, with the shadows from objects outside the window passing over the room in the moonlight, they found the other through the answers; and at times, they found their own selves in what they confessed. Both questions and answers had become their way of communicating. The only way between the two of them was to surrender information freely to the other, and they each knew this. No topic was untouched, no subject too sensitive. Matt learned of Liz during these nightly interviews. And she him. They would pry these thoughts free with each question, one at a time—one answer before the next until they fell asleep with their hands and arms entwined so that you could not tell one body from the other.

Many nights after they fell asleep, Matt would wake and turn over on his side so as to face her; there, he would find her in the dark maze of pillows and sheets—a mountain within the vast plain of fabric. He would rest his hand gently on top of her chest. The feel of a beating heart within this body continuing its work even in the darkest parts of the night fascinated him. She became more real to him at these moments than at any other. His mouth would work in continued conversation, though no sound would be heard. After a while of this, he would stop and wait for a response that would not come. Yet he would listen for it each time, and he would smile. Even the silence had a voice to it.

One night, with rain hitting hard on the window beside the bed, sounding in ticks and splashes and creaks, she asked Matt about God. He turned to face her and saw only the dark of the room, only the rough outline of her face; he knew there would be her cheek, and there her eyelid, and there, too, just below, was her jaw and the scar on it; he knew that he could close his eyes and be able to see her clearly in his mind, but he refused to do so. Instead, he wanted more than anything to see her as she truly was in that moment: a dark beauty hidden in the world, hidden even to her own self. He smiled then, as she asked him about God, and then he shook his head. The sound of the pillow answered her before Matt's voice. "I don't know if there is a God," he said, quietly. "I don't think so."

There was a silent pause for a while and Matt wondered if he said something wrong. Outside, the sound of rain continued its melody on the glass, the ruffle of sheet fabric adding a silent harmony to the percussion-song as Liz moved her legs back and forth. "I think there is," she said. And she smiled at this, remembering.

After leaving home, Liz traveled south, exchanging the snow of the Upper Midwest for the warmth of the Gulf Coast. When she stepped off the bus, she found herself in a place she had only heard of in stories. Slung over her shoulder was the small bag she had brought—inside were a few changes of clothes and her high school diploma, which she had just received in the mail two days before leaving the house. The wallet in her back pocket held her driver's license and several hundred dollars that she'd taken from her mother's nightstand.

Liz had no direction planned when she started—still didn't. Instead, she believed that there was some kind of order to the world that would show her where to go.

After walking several of the streets of the small Alabama town, she made her way to a park. Much of the area was shaded by trees, the foliage heavy and dark. She sat on the grass under one of these trees and laid back. Her eyes closed heavily; she had not slept the whole drive, and she now fell asleep quickly, the sounds of children's laughter from the playground echoing all around her.

When she woke, the sky had grown dark and the park was nearly empty; there were a few couples walking the winding paths, holding hands and smiling to each other. Just across the way from her was a small family: a mother and father and two young children who looked to be eight or nine. They all sat on a spread blanket, eating sandwiches, grabbing handfuls of chips from a bag. An evening picnic. Liz watched this family for an hour; though she could not hear their conversations, she replaced their words with her own. She imagined how it might feel to be loved, to share a true laugh with someone, to be part of a family, to be something more than just herself.

These phantom conversations played within her mind as she watched the family, and she realized then that she had been crying. She wiped the streaming tears from her eyes and then laid back down, her hands now covering her face. Then, from somewhere deep in her mind, she heard his voice. Minister Felston and his sermon from several months before.

Liz's mother, despite all her personal and family troubles, had always claimed to be a devout believer in the faith, a "True Christian." They, mother and three daughters, attended church every Sunday morning and participated in the church bake sales, Bible study, and other fundraisings and events. Since Liz turned fourteen, she would closely watch her mother outside the walls of the house, silently calling the woman a hypocrite under her breath and hoping that one day her mother would be brought to some kind of spiritual justice, though she didn't know what kind. Liz always felt guilty for these thoughts but would just as quickly shrug them off and move on with whatever she was doing.

While her mother showed herself to the world as a Christian, Liz always kept a skeptical mind, hearing the preaching and the stories of the Bible and questioning their validity rather than simply accepting what she was told. When she was nine, Liz was pulled across her mother's lap and spanked ten times when the girl refused to say a blessing over dinner. Liz couldn't sit down without wincing for the next two days. After that, the girl recited the memorized words when asked to bless the food, but Liz had, in her mind at least, turned from any form of religion. She kept the hope that there was indeed some spirit that watched and guided her along the way, but she did not know if she could rightly call it *God* or believe that it was something that cared for her at all.

One Sunday morning, nearly six months before Liz left Michigan, Minister Felston stood up in front of the small Presbyterian congregation and spoke of hope and signs from the Lord.

The man began quietly—almost in a whisper—saying that many people nowadays do not trust that things will be all right. As she listened to the words from the man's lips, Liz felt as if this sermon was directed at her, as if she was being singled out from the rest. She looked nervously around her at those people seated on the pews in front and behind where she sat, searching for eyes that might be looking scornfully at her, as if they knew her secret truths. But she saw no one paying her any attention, and so she brought her eyes back to the minister.

He said in a cool but aged voice: "Carried through the air, at any one second, are millions of prayers, hopes, wishes. All spoken in silence or called out at the top of lungs or recited with tears. They're out there," he said, waving his hand through the invisible words. "And each of these prayers is a message sent. Some to God, others to loved ones and friends. Most of you do this, I imagine. And these whispers can even be directed at yourself, now or in the future, a commitment to the person you wish to be." The man was silent for a moment. He walked out in front of the podium that he always seemed to hide behind; the wooden podium always seemed to shrink the short man more than he already was.

The minister looked out, moving his eyes over the congregants. Normally, Liz would have seen this action by the minister as an elaborate show, a playact meant only to increase the dramatic tension he had already created, but on this morning, it was different. She sat there with rapt attention, awaiting what next would be said. The man continued in a quiet voice, yet it had grown soothing in some way. "Still, in the end, it doesn't matter who hears these prayers. It only matters that they are said to begin with."

"Close your eyes. Everyone," he said. His voice was now just louder than a whisper.

The members of the small church did as they were asked. Liz leaned forward even more, dropping her head slightly and cradling it in her hands.

"Good," Felston said. "Now, I want you each to send a positive prayer or a message, anything you want. Send a silent word out into the world. I want you to dig deep within yourself and find something you hope will happen for the future. It begins with you, right now. It begins here and in your mind. Look inside yourself for something important." He was silent for a minute before he continued. "Once you have it in your mind, I want you to whisper it. Whisper your words, though whisper it to yourself. I want you to direct these whispered words to yourself, to your future self. It doesn't matter what you say. Just focus on the hope that it will bring in the future. Good," he said, smiling as he watched the members at work. "Once you say it, you can open your eyes."

Liz finished and then looked around. Like dominoes in reverse, she saw the others' heads lift up. Many of the congregants wore smiles on their faces, and a buzz generated from the small room as people whispered quietly to their neighbors what their prayers were.

Felston walked back behind the podium and set his hands wide on the wood, gripping tightly each side of it. "Some day—I can't tell you when it will happen but I can promise that it will—you'll hear your words of hope again. They'll come back to you in the wind. And you will need to listen to the wind, listen for your one prayer in the millions that are out there with it. Listen for that reassurance that you're giving your future self now. And know that your words of hope are only meant for one person: yourself. But listen for the wind first, because the wind will talk to you. The wind will talk."

When Liz opened her eyes again, she found herself once more on the grass. The family across from her was just finishing its picnic, the father gathering the trash while the mother folded the blanket. The children ran around their parents in a game of tag, their giggles coasting over to where Liz sat.

She lifted her head to the darkening sky and listened. She searched the air, feeling the gentle wind that stirred the trees and bushes around her. Later, she would look back and wonder if it was just her imagination that made her hear the words or if it was truly as the reverend had said, but whatever it was, she came away from the park smiling, knowing for the first time that she was doing the right thing. And she had hope.

In the wind, as she sat there, she had heard her voice from months before. A whisper that said simply, "Good morning." She had said those words over and over again with her eyes closed in that small church, knowing that when she heard those words again she would no longer be sitting next to her mother or her sisters. She knew when she heard those two words again that she'd be happy and free.

She knew in that moment that she could finally wake up and begin her life.

Chapter 7

This is a road trip. A chance to experience a world unexplored. It's a chance to learn through the geography, the changing landscapes merely markers for the journey, though it is a journey that transcends merely driving. For Matt, this trip is something far more than he can understand or explain. The land that passes beneath the tires is new for him; he sees parts of the country he has never known, moving through places he has only read of in books or seen on TV, heard only in stories.

The western valleys are lands stretched like oceans. Eventually, he will come upon plateaus and mountains, areas forged from clay into dusty regions of desert.

Can I create man from dust? If so, then is that what you are? Dust from creation returned? To what?

He must pass through rain-drenched grasslands only to find himself in a place where water is simply a fantasy, where all that survives must drink from the nectar of cacti and live in the shadows of night. He sees this on the map. This path that he drives will take them through hell; he only hopes that the Eden he believes awaits them on the other side will be there and that its gates will remain open long enough for them to pass through—for Liz, if no one else.

What are you? He rolls this question around in his mind like a cigarette between lips. How should he refer to this thing?

Her? She? It? When he looks at her, she smiles. He knows this smile. It is her smile, just as he remembers it from before, though it cannot be. *Ghost. Specter. Spirit.* He has only heard of these things in fictions, but they can't.

At night, when he was younger, he would see dark forms cross his bedroom only to disappear when the lights came on. He would close his eyes tightly and tell himself not to be afraid, that they were not real. Not real. But if they were not real, what of her? He needed to believe she was Liz. Needs to. So those shadows from his childhood must have been real.

Still, why has she returned?

Matt had only been on one road trip before this—the summer after he graduated from college. Jeff Tilston had been his roommate for all four years of undergrad; they lived the first two years together in a cramped dorm room, struggling with each other to find personal space; several times, they almost came to blows over some small argument. Like Matt, Jeff studied biology, chemistry, all classes that looked good on medical school applications.

They became fast friends but decided at the beginning of their sophomore year that the next year they would find new roommates. It was nothing personal, they just wanted the change. Both Matt and Jeff kept that deal to themselves, each holding the other accountable, until one day late in their second year.

Matt had bought the small bag of weed from one of the graduate students he saw everyday at the small campus café. When the R.A. came into the room unannounced and saw the bag laying on the table, he immediately blamed Matt, but Jeff went directly to the R.A. and said that the bad belonged to him, not Matt.

When Matt asked Jeff why he lied to protect him, Jeff smiled and laughed, and said it was the right thing to do. They were friends, he said. Matt knew that it was because Jeff's parents were rich whereas Matt came from a poor family; Matt's only way of attending school was through scholarship, which would be worthless if he was caught with drugs.

Jeff met with the Dean of Students on several occasions over the bag; he was threatened on each occasion of expulsion, but instead, Jeff was put on academic probation and required to submit himself to random drug testing throughout his attendance at the university.

Not long after that, Matt asked Jeff to room with him for another year.

They moved into an apartment for their third year. They shared the place with two other students they had known from different classes. For the most part, though, Matt and Jeff kept to themselves, only seeing the other two at breakfast and dinner hours. After their third year, they kept the living arrangement as it was, realizing that they had indeed become brothers, knowing that they each needed the other for support as much as they needed food.

If you looked at the two of them, you would have guessed them to be complete opposites, though this was not so. Often around campus, they were called Lennie and George, Matt the smaller while Jeff was the larger, more deliberate, and quieter speaking of the pair. Neither minded these names; Jeff even seemed to embrace the designation of the kind-hearted idiot, often introducing himself as Lennie at bars and parties. Sometimes, Jeff would walk around drunkenly, winding his way through the clusters of moving bodies and asking about the rabbits. Those who understood the joke laughed, and those who didn't just ignored him as a drunken fool.

Matt and Jeff began talking about the "after" during their senior year. The plan they decided on was to follow each other to med school, room together there and continue whatever type of friendship this was. But when Jeff's scores on the

MCAT were too low to admit him into any of the top tier schools, they found that it was true: plans were only made to be changed. Matt told Jeff that he wouldn't go to Creighton—he'd just received his acceptance letter with an offer of a near full scholarship—but Jeff laughed and patted his friend on the back and, with a serious face and a stern voice, told Matt that if he passed on the chance to go to Creighton that he, Jeff, would never be able to forgive him. Matt could only nod his head and thank his friend, knowing that Jeff was right. They went out to the bar that night and bought each other rounds until neither could remember the reason they went to the bar in the first place.

By the end of that last spring semester, Jeff had been accepted to a small med program in St. Louis. Though he was ultimately disappointed in the school, he made sure never to show this to Matt. He would instead remind his friend that they would only be two states away from each other.

Jeff asked if Matt would stay the summer after graduation with him and his family at their home in Connecticut. When Matt agreed, Jeff said that there was only one condition: since Jeff's parents took his car from him after the drug incident, and since Matt had a car—a beat up Toyota Corolla, the once black paint now scraped from most of the body so that most of the steel grey skeleton of the thing showed through—Matt needed to drop him off in St. Louis at the end of the summer. So, in late July, the two set out on the road driving back to the Midwest. In the trunk and back seat were suitcases and boxes stuffed to the brim, books they had collected from undergrad classes, and Jeff's guitar—something he refused to leave behind.

Now, driving under the late morning sun, Matt thinks back to that trip with Jeff and remembers the small towns they passed through along their way. Abandoned shacks, old mills dried up and deserted. These places reminded Matt of Corvin

Valley. As they drove, he thought of his home and his father, wondering if there was any way to salvage something that seemed so broken.

On that drive from Connecticut to Missouri, they passed cities shining bright into the night and towns destroyed from time and overuse. Yet, in each of these places, Matt noticed how they all shared one thing: each had a cemetery. *There's not a place on earth that doesn't have its share of the dead.*

There was one town in Ohio that both he and Jeff stopped their conversation as they drove past; Jeff even turned the radio off as if that would help them process the place that they had found. No other cars drove behind them on the interstate, none passed them; it seemed as if the rest of the world knew of this place and chose other routes to avoid being trapped, if only for a few minutes, in this town—as if even the sight of this dead place was too much to take.

So many of these towns exist. Fossils from some time long ago, before the raw earth dried and refused to yield any more minerals from the ground. This one town was many towns—deserted, abandoned, destroyed. Like so many towns that line the highways, this was one whose name no longer was important enough to be written on maps, its existence only shown in the dusty and faded signs that line the back roads and interstates. When these signs fall, does it mean the town is no more? That it cannot be saved or remembered? Matt wondered how long until Corvin Valley would become like this—a nameless place to drive through, to hold your breath from the stink of disuse as you went on your way.

Matt stopped the car along the side of the road, and they both looked at the ruined place. Yellow grass stained the ground in all directions, both within and on the outskirts of the town. On one of the streets, they could see a tipped-over cargo trailer of a semi. Graffiti covered the red metal of it that had rusted dark and black from the sun.

Neither Matt nor Jeff spoke as they sat there. They merely watched the town, searching for some reason for its death. They looked at the houses—abandoned shacks now. Most had fallen to pieces and cluttered in heaps and piles that reached up to the sky. Other houses showed various stages of decomposition.

From one of these houses four small children came running outside. Jeff tried to follow them with his eyes—these mongrels forgotten by a dead town, overlooked in their poverty and filth, these small people who had created their own society that no one except themselves could be part of—but they ran behind a house and disappeared.

When Matt started the car again, pulling out onto the road, he felt a sense of guilt from leaving the town and its few inhabitants behind. The place was relegated to the past, a memory now. A story to be told someday, maybe.

Chapter 8

Hidden moments exist each day, answered truths to the most important of questions: the reasons of the universe, its workings, the presence of love and hatred among us, their shared qualities and differences, our understanding of each. The identity of the world. Its maker, its soul, ourselves.

The wind outside your window carries these small things, these truths. See for yourself. Look there, in the growth of the grass, delicate and fine, hidden from your eyes' perception, the movement of shadows over an hour's time. We sense these things, but we look away; we have not the patience to wait for and recognize these aspects of the world. A red bird digs within the earth; it spits out dirt and mud to find its prey; it carries the worm to its perch above the earth and vomits the wriggling thing into the mouths of its young. This is not some accident nor is this some master plan. It simply is. And we call it life and nature.

When a woman asks her lover if he is an angel, he must simply answer that he is not. He is simply a man, though she does not believe this, not when his touch creates such a feeling of calm and comfort. Shivers run through her body, over her skin. He breath quickens and her heart beats stronger, and she thinks that possibly this man is both angel and human, salvation meant only for her.

You can find these events, these actions, these quiet truths, if you look close enough. Though if you look too closely at something, then you might miss seeing the whole of the thing. In so doing, we forfeit the complete for the specific and lose our bearings only to become adrift in potential: in what could be and not what is.

Matt always had an understanding of all this.

One afternoon, after he came home from a twenty-hour shift at the hospital, he opened the front door and called out Liz's name. There was no answer. Behind him outside, the late-afternoon shadows of the trees stretched a far distance along the grass. Children played basketball and football in front yards; streetlights were preparing to turn on.

He made his way through the small house, peeking tiredly out each window, looking in each room for her. As he neared the back of the house, Matt heard heavy breathing. The door to the back room was cracked open just far enough for him to see through with one eye, and he brought his face close to the open space.

The ground of the room now had a dull, stagnant color to it, and Matt needed a second to realize that the carpet had not changed but rather it had been covered by a large, beige cloth tarp. The furniture that once spread over the small room—a small wooden desk, the old couch from his dorm, plastic boxes of unpacked items—were now gathered in the far back left corner. It was the shadow that first caught his attention. He could not see her except for her shadow that moved around the room, passing darkly over the walls. Opening the door a bit more, Matt saw the rest of the room.

Liz was in the corner. In her right hand was a paint roller. Before her was a half-painted wall; it had been an off-white color, but now there were splashes of bright blue across it. Streaks of color stretching in various directions on the wall. It looked as if she could not spend her effort in one place but was too caught up in the tribal markings that she could make with the paint. Endless possibilities of creation.

Liz wore a blue bandana tied loosely over her hair; her ears were covered by bulky headphones. The cord stretched to the small mp3 player she had stored in her pocket. Her body moved in circles of dance; her bare feet twirled in place, propelling her body around and around. Matt ducked himself back into the hall, hiding behind the still-closed door. He was afraid she might see him and end her dance and this moment for him. And so he watched her.

Her eyes were closed, her head tilted back. There was a simple smile on her face, as if this one moment was as natural an act as breathing or taking a step. Matt could not tell the song she was listening to, but figured it to be a Tom Petty song, her favorite.

Matt could not have said how long he stood there, his back cramping from the angle he stood, but he did not care about his tight muscles. He could have watched her in this moment forever and been content with his life. This woman he loved. This woman whose long, dark hair fell from the bandana with each passing circle she made. This woman who flung paint from the roller out to the farthest reaches of the room, not caring where it landed. Her skin and clothes were covered in spots of blue, an alien woman alone before him.

This is how he will forever remember her.

Matt turns and looks over at Liz, the image of her next to him in the truck. She is looking out the window now. Prairieland passes by outside, and she watches through the window as this landscape slides past her. If you keep your head fixed, your eyes straight ahead as you look out the side window, all you can decipher is color and its changing patterns and shades. You try to make sense of this, but you cannot. It simply is. To someone outside looking your way, the car that you travel in is merely another color, as well; it passes by briefly and then is replaced by whatever follows.

They have been driving for nearly five hours. The sun is at their back still; few clouds scatter the blue above them. Glancing down at the map, Matt sees that they are nearing the border to Colorado. He looks back at the seat next to him, watches her a bit more. He wonders if there is music playing in her mind. Or thoughts. Memories of their past, reminders of who she was.

Chapter 9

His class had just finished a lecture in one of the many closed off rooms of the ICU in the hospital. Dr. Ramsey took them there, showing the students a body laying on a metal table. The body, she said, belonged to a man who was in a PVS—persistent vegetative state—and had just been taken off life-support. Surrounding the corpse was a series of machines with wiring and tubes connected to various parts of the body. "The ventilator here keeps the cardio-pulmonary functions of the cadaver sustained," she explained.

The students filed around the table, careful not to get too close. Though being in the room with a dead body was nothing new to the students, especially at this stage of their schooling, there was still a thrill to it. A strange rush that made the hairs stand up on their arms and a cold feeling sweep over them and stay pitted in their stomachs.

"With the ventilator," Ramsey continued, "the organs—heart, lungs, kidneys—all continue to function as if the person were not deceased. We can then more easily transfer the organs to donor recipients. A cycle, in short," she concluded.

From a distance, the body on the table—a middle aged man—would have looked to be alive. It was not until you went close to the table that you realized he was dead. There is a certain feel in the air around a dead body, an imperceptible smell, maybe. Matt couldn't put his finger on what it was, but there was a definite difference between the living and the dead, and he was beginning to know how to quickly distinguish the two. He could look at the eyes of a patient and know if she would be all right or whether he should stay close and listen for the echo of the flatlining to begin. Matt could now sense when a patient had given up, when the attending doctor needed to call the time of death, when it was all over. These were the untaught things he came to learn along the sad, neutral-colored hallways of the hospital.

The previous week, Ramsey had brought them all to the lower floor of the hospital. The morgue had always been a place of ghost stories, even to medical students. They anticipated the trip to the morgue weeks in advance, knowing what lay ahead of them.

When the elevator doors opened, they made their way through a small maze of short corridors, arriving finally at a large room. Fluorescent bulbs buzzed overhead. There was a ticking sound somewhere above them that the students eventually grew used to. Three bodies lay on metal tables. The cadavers were uncovered, the skin a pale white that seemed to glow in reflection from the lights above.

Ramsey separated the class into groups and directed each to one of the bodies. She spoke slowly, hushed, as if she were afraid of interrupting the quiet of the room, the sanctuary of this place. They were to look at the heart today and perform a removal of the organ. Stephanie Thibold, the only female in Matt's small group, was selected to perform the initial incision. Her hand shook as she dragged the scalpel down the dead woman's chest. Stephanie stopped after a few inches; Marcus, one of the other members of the group, pointed out to her that the cut was nowhere deep enough. Stephanie giggled slightly under her surgeon's mask and then started again, retracing her earlier lined mark; this time, she pressed down hard on the tool.

The cut started just below the throat and stretched down nearly to the navel. Matt and Marcus took either side of the now divided chest and separated the sternum, spreading the white bone apart. Underneath was the heart. Matt and the others circled closely around the table, pointing silently and marveling at its size—though they had seen hearts in photos and within jars, the organ looked so much smaller when it was lodged inside its normal surrounding. Matt balled his fist up and looked down at it, comparing the size of the heart and his hand; there seemed no difference.

Ramsey continued her lecture, explaining that for a normal transplant procedure, tubes would need to be inserted—blood would need to be pumped from the body into a cardiopulmonary bypass machine—before the removal of the heart could be achieved.

Matt and the others in his group began cutting through the stringy tissue, separating arteries and valves from their connections with scalpels, each student taking a turn at working within the open cavity of the body; the whole while, Matt kept wondering why this organ, whose only function was to pump oxygenated blood through the body, was said to be a place of pain during loss, the place that controlled love and desire.

Matt thought of his past two classes with Dr. Ramsey as he walked through the sliding front doors of the hospital after the lecture. His mind was still on the heart that lay dormant within that woman's chest the week before. He then thought of what he'd just seen: the corpse that lay on the table, the strange buzzing machines that circled around the dead man like fortune tellers. He could still see the man's body, the cords that ran from the corpse like tendrils from a plant. *Everything in this world is the other.* The organs of the cadaver were still alive, though the man was dead. Matt shook his head, wondering quietly how that could be: how could someone whose body still functioned not exist anymore? What, then, is death or life but a state of being, a mental presence? An understanding of self and others. And what happens after you leave that body?

His head was down as he walked, and he casually glanced up when he made it to the street. That's when he saw her standing there, a short distance off—the bag at her feet, the nervous wave hello. He turned away quickly, closing his eyes tight, trying to force the imagined girl from his mind. He continued walking down the street toward his apartment. It was not until he heard the sound of shoes chasing after him that he turned again and saw her for who she really was, not a memory at all. It had been five months, but he knew her face. It was the one constant for him, the hopeful thought that got him through the moments when he missed Trisha the most. During those times, Matt would close his eyes and focus on Liz's face; knowing that she was out there somewhere in the world living her life made things all right for him somehow. With that knowledge, he knew he could move on and be okay.

But when he realized that Liz was actually there in front of him, Matt found that he couldn't speak. What was there to say? Sweat beaded on his brow, and he felt his pulse quicken.

She looked shyly away. Nervous. Then she spoke, breaking the thick fog of silence that hung between them. "This is probably all wrong, I know."

Matt shook his head slowly, a smile only now beginning to form.

She spoke again. "Since the beach, I can't stop thinking of you. It doesn't make sense. I barely know you, but here I am."

"Here you are." He let out a silent laugh and looked around the street, trying to understand what was happening. It didn't seem real—this couldn't be.

"I didn't tell you anything about me that night on the beach because I haven't told anyone. But here, here's all the questions you asked me and all the answers I didn't give you: My name is Liz Simmons. I'm from a little town in Michigan, just south of Canada. I don't have a job. I don't have a home. I ran away from my mom and sisters when I was seventeen. When I was little, I wanted to be two things when I grew up: a photographer and someone who helps somebody, but I've never had a camera and I don't know anyone to help. I've never had anyone to trust in my life, and I've never played anything safe. And I realized after you left that night that my life needs safe. And I realized, somehow, that you are safe. You're safe to me."

Matt shook his head, confused. Men and women walked hurriedly along the sidewalk around them. No one on the busy street noticed the two of them standing there talking. Matt and Liz were lost within the crowd, alone inside the lives of others. Down the street, a small girl ate from an ice cream cone, her hand being held by an older woman, a grandmother, maybe. Matt saw the girl and watched her living in the safety and quiet of her own world. Nothing else mattered to her.

"This is wrong, isn't it?" she asked after a few seconds of waiting for his response. Liz shrugged her shoulders as tears welled in her eyes and began to fall down her cheeks. "I should go. I'm sorry, Matt."

As she turned to walk away, Matt reached out and grabbed hold of her arm. His grip was soft, like he was unsure of what he was doing. And that was how he felt. Liz turned back to him. Her eyes were red, lips wet from where the tears had run.

"There isn't a day I don't think of you," he said quietly.

She smiled and sniffed back tears, laughed nervously. "I don't know what to do. I feel like I've got nothing left. And I can't keep running."

"Then you stay with me. We'll figure this out as we go."

Chapter 10

They are nothing but invisible boundaries that divide territories fought over long ago and bought and sold with gold and blood. And despite the fact that these state lines that populate maps exist only in ink written an arthritic scrawl, there is a definite change in geography to each new state. You can say that one state looks like another, but there is still a marked difference, though you cannot say exactly how or why.

Colorado came on him sooner than he realized. Matt had been focused only on the road before him, hypnotized by the black path that seemed to lead up into the skies, into oblivion. For the past hour or so, he had been trying to see the faces inside the cars that passed by; he looked through the tinted windows, peeking into other people's lives, to escape his own and rid himself of the hurt and fear if only for a fleeing moment in time. Matt saw children smiling and laughing in back seats, wives and husbands, lovers, friends, people he would never know, arguing over spread maps, over cell phones. He nearly missed the large sign that welcomed him to the new state. Not long after passing the sign, Matt realized that this was the farthest west he had ever driven.

His body feels tired, his eyes heavy now, dropping almost mechanically. The truck drifts slowly to the right before he catches himself, jerking the wheel back into place. He shakes his head, his lips feeling loose on his face. A few hard slaps to his face now, some pinches on the skin of his legs and arms, a readjustment in the seat, now sitting taller, his head reaching near the truck ceiling. *Stay awake,* he tells himself.

He glances over at Liz. She is looking directly at him, and he turns quickly so as to face the road again. Matt is about to turn the radio on but stops when he hears his phone ringing loudly in the cup holder. Picking it up and feeling the gentle vibrating of the phone, he reads the name on the screen. Travis. He flips the phone open and hits the red ignore button with his thumb. The phone goes silent and calm, and he reaches out and turns the radio on.

The TV was on when Matt opened the door of the hotel room. The volume was turned up loud. A comic was doing a stand-up routine on one of the late-night talk shows that played on repeat. Laughs from the audience blasted out of the small box. The sound made Matt feel as if they were in the room with him, laughing at him. With him? He didn't know.

Travis had been asleep for over an hour, and Matt didn't want to wake his brother. He crept across the darkened room that was lit only from the television screen across from where he was. Inside the bathroom, Matt brushed his teeth and looked at himself in the mirror. The brightness of the light bulb over the sink made him squint. He spit and peed, not flushing the toilet for fear of waking Travis. After he turned off the bathroom light, Matt walked quietly over to the second of the twin beds in the room. He had just picked up the remote and hit the power button, turning the room to complete black, when he heard the sound of Travis sitting up in his bed.

"Where you been, man?" Travis's voice was still full of sleep, marbly with saliva.

Matt sighed. On the small table opposite where he lay on the bed was a coffee maker; a small red dot of light glowed from the machine, something Matt hadn't noticed during the previous six nights there. "Been out, I guess."

"Shit, dude. What time is it?"

Matt could tell Travis was waking up more and more. He heard the sound of Travis's body rolling over the heavy hotel bedspread—the synthetic material scraping loudly—as his brother checked the clock on the side table.

"Damn, Matty. It's three o'clock."

There was the sound of the bedspread again as Travis laid back down. The room was cold; Travis had turned the thermostat all the way down, and Matt pulled the blankets to his chin. He didn't feel tired. Instead, there was a restless feeling that ran throughout his arms and legs. He wanted to go back out into the night. "I know," he answered quietly.

"Our plane leaves in a couple hours. I was worried about you, especially with you not having a phone, you dumbass." Travis had not stopped joking with Matt for leaving his phone in Omaha, though Matt told Travis that he left it there on accident.

Matt smiled at his brother, though he could not see Travis in the darkness. He and Travis hadn't been close growing up—when they were kids, the three-year gap between them always seemed bigger than it really was—but they had come to terms with each other as they grew older, becoming an odd pairing, friends who didn't have anything in common except family blood and a similar smile.

Matt fell asleep with the memories of the past playing like a night film in his head.

When the clock alarm sounded in the small room a couple hours later, Matt opened his eyes and stared at the ceiling above him. Travis, already dressed, threw a pair of jeans and a shirt at Matt, who sat up and rubbed the sleep from his eyes.

The sunlight came through the window and Matt saw that Travis had already packed both of their suitcases. Travis was waiting by the door for his brother.

On the way down the elevator, Travis reached his arm around Matt's neck.

"Late night. Must've been fun, huh?" Travis smiled.

Matt shook his head and returned the smile. His cheeks began to blush, and he looked away. "I know. I know. I'm sorry, man. Last night here and I bail."

"It's all right, big brother. I don't want to know anything about it." There was a silence between them. The elevator bell dinged when they reached the lobby. Just before the metal doors slid open, Travis let go of his hold around Matt's shoulder. He looked at his brother and laughed. Matt smiled over at Travis.

"Haven't seen you this happy in a long time. She must've been worth it." Travis patted Matt on the back playfully.

The elevator doors opened, and Travis walked through them toward the front counter to check out. "She was," Matt whispered to himself. His smile widened from the memory of Liz and the night before. He lifted his suitcase and walked through the elevator doors, making his way over to his brother.

Chapter 11

The walk back to the apartment from the hospital was quiet. They were both afraid to say anything and ruin the moment. Matt carried her bag while she walked with her head down, her hands stuffed deep into her coat pockets. Matt lived in a studio apartment four blocks from the hospital, and they made their way there over the crowded lunch-hour streets.

Matt asked Liz if she wanted to eat anything, but Liz shook her head, saying quietly that she wasn't hungry. When they walked into the apartment, Liz was taken aback by the small size of the place, though she tried hard not to show her surprise. There was just enough space for a bed, a couch, and a small TV in the living area that bordered an even smaller kitchen. Just to the right of the front door was the bathroom. Liz wondered if she was crazy for being there, but she pushed the thought from her mind and instead focused on the fact that she was there at all.

Matt set the bag down on the bed and turned to her. His smile showed many things but mostly surprise and happiness.

"How'd you get here?" He shook his head as he said it.

She shrugged her shoulders, looking around the small room. "I lived at the beach in California for a little bit after you left. Worked at this little shop there. After that, I drove around, up towards the mountains in California. On my way there, like a month or two after I saw you, you, my car broke down, and I ended up selling it and buying a bus ticket to Omaha. I don't even know why. The whole drive here I didn't know what I was doing or how I'd find you here."

"How did you find me?"

She smiled. "I remember you said you were in school to be a doctor. I hoped you were still in school here." She shrugged her shoulders playfully. "So I stood outside that hospital for four hours, watching everyone that went in or out, looking for you. I wondered if I'd remember what you look like. But I did."

He shook his head and sat down on the bed next to where he had set her bag. "What if I wasn't there?"

Her smile turned serious. "I don't know. I guess I would have stayed there all day and gone back tomorrow."

For the first month, Matt slept on the small couch while Liz, despite her many objections, took the bed. The first week was awkward; neither knew how to act nor knew what to say or what not to say. For the first week, they remained strangers living in the same small room. They each found themselves trying to understand the other's mannerisms and ways. Sometimes they would catch each other staring and both would look away, giggling silently. After a few days, though, they loosened up, showing themselves who they really were. They soon found that neither was the same person they had known that night on the beach. The Matt and Liz from the beach were dry façades of the real people, and they each found that there was so much more to know and learn.

In his mind, Matt wanted more from her, but he kept these things secret from her. From the first day, he told Liz the first day that whatever there was between them, whatever there could be, he didn't want to ruin it by pushing things too fast. "Let it come when it does," he said.

Liz smiled at Matt for this, smiled at his overprotection of her, his worry for her comfort. Matt would ask her time and time again throughout each meal if she liked the food he made, even if it was just pasta with canned sauce on top. Every night, he would lay out a stack of blankets at the foot of the bed, reminding her that they were there if she got cold in the middle of the night. In the morning when he woke and went to class, he would tiptoe around the apartment, afraid to wake the sleeping stranger in his bed. She would watch him with her eyelids open just enough to see how much he cared. He was a good person, she realized; this was something she knew very little about. After he left for class in the mornings, she would lay awake in bed and try to think back to another person as genuinely caring and loving as Matt, but she couldn't think of anyone.

Liz stayed in Alabama for two months. She found a job at a clothing boutique. The money she made there, combined with what she had saved from home, gave her enough to buy a car.

She went to a dealership and asked to see the used cars. She glanced over the selection briefly, spending more time looking at the size of the back seats than anything else. She eventually settled on a haggard-looking Cadillac model from the late 80s. She bought a pillow and a small blanket and slept in the back seat. In the trunk, she kept what few clothes she had, along with a towel and water pail she would use for bathing in public bathrooms. Once or twice a week, she would drive to the beach, soaking her body in the Gulf and letting the salty water cleanse her.

After she left Alabama, she made her way north, stopping in North Carolina for a little while. She found a small town at the base of the Smokey Mountains where she worked at a grocery market. It was there that she met Brad, one of the other cashiers. He was several years older than her, and he lived in a trailer in the woods. She stayed with him for six months, never feeling a true connection with him, though she didn't want to challenge the good-enough thing she had going with him. It wasn't until he came home drunk from a night out with his friends that she realized how she was only falling into the same kind of life that she escaped from in Michigan. Looking back on it, she only wished it had not taken the black eye, cut lip, and broken rib to realize what she knew all along: Brad was a mistake.

Over the next several years, Liz drove the country. She made her way to upstate New York, then down to Georgia, and over to Texas and New Mexico. She would remember various parts of the different places she visited: the sunrises and sunsets in New Mexico, the purples that seemed just darker shades of red and orange—all things one and the same—or the humidity of Georgia in the summer and the cold of winter in the Northeast.

Liz worked all types of jobs, from bartending to hotel cleaning, retail stores to diners; anything that put gas in the Cadillac and gave her enough money to buy food. There were several men, like Brad, that she thought she loved, though each one of them found some way of disappointing her.

She was headed for the Pacific Northwest when she stopped in California, wanting to see what a West Coast beach looked like in comparison to the Gulf. She had just driven in that afternoon, just set her beach towel on the sand, when she saw Matt in the water. She would later tell him that it was his eyes that first caught her attention, his smile that kept her interest, his love the made her fall for him under the moonlit night.

During those first months living together in the studio apartment, they stayed awake until morning, talking of things both important and not. They would talk until one or both of them fell asleep. Matt came to know her by these conversations, though there always seemed to be things she was afraid to tell him, aspects of her life that she still kept secret from him. When she slept, he would look at her caringly, watching the flicker of her eyelids from a dream; there were so many demons, so many ghosts hidden under those lids.

Many nights, he would wake to the sounds of her dreams. She would talk in her sleep, lucid speech that at first frightened him, though he came to feel comforted by it somehow; he would wait at night for the dream-words to come. He would answer her, ask her questions. He never knew if the things she told him in her dream sleeps were truth or not, though it did not matter: these words were hers, and he remembered them as such.

During the days while he was in class, Matt would think of the woman at home. He found himself constantly worrying that he would open the door of the apartment and find her missing as if she were just a figment of his imagination, a ghost from another time haunting his thoughts.

Though he didn't have many people he considered friends, Matt didn't tell anyone about Liz. He was most concerned about keeping quiet about her during the days when he and Trisha shared a class together. The two of them had remained friendly with each other after the breakup, though there was an obvious tension between them, and neither wanted to strain that tension by becoming wrapped up in a long conversation.

After classes or shifts in the hospital, Matt would hurry back to the apartment. Though they had established early on that there would be no physical relationship, at least not immediately, he still found himself wanting her throughout the day. He could see the start of passion: an accidental touch of skin, their legs touching briefly as they sat on the couch together while they watched a movie. When this happened, one or both of them would pull away from the other quickly with a nervous smile and laugh.

It was not until she had been there two months that she noisily threw the covers off herself one night and made her way over to the couch. She knelt down, bringing her face level with his. She kept her face there, just out of reach of his. He had been trying to fall asleep but was finding it hard to do in the cold night. Her long, brown hair brushed gently against his face, and he opened his eyes. Matt never understood why, but when he opened his eyes and found Liz staring at him, waiting for him, he felt a sense of expectation, like he knew this was going to happen.

Outside was the first snowstorm of the season.

His heart beat quickly as she slowly brought her face closer to him. Finally, after what seemed an eternity, Liz brought her lips to his. They kissed for several minutes, their tongues exploring each other's mouths. Her lips traced the skin of his neck in soft kisses that made him pull back from her. Matt brought his hands up underneath her shirt and explored the flesh of her belly, her breasts; he felt her nipples hard in the cold night. She pulled away and took off her shirt and laid down on the carpet next to the couch. Matt rolled off the couch, catching himself with his thin arms, keeping himself just above where Liz lay. They kissed again, taking the rest of their clothing off as they did so, sharing the warmth of each other in the cold night while outside the snow fell and covered the ground and everything else out there in a fresh blanket of white.

Chapter 12

Bad weather makes him think of her. Whenever he looks up and sees the clouds darken, he always stops what he is doing and reaches down with his right hand, moving his fingers gently over the gold band on his left ring finger.

Liz always joked about it, saying that the bad weather outside was what kept their relationship sunny. Though there were always storms that seemed to linger just beyond their knowing, Matt would constantly remind himself of the sun that shined down above those storms.

The rain begins to hit the windshield first in small patters, sounding more like bugs against the glass than water. The storm is coming. He knows it.

Above him now, though, the sky is clear. Birds fly high, their shadows passing over the road quickly, their movements graceful and sharp. He wonders what it must feel like to be up there, lost above the world. The wind against his skin. Cold. Free and peaceful.

Matt brings his eyes back to the road, and he watches the cars passing him in the opposite lanes; the hoods and windshields are beaded with rainwater, wipers moving fast, blurring the faces of the passengers inside. He drives on for several more miles under the cloudless sky. It is not until he makes his way around the bend in the interstate that he sees the gray and black clouds. They are still some miles away yet, but the stray drops of rain continue. He slows the truck, noticing the straight road ahead of him; there are no more curves in the interstate that he can see, and he does not check the map to confirm this. The road leads directly into the heart of the storm that sits calmly ahead; it is as if the storm is waiting for him, beckoning him on with its thunder voice. Challenging him, even.

Pushing his foot down heavy on the gas, Matt forces the truck to speed up. He knows that in a few minutes the storm will be all around him, trapping him inside. He can see several crackles of lightning, the bolts flashing brilliantly against the darkness that surround it. This only makes him drive faster.

They were coming back from dinner that night.

They had been living together in the small studio apartment for nearly eight months. It was late, and there was no moon in the sky. Liz was in the passenger seat of the Corolla, looking out the window at the dark night lit only by scattered streetlights. Matt was about to turn into the apartment complex when he heard Liz gasp. Turning to look at her, Matt saw a bright flash of light in the distance. He could clearly make out the jagged edges, the limbs of electricity branching out from the main stem of the lightning. With each explosion of light, her smile grew wider.

Liz turned quickly to Matt. “Follow it,” she said, turning back to the window.

Matt looked past her, watching the next bolt break in the open sky. Next to him, Liz giggled. He continued past the apartment complex and made his way to the east of the city.

After several minutes of driving, Matt parked the car on the bank of the Missouri River. He turned off the engine so that no light showed on the dash. All around them was darkness. They sat like this, watching the dry lightning crack over the earth like they were watching fireworks explode on Independence Day. After several minutes, Liz opened her door and stepped out into the hot night. Matt tried to talk her back into the car, but she waved him off. "Come out here," she said to him and then turned back to watch the sky.

Matt got out and walked over to where she was, and they both sat on the hood of the car. A sharp crack of lightning sounded continuously in the distance. Liz wondered if the sound of war was anything like this, though she tried not to think of war or death or sadness—not in a moment like this. She had found her peace; she had found what she was looking for, something she didn't think truly existed. *Hope*, she thought. She leaned her head against Matt's shoulder as the lightning continued to shoot down from the sky and make the distant world momentarily bright.

Matt put his arm around Liz and moved his body closer to her so that their hips touched. He looked down at her and then back to the sky. He smiled and, in a quiet, calm voice, asked if she would marry him.

She didn't look over to him when she heard the question. She kept watching the lightning in the distance, thinking how the sounds she heard were not those of war or destruction but of her heart beating in her chest. Her eyes welled with tears, though she did not wipe the tears away, did not look at Matt. Instead, she simply whispered her answer. "Of course."

He pulled her tight to him. They continued to watch the lightning erupt in the darkness until the early hours of morning when the new day began, and they both realized that what had happened that night was not a dream. It was something real, something true.

Chapter 13

After graduating from Creighton, Trisha and Matt worked together in Pediatrics. She had wanted to become a surgeon, but Matt talked her into working with kids after the two had gone to the county fair. Trisha helped a lost four-year-old girl find her parents. Matt watched from a distance as Trisha knelt and placed a gentle hand on the child's back, drying the girl's tears with a napkin. Trisha was so kind and gentle with the girl, and Matt saw the look of joy on Trisha's face after the girl's mother came and, crying and thanking Trisha a dozen times, carried her daughter away. "You ever think of being a pediatrician?" Matt asked after she made her way back over to him. "You should."

Matt dreaded the thought of telling Trisha that he was engaged, especially since he hadn't told her that Liz even existed; for all Trisha knew, he was living alone, still mourning their failed relationship the way she was.

He told her in the cafeteria of the hospital when he knew that Trisha would be alone. It was a short conversation, and even though Trisha congratulated Matt, he knew from her long silence that she was heartbroken. She stopped eating her lunch, and, after a short while of sitting there quietly, Matt smiled sadly at her and then left her alone at the table.

The painful reality of Matt's words didn't fully sink in for Trisha until she got back to her apartment that night. She had finished the day in a trance-like haze, not hearing clearly what anyone said to her. When Trisha got home, she fell on her bed and buried her face in her pillow and cried; she told herself over and over that what there was between herself and Matt was over, that she should be happy for him. But she always hoped in the back of her mind that they would still end up together somehow. They may not have been the best couple, she would always think that, but Matt was all she had ever known. The thought of him not being there for her, of her having to start over with someone else, it all terrified her.

The phone rang several times throughout the night, all calls from her parents, but she didn't get up to answer them; Trisha stayed on her bed, napping on and off in a fitful sleep, her face wet with the tears.

The day after Matt proposed to Liz, the two of them went to one of the jewelry stores in town. It was a small shop in the older part of town. At first, Liz refused to come along, saying that it was Matt's choice, that she wanted to be surprised with what he picked for her, but Matt only laughed at this. He surprised her the next evening after their celebration dinner when he pulled the Corolla up to the small shop just before it closed for the night.

Liz walked inside with Matt, looked around at several of the rings in the glass cases. Then after a few minutes, Liz quietly walked out of the store and sat in the car. Matt came out, asking her what was wrong, and she smiled. "Go inside and pick me the best ring. The one that you like," she said.

Matt shook his head and then returned the smile. "Okay," he said. He went back in, and a half hour later, he came out of the store carrying a small bag.

Liz watched his every movement, waiting nervously to see what he had chosen. But when he got into the car, he started the engine and drove home, never once mentioning the ring or what was in the bag. When she asked, Matt simply ignored her, turning the radio up louder and smiling to himself. He didn't look over at her, knowing that if he did, he would see her face, full of excitement and anticipation.

It wasn't until the next morning that Liz saw the ring. Matt had already left for class when she woke up. She walked into the bathroom to brush her teeth but stopped when she looked at the mirror. With soap, he had written the words "Marry Me" on the mirror. Just under that, taped onto the glass, was the ring. She pulled it from the tape and put it on her finger. Under the bathroom lights, the ring sparkled brightly, sending out a dozen different prisms on the walls—strobe lights to celebrate, patterns made only in nature. She held it up close to her eyes so that she could see it better through the tears that fell down her cheeks. It was exactly the one she would have picked herself.

Travis and Jeff flew into Omaha the following Thursday. Travis had just started teaching ninth and eleventh grade English at Corvin Valley High School, where both he and Matt had graduated from. Though Matt couldn't understand why his brother would go back to the dying town, he never questioned Travis on his decision; he only smiled and congratulated him when his brother told him of the job.

Travis had been dating Sandra McClellan for just over a year. Matt remembered Sandra from high school; she was in his graduating class. As he waited at the airport for Travis to arrive in Omaha, Matt remembered when his brother called months earlier to tell him about Sandra. She was also teaching at the school, Special Education, he said. The two had only been dating for a few months when Travis called, and Matt didn't know what to ask or say to his little brother about Sandra. Instead, Matt and Travis talked of other subjects over the phone. They made jokes about each other, about themselves, and they laughed for a half hour. But when Travis told Matt that he had gone to see their father in prison a few weeks earlier, Matt's voice grew serious, and he changed the conversation quickly. Matt didn't want to rehash the disappointments of the past.

As for Jeff, he only lasted a semester in med school before he dropped out. He met Kathy at a bar in downtown St. Louis not long after the semester started. She was finishing up her MBA at one of the schools there. After a month, though, she came to Jeff and told him she was pregnant. It was a quick engagement and a small wedding; Matt was Best Man—it was the last time Matt had seen Jeff before the latter flew into Omaha. Jeff hadn't bought Kathy an engagement ring, only the wedding band; they needed to save money for the baby and the other expenses that they knew would come. Though she never admitted it, Jeff could always see a disappointment in Kathy's eyes when she looked at her left hand.

Jeff wouldn't say it out loud—always telling Kathy that he never enjoyed medicine and that he quit because he couldn't stand working so hard at something that brought no excitement to him—but he dropped out because of the baby, because of his mistake, he would always think. When Jeff called and told his parents about dropping out of the program and his sudden marriage to Kathy, they hung up the phone quickly; two weeks later, he received a card in the mail: a simple note of congratulations followed by a postscript reading, "You made your life, now live it. We won't be helping you out anymore."

There were plenty of nights when Jeff would lay awake and think of what his life would be like if Kathy and he didn't have Kylie: he would be a doctor, still working long hours but doing something he wanted to be doing. Instead, he was now working late into the night at a low-paying job, one that in no way could cover all the expenses they had, especially with Kathy out of work because of the baby. He hoped that Kathy would go back to work when Kylie started school, but that was still several years away.

On those nights when he thought of that other life, Jeff would reach his hand across the fabric and touch Kathy's hand as she slept. He would have still married her, baby or no baby, he knew that. He loved her, even with the problems between them. But he knew that if he had stayed in school, they wouldn't be living paycheck-to-paycheck, eating soup and pastas during the weeknights when money was tight and bills were due.

He had put the flight to Omaha on the credit card that was nearing its limit, but he loved Matt like a brother; Matt was the only true friend Jeff ever had.

Matt had arranged the flights so that Travis and Jeff would arrive at the airport near the same time. Matt was waiting at the luggage turnstile for both of them. He hadn't told either why he needed to see them; Matt just said that it was important. The three of them went straight to the bar, a local hangout. Though they asked several times, Matt refused to answer what the occasion was—what was so urgent that he had called four days earlier and demanded they be in Omaha on Thursday. It wasn't until after the third round of beers that Matt said quickly, with a smile on his face, "I'm getting married." By that point, Matt was already lightheaded, laughing and smiling at most of what his friends said.

Both Travis and Jeff sat quietly on their barstools, watching Matt, trying to decide if he was joking or if this was for real. They exchanged glances quickly before Travis asked if he was serious.

Matt put his arm around his brother, smiling the whole time. "It's the girl from California. The one from the last night there. Remember? The one I never told you about."

"Bullshit." Travis smiled, embarrassed, as if Jeff might think that Travis was in on some scandalous secret that Jeff was not privy to.

"Seriously," Matt said. He looked over at Jeff. "Tomorrow. We're going tomorrow, and you're my Best Men."

"You are serious." Jeff said, beginning to smile. From Matt's now straight face, Jeff realized that there was no joking.

Matt nodded his head.

"Well, shit," Jeff said, raising his beer glass high in the air. "You're a stupid-as-fuck idiot, but congratulations." He laughed.

Travis stood from his barstool and walked over to his brother. He hugged Matt tightly, playfully pushing his brother around. "Well, shit, man, it's your bachelor party, then," Travis shouted loudly, so others around might hear. Several people sitting at a table nearby raised a loud cheer and lifted their glasses. "Let's celebrate," Travis shouted, a smile spread wide.

Travis and Jeff met Liz for the first time at the apartment after they finished at the bar. She had been waiting at the apartment for them; it was later than she expected. The three men were all nearly drunk, though they were not as bad as she thought they might be. Liz had seen Matt drunk only twice before, and this was nowhere near what he had been on those other occasions. Both Travis and Jeff introduced themselves, their eyes darting quickly between Liz and the floor. After they shook her hand, there was an awkward silence while everyone tried to find something to say. This didn't last long, though. After an hour, the four of them were spread out on the couch and floor of the studio apartment, sobered up and laughing together. They talked until morning, telling old stories as if they were new. You would have thought them all to be friends who had known each other in a previous life.

The next morning, the four of them drove up to the courthouse in the Corolla. The three men were dressed in black suits while Liz wore a light, cotton, white dress. They walked in and asked where they could find the Justice of the Peace.

An hour and a half later, the four walked out of the building. Matt and Liz held each other's hand while Travis and Jeff followed behind. The two of them looked at each other and shrugged their shoulders and smiled in a mutual thought: "As long as Matt's happy, and he really seems happy for once."

Chapter 14

The stories we tell ourselves to make sense of the past.

Liz once asked Matt what the worst thing he ever saw was. They had been married for a little over a year and a half, having just moved into the house. It was a small place: three bedrooms, two baths, a front family room that connected to a kitchen, and a basement below.

Liz asked him this question as they explored the basement; the previous owners had apparently used the lower level as a storage place, keeping scraps of metal and wood piled high to the ceiling in various corners. Liz and Matt navigated the labyrinth that led through the basement, listening to the scurried scrapes of mouse-feet, chirps of crickets, water running in pipes that seemed to surround them.

They talked about what they could make the basement into: a game room or a gym, an office area, a craftroom for Liz. They laughed at the possibilities, each suggestion crazier and more fantastic than the one previous.

It was dark down there, lit only by a running fluorescent bulb that stretched the length of the ceiling; the bulb cut the room perfectly down the center. The corners of the basement received no light and stayed dark like patches of a different world that surrounded a brightly lit kingdom.

After spending a half hour down there, they made their way back through the mazes toward the stairs that led up to the main room above. Liz turned and sat on the third step, and Matt sat below her. He rubbed his hands over her legs, his palms feeling the roughness of her jeans. Liz reached down and ran her fingers clumsily through his hair, swirling strands of it around her fingers. They were silent as they stared into the cluttered basement.

"Think of being down here with the lights off," Liz said.

"I could go cut them off." Matt looked back at her and smiled. He raised himself up a little, pretending to go flip the light switch.

"Sit down," she said quickly, reaching up to stop him from getting up.

"You aren't afraid of the dark, are you?" Matt asked jokingly. He laughed and then smiled up at her, wanting her to show emotion, show anger or fear, some indication that he was getting to her.

"No. Just afraid of what's in the dark." Liz's voice was sarcastic, an equal to Matt's taunt. She playfully pushed him away from her and he played along, pretending to fall down the stairs, landing with a thud on the floor of the basement. When he climbed back up and sat down again, Liz laughed and brushed the gray dust from his shirt.

They stayed like this for a minute. She was the first to break the silence. "What's the worst thing you've ever seen?" Her voice was calm and distant as if she were speaking to him from another room in the house.

Matt had been working in the hospital for a little while, having graduated just a few months before. And though he was a pediatrician, Liz assumed his answer would come from the hospital, either from school or from work; she could only imagine the pain and suffering and death that he saw in that place. But his answer didn't come from the hospital; instead, he spoke of a time long ago.

"It was 1992, and I just turned eight. My mom was still alive then; it was just a few months before the accident. When she died." Matt shook his head as he said these last words; that was a time and memory he'd tried to forget.

Liz put her hand on his shoulder, though he didn't seem to feel it. He continued on, speaking out to the empty room, his voice quiet and shaking. The words echoed about the place, reaching the far walls before coming back: these words spoken from the past. "We were on summer break from school. I remember that summer—it was the hottest summer they'd ever had in Corvin Valley, a heat storm no one ever saw before. It was also the summer a little girl ran away from home there in town. She was about my age, I think, but I never knew her. I remember how the whole town went out looking for her, we all spread out and walked in a line across town and the woods out there. My mom dragged me and Travis with her to help look for that girl. They never did find her, said she just took off in the heat, but I don't think she could have survived it. It was that bad.

"Anyway, Travis came up to me one morning and asked me to come with him and his friends. He was five or six, I guess. We never spent time together then; I couldn't stand him always bothering everyone. But I went with him that morning; I didn't know what was going on. I still don't know why I even went, but I did. He seemed all excited as we walked into the woods out back of where we lived. It was so hot, even under the shade of all the trees. I remember how we were sweating from it, our shirts all dark with the sweat. I kept asking Travis what was going on, but he was quiet about whatever it was. Wasn't till I got there that I saw what was happening.

"There were four or five other kids Travis's age, all his friends—he always had so many friends—and they were all huddled in a circle, all staring down at something on the ground, but I couldn't see what it was. We went up to the group, pushed a couple of the kids out of the way so we could see it too." Matt took a breath and then turned his head so that he could just see Liz above him on the stairs; her face was serious and focused on his story.

"There on the ground in front of us was a yellow and brown dog. And it was moving and wriggling around, turning over and trying to get up and then falling—barking so loud I thought I'd have to cover my ears. I didn't see it at first, but there was a rope around its neck and one around its back feet; two kids—one on either end of the dog—were holding the ends of the ropes. I remember looking down at this thing, at first excited. I'd never seen a dog this angry or wild before. I thought it would bite one of us, and I remember feeling all this adrenaline from that. But I felt bad for it, too. I knew it was scared, knew it was being tortured by them, but I didn't say anything. God. I didn't do anything." His voice cracked as he said this.

Matt took a deep breath and then shook his head. Liz thought she could hear a deep, pained laugh come from Matt, one mixed with hurt, but she wasn't sure. He sniffed deeply, a loud sound of wet air through his nose and then wiped his face with his shirt sleeve. Liz knew he was crying, something she'd never seen him do.

"After a few minutes of us all standing around the dog, one of the kids, Travis's best friend then, Caleb Rawlings, he pulled out this little steak knife. He told us afterwards that he took it from the dishwasher the night before and hid it under his bed."

Matt turned back to her, his eyes red and wet. "I guess they caught the dog the day before and had it tied to a tree or something through the night. I don't know how it didn't just get away or let go by someone, but it didn't; when they went out there that morning it was still there where they left it, all tied up." He moved away from her a little and put his head down in his hands. He laughed the same pained laugh again. "God, I haven't thought about this in a long time." Lifting his head up, Matt ran his fingers through his hair and took another deep breath.

"But, yeah, so Caleb pulls out this steak knife, and I finally said something then, asked what they were doing. Even though I was older, I was always scared of them, like they thought I was an idiot or something—they treated me like one. I didn't want to be the scared one or get made fun of. But they told me to shut up, a little five-year old saying it, I know. Then Caleb asked if I had ever seen anything die. I told him no. And he said they all wanted to know what happens after you die, that they were gonna kill the dog, watch it die, and then see what happens to it, like if a ghost would come up from it or something like that, I guess. I'd always wondered that too, so I didn't say anything else. I wanted to leave, run home and tell my mom, but I wanted to see it. I don't know.

"Anyway, the two kids with the rope ends backed up a few feet, pulling the ropes tight. All of us around the edges backed up some, and then Caleb took the knife and stabbed it into the dog once. Right in the left side of the thing. He did it quick and then pulled the knife out. There was a little blood on the blade, but I think we were all expecting more.

"The thing let out this sound, like a scream. I don't know how," he trailed off for a second. "It wasn't loud or anything—maybe I just imagined it, I don't know. But it flinched quick and started moving fast, falling over itself. I could see blood start coming out of the gash Caleb made; it was soaking out onto the dog's fur. Caleb dropped the knife and knelt down, and all of us did the same, getting lower in hopes of seeing better what would happen. I watched that thing moving around; I knew it was in pain, that I was watching it die. I wanted to leave, to run away, but I couldn't. I remember crying, and I was worried that the others would see me and make fun of me. But then I looked around and all of them were crying. Even Caleb. I remember him talking quietly, telling the dog to just die.

"After a few minutes of it, the dog finally stopped moving around. It laid down all the way on the hot ground—it was so hot still, hotter than earlier, and sweat kept getting in our eyes. When it laid down, we could still see its breath, but those breaths were getting further and further between, coming shorter and shorter. A little bit later, the dog took one last breath and then it didn't move anymore, didn't breathe anymore." His voice had become a whisper by this point.

"The two kids holding the ropes let go, and we all stayed there for a while, not knowing what to say to each other. Later, as we were walking back home, we all said that we had seen something come out from the dog just after that last breath, but we all knew we were lying, trying to make up for what we did. Try to make it right somehow."

Matt turned his body so that he faced Liz completely. He moved forward on the stair and rested his head against her leg. She gently bunched his hair up in her hand and massaged his head, trying to push the memory away from him.

After a minute or so of him sitting like this, Matt sat up and looked at her.

"I'm sorry," she said. "I didn't mean for you to think about that."

"It's okay. It was a good thing."

"How?"

He smiled sadly. "It was when I saw that dog like that that I knew I wanted to be a doctor. I wished I could have stopped it or fixed it. Wished I could have saved it."

Liz told him that night, after they had sex for the first time in their new house, what the worst thing she ever saw was.

Matt was laying on his back with her head resting on his chest. He could feel her breath against his skin, her hand resting gently on his stomach. They were quiet, lying like that for a long time. Statues in meditation.

Eventually, she asked if he was still awake, and he said he was. Then she told him of when she was nine or ten. She couldn't remember exactly, she said, but she could remember what she was wearing, the temperature outside, the thoughts that ran through her head when she watched it happen.

"I was in a dress; it was light blue and had these random dark blue shapes and lines on it. That was one of the only times I dressed like that—I always wore jeans and a T-shirt, but it was nice every now and then to be dressed all pretty. But I was only wearing it that day because it was picture day at my school." Liz's voice was so calm as she said this, and it made Matt close his eyes and picture this young girl that he did not know—she had no photos from her childhood, no way to show Matt her past: where she came from, who she was. He had to paint these memories of her from his own mind, only relying on the woman he now knew.

"Our neighbor, who lived just a little bit down the road, came to the front door and asked if we'd seen Tony, her son. I had just gotten home from school and my mom was there at home—a day off, or something. My sisters were in their room.

"We told her that we hadn't seen Tony that afternoon. She was about to walk away from the door when I told her he hadn't been at school that day—Tony wasn't in my class, but I knew him from being neighbors and I remembered I hadn't seen him at recess. Mrs. Castillo—that was the neighbors' name—turned back and asked if I was sure. I told her I was, and that was when I saw her face just go white. God . . ." She was quiet for several seconds, and Matt didn't know what to say or do. Then she continued: "She asked my mom if she could use the phone to call the police; my mom said yes but asked what was going on. Mrs. Castillo said that that morning was the first morning she let Tony walk to school. She usually dropped him off, but she had to go into work early and Mr. Castillo was out of town, so she let Tony walk. She thought he was at a friend's house after school, she said.

"After a while of my mom and me sitting at the house, the police came and asked me some questions about when I'd last seen Tony. They asked me again if he was at school, and I told them the answers. I was so scared talking to them. They left, and after a few hours of sitting there with the TV on, I decided to go outside. I could see seven or eight police cars in the street; in the back, along the edge of the lake, were a few cops walking around, and I could see some out on the water in a boat. The sun was almost down, I remember, when I started walking down the street toward the school. The police had blocked off the street. I don't know why there were so many cops there, but it was a small town, so I guess they didn't have anything else to do.

"I'd walked almost to where the street was blocked off when I looked along the side of the road. The street had pine trees on both sides, and I could just see through to where there was a group of cops standing there. They were all next to the old well—the family that owned the land on that side of the street had put a water well in for the horses they owned. God, I can remember them always riding those horses all up and down the streets and in the woods. On the ground, I could see this big bump of something, and I walked through the trees to get closer.

"Then I saw that the bump was Tony. His face was blue, and there were cuts and marks on his face. I couldn't take my eyes off him laying there on the ground like that. He just laid there, not moving. When I first saw him, I relaxed a bit because I thought he was okay, but then I realized he was dead. That was the only dead body I've ever seen. They never found out how he fell into the well there. I don't know."

"My God. I'm so sorry," Matt said quietly. He moved his arm up and down her back.

She readjusted her head on his chest.

"That wasn't the worst part, though. The worst part was when Mrs. Castillo came over. One of the cops had been walking with her from her house, but when she made her way through the trees and saw him there, she started running and screaming. I remember how she tripped and almost fell down as she ran. When she finally got to where Tony was, she fell down on her knees hard next to him, almost like she was sliding on the ground. I think I would have laughed if it was any other time.

"When she got there, the cops moved away a few steps. I watched as she just held Tony's head. She was crying and screaming at the same time, rocking herself back and forth. Back and forth."

Matt felt the tears falling onto his chest and wetting his skin. Then he felt as she took a deep breath.

"But then she started straightening his jacket he had on. She zipped it up, making sure it was straight on him, and she pulled his pants' legs down so his socks wouldn't show. The whole time she was crying so hard.

"After that, she wiped some mud off his face and moved her fingers through his hair, combing it to look nice.

"I don't think I'll ever forget that. It was the worst thing I've ever seen, but also the nicest, most caring thing. There was so much love in that moment. I remember turning and bending down, my back against a tree. I cried so hard with her."

Liz was silent, and Matt wondered if she had fallen asleep, but then she whispered quietly. "I knew my mom would never care about me that much."

Matt moved his fingers slowly through her hair. On his chest, he could feel the warmth of tears as more of them gathered; he moved his hand down, pressing his palm gently against her eyes to brush away the tears away.

He lifted her head with his hands; she turned her body over in the bed so that she could face him. Her eyes were puffy, and he gently kissed her eyelids; then he kissed her on the cheek and moved his way to her lips, kissing her there once more. She laid her head down again on his chest; she could make out his thin face in the darkness, his silhouette black against the bed frame.

Liz closed her eyes, and just before she fell asleep, she heard Matt whisper quietly. "I promise I'll care that much about you. I promise. I'll love you forever and always." And she smiled.

PART 2:
DEATH

Chapter 15

Cut through this land's center. It's my land, and yours. Dissect it from navel to sea. It folds around me, envelops me within its peaks, lowering me to its valley floors. I scuff my knees on rock, slice my hand on glacier. Pour sand on my wounds. Struggle to climb out, find peace within. The basins and streams, the water in rivers wash my dirty feet. These feet have been soiled by mud and shit, the stuff of my past.

You surround me, and I am small. How do I look from up high, where you are? A speck? Smaller? You see me. Am I who you wanted me to be? I can only hope. I miss you too much to think. It's dumb. My love hurts. I didn't know what that meant until you were gone. Is it you, this thing that sits beside me now? I don't know what scares me more: Yes or no.

Matt turns around. His walk is drunken, his eyes filled with tears, the first tears he has cried since before she appeared to him in the kitchen months before. He sees where he is now; he has walked several yards away. The low hills of this place surround him in the far distance. Red hills. They stand guard over him, protecting them both. The truck is where he left it, its door still open from where he staggered out only a minute before.

They are a quarter mile off the interstate. In the distance, the sounds of cars and giant eighteen-wheelers rattle in the late afternoon air. There is no breeze, and the sun is still bright in the western sky, though it is sinking more rapidly now that he's walking around. Soon it will be gone, and the air grows colder with each minute he stands alone.

Above the fading sun, Matt can see darkness edging its way just over the hills that surround this valley. Wiping away the tears that fill his eyes and stain his face, he sees her. Her body is dark in the long-cut shadows that stretch toward him from the surrounding hills and trees, though there is no shadow cast from her body. She watches him wander the dusty parts of this country; he sees this, but he no longer cares. There's little left now.

He falls slowly to his knees. Bringing his head down to the earth, he rocks back and forth, swaying to the turning of this world. Lost. Flowering weeds surround where he kneels, and he can hear the buzzing of bees around him. He tries to shake them away with his head, fling them away with outstretched hands. They bring back the memory, though he does not want to remember, but it is too late. And he cries.

In the darkness of his closed eyes, Matt sees the picture that hangs in the guest bathroom of the house. He remembers the morning he hung it on the wall. That was almost two years ago now, but it seems so much longer ago than that—another life, even.

Matt had tried to be quiet, but the hammering of the nail in the wall echoed through the house and woke Liz. She came in, eyes tired half-closed and puffy, and saw the picture. The T-shirt, one he had kept from high school, stretched down past the gym shorts she slept in. He always loved seeing her in that shirt; it reminded him that she had a past, that she hadn't just dropped out of the sky one day.

The photo was his favorite of hers. He had taken the film strip to a small photography shop in town the day before and had the image enlarged. There, he also bought the large black frame. Matt had wanted it to be a surprise, but she came in just as he was hanging the frame up. He glanced over to see her standing there and then took a step back to look at the mounted photo.

She had stayed nearly an hour in the field the day she took that picture, tilting her camera every which way, trying so hard to capture the right light, to eliminate any shadow. They had picnicked there, on the grassy spot next to the Missouri that they had come to call their own. After eating the packed sandwiches, Matt laid back on the blanket and watched as Liz took her camera and walked out into the knee-high flowers that surrounded them. It wasn't until she had walked out to the middle of the flowers and plants that she saw them all around her.

Large bumblebees hovered in various directions, perching themselves lightly on flowers to drain the nectar before moving on to the next. The low buzzing seemed to come from every direction, and she became lost in that moment. Bees hovered around her arms and legs, at times landing on her skin before setting off in flight again. Hidden on the green leaves, delicate and lucent in the falling sunlight, grasshoppers and brown crickets sat perched. These things remained motionless until she passed by them, as if she held some mystical life-source that brought them back to life.

Liz knelt down with the camera at her eye, focusing on the bees as they set themselves down on the flowers. She took nearly a hundred pictures there, all at different angles, different levels of zoom. After she had the rolls of film developed, she looked through the photos, frowning. With tears in her eyes, Liz told Matt that none of the shots were good, that not one was worth the hour she wasted in the field. Matt could only smile at this; he told her that there were plenty of good shots, but she wouldn't hear him. Liz knew what she thought, what she believed to be truth, and she would not let anyone say otherwise.

She left the pictures on the couch and walked away.

After she left, Matt took the stack and looked through them again, stopping for a long time on one particular photo. It was a simple image: a bee hovering just above a flower; both objects were slightly out of focus; the lighting was dull in that afternoon sunset, and in the back of the photo was a dark shadow that could have been from Liz or a cloud. Matt focused on the picture for several minutes, watching the bee as it seemed to hover in his hands—it seemed so real to him, so unpolished. The thing looked raw and human in some strange way that he couldn't make into words. The beating wings turned a faded yellow in their movement, becoming nearly invisible against the shadowed backdrop; the fine yellow and black hair, tiny in reality was now magnified and given a glossy texture. It reminded him of life, this photo. The bee seemed inviting in some grotesque way. It seemed surreal.

Matt took it from the stack and kept it with him, looking at it on the long days at the hospital, staring at the flower and the bee, remembering Liz in the afternoon glow of that day. He also took the negative film strip, hiding it in the drawer of his desk.

Liz came over to where he stood in the bathroom and looked at the framed photograph on the wall. A smile was on her lips, her eyes wet, though he thought that might have been from sleep still.

"Remember how you thought none of them were good?" He smiled. "Your pictures are good enough to hang on a wall. You just have to look close to see how beautiful they are," he said.

She kissed him then, whispering a quiet thanks as she did so.

When Matt lifts his head from the ground, there is red dust that sticks to his forehead; his tears are turned muddy on his cheeks. The bees still buzz around him, but he no longer tries to fling them away. He wipes his face and stands, sighing heavily as he does so, and begins to walk back to the truck, back to where the phantom of Liz stands waiting for him. There is a sadness to her face, though he does not see this; he is too busy looking at his hands, his palms upturned in front of him. They shake gently, and he cannot control their movements, even when he clenches his fists tightly.

What more is there? If I lay within your arms, will you take me under? He looks quickly at Liz and then back to the ground at his feet. *Are you a memory still? Or not? A polaroid not yet finished developing, with colors coming through still in dark patches so I can just make out a dark form?*

Nearly an hour has passed since he saw the lights flashing brightly behind him, but it seems like seconds ago. Matt's heart beats fast in his chest; his pulse is quick, and his hands are damp from sweat. When he saw the lights in the rearview mirror, he hadn't known what to do. He didn't know how long they'd been behind him. Matt checked his speed and saw that he was just over the limit, and he slowed the truck, the whole time keeping his eyes on the mirror.

For the hour before, his eyes had been growing heavy, the lids closing shut and staying this way longer until he roused himself. The storm had passed a while back, but there was still the smell of it in the air that came whipping in through the half-opened window. The ground was wet, the normally dry dirt of the land now muddy in parts that stretched out to the mountains in the distance. The low, steady rush of the interstate under the tires, the monotonous tune of it played on and on, a lullaby which he could easily have fallen asleep to. And if he were to never awaken from that sleep, he would have been fine with that.

When he saw the lights behind him, Matt glanced quickly over to Liz. She sat there with her attention focused on the side mirror; he could see a look of fear on the side of her face, an expression he'd not seen in a long time—not since she was alive, at least. Matt looked into the rearview mirror and saw the flashing red and blue; the patrol car was still several miles behind him, though it was coming fast. Matt looked back to Liz and then leaned himself over the middle console of the truck, moving his body toward her. In the side mirror, he could see no reflection of Liz, just an empty seat; he could see his face in the corner of the glass and the road and highway behind. He wondered briefly if he was crazy; this thought had been constantly on his mind since she appeared to him in the kitchen all those months ago. He tried to talk himself into his sanity, make himself believe that he wasn't just seeing things, that she was actually there. *Isn't that what crazy people always say, though? They rationalize their delusions?*

Matt's eyes shifted back to the road, moving frequently to the mirror so that he could see the lights growing brighter behind him in the late afternoon. Sweat began to form on his palms—he could feel the slick on the wheel; this only made his grip tighter. His body was now completely awake, alert to the approaching highway patrolman. There were no other cars ahead of him on the road, none behind. Matt slowed the car and wondered how they had found him so quickly; he had assumed it would take a couple days after finding the grave to track him down, and, even then, how would they know he had done it? Or better still, how would they know he was in Utah now? It didn't make much sense, but he continued to slow the truck, directing it to the shoulder of the road. After coming to a stop, Matt put the truck in park. He sat quietly and watched the patrol car come up the highway behind him. His breath came in short spurts, and it hurt to breathe.

After a minute or so, Matt watched as the patrol car raced past him. He hadn't realized until after it drove by that he had been holding his breath for the past several seconds. He now let it out and sat there for a while, his eyes focused ahead of him on the road, watching the other car shrink smaller and smaller, its lights fading in the distance.

He felt like he couldn't move, and so he sat there for a while before putting the truck into drive. But instead of pulling back out onto the interstate, Matt turned the wheel to the right and drove into the open area that existed between the road and the mountains. He could feel his body shaking still; his muscles felt tired, and he wanted to lay down and cry. After a quarter mile or so, Matt put the truck back into park and turned off the engine; he stumbled out of the cab, walking without direction, without thought into the open space before him; the only thing he knew was that he needed to get away. He needed to forget, if only for a moment: forget everything that had happened and everything that still lay ahead. As he walked, he looked at the low mountains before him and the land that stretched out from his feet, and he began to cry. It was the first time he had done so since Liz's funeral, when he found himself under the shade of the tree in the park alone.

Chapter 16

In the beginning, they had arguments and fights just like any other couple, but these problems seemed to become worse and more frequent as time passed.

Early on, they would rebound from whatever it was they fought about, moving past it with smiles and forgiveness. There were times that she would call him names, moments when he said stupidly that he didn't love her. There were times when one or both of them questioned the relationship entirely. When this happened, they would each go their separate ways for a while—sometimes five minutes, other times for a few hours—and then they would come back to each other. They would sit next to the other, trying to be serious, to stay angry, though each argument, each fight, always ended the same way: one of them would look at the other, their faces remaining stern, showing a feigned hurt and hoping that with that face an apology would come, though this never happened. Instead, once they each looked over and saw the other acting the same way, they would fall into laughter. Matt would pull Liz close to him, or she would run her head playfully into his chest, and they would reenact the entire argument again with laughter instead of anger, pointing out the silliness in it all, making fun of each other's reactions, mocking their own part in the battle. At those moments, they would realize that there was no point to staying angry; they found their way past it, looking at the spot of blue sky in the storm.

After two years, though, reality seemed to set in. No longer were they able to simply laugh off the issues that plagued the relationship. Recovery from these upsets began to take longer than before, and there was rarely a day that one of them would not be angry with the other, and those rare days were usually the ones when Matt worked through the night and Liz was left alone, a phone call being their only form of communication for the day.

Many nights, they fell asleep quiet, each facing the opposite direction, sometimes with tears on the pillow, other times in anger. On these nights, there would be no "I love you," no "Goodnight" or "Sleep good," no kiss.

Yet no matter how bad the night before was, no matter how much they might have hated the other only hours earlier, they would each wake up in the morning and look over at the other and smile. They still saw their own happiness in the other. There was still home there. And hope.

Trisha invited Matt and Liz to her wedding. Like their own, Trisha's was a quick engagement, though her wedding took take place at the First Methodist Church in Omaha. Matt remembered going to the church on occasion with her, when Trisha felt a desire to seek faith on random Sunday mornings. Though her parents were devoted to attending every service, Trisha only found it necessary to go to church when she felt particularly lost or guilty.

The first time she and Matt had sex was on a Friday afternoon, and two days later, Trisha dragged Matt to church.

Liz opened the invitation and stuck it on the refrigerator door. She had met Trisha several times at the hospital when she stopped by, but each meeting was only in passing. Matt told her that Trisha had gone to med school and worked at the hospital with him but that she now worked at the county hospital. He hadn't told Liz why Trisha worked at the county now, hadn't said to her that it was so he and Trisha wouldn't have to see each other every day.

With Liz, Matt had carefully kept from her the truth about his past with Trisha. Matt always found it hard, the thought of explaining how he and Trisha had been lovers; he could never find the right words to tell Liz that he had been in a relationship when they first met on that beach. He didn't know the right way to tell Liz that it was not until after he returned home from California with images and memories of her stuck in his mind that Trisha ended the relationship. In truth, Matt thought there would never be a real reason to explain any of that. On the rare occasion that Liz did see Trisha, the former got a strange feeling from the other. A quick hello and goodbye was all Trisha would give—no small talk, no questions or answers, no invitations to parties or lunch. That all seemed strange from a friend of Matt's, though Liz never connected the dots.

Looking at the invitation, Liz thought about how she had never met Derek, the groom-to-be; she wondered if Matt knew him. Liz studied the picture of the smiling couple as she put the magnet against the fridge. Trisha was beautiful, a wide smile with straight, white teeth and deep green-brown eyes. All these seemed in contrast to Liz's simple features, the freckled moles that dotted her neck, the dark brows that arched low over her eyes; Liz had thought all this the first time she met Trisha. She looked at the photo longer, studying the image. She hadn't remembered Trisha's hair being long before, but now the soft blonde hair stretched down her back, just about the length of Liz's hair. In many ways, the strange woman that looked back at her from the photo somehow reminded Liz of herself.

Throughout the day, Liz walked back to the refrigerator and looked at the invitation, wondering why she and Matt would be invited to the wedding of a relative stranger, someone she knew so little about and someone whom Matt had said was only a friend from school, and so Liz decided to ask Matt this later, after he came home.

She forgot all about the invitation, and Matt failed to see it taped to the refrigerator door when he came home. It wasn't until the middle of the night when Liz woke and remembered what she was going to ask him, that she nudged Matt awake and questioned him about how he knew Trisha.

There was a silence, a pause that seemed to last longer than it should have, and Liz wondered if Matt had fallen back asleep. When she asked again, this time in a quieter voice, afraid to wake Matt, he replied with a deep sigh.

"Why?" he asked.

She told him about the wedding.

His first reaction was of surprise. He'd known Trisha was dating one of the other doctors at her hospital, a radiologist he'd met only a couple times, but Matt didn't think the relationship had been anything serious.

Matt rolled over onto his side, facing away from Liz. "I didn't think it was important, but I guess you should know." There was another pause. Then, he said, "We used to date, me and Trisha."

"Oh," Liz said. She was quiet. The air seemed to grow tight around her, like she was caught in some dense fog, and she wondered if she was only dreaming, but the sound of Matt next to her assured Liz that she was awake.

Matt rolled over so that he now faced her. He could hear Liz scratch her head.

"Why didn't you tell me?"

He shut his eyes tight, trying to block away the worry of what was to come. Then he relaxed himself, opening his eyes to the darkness of the room. "I don't know. I didn't want you to be weird about it. It wasn't anything between us."

Matt could hear Liz moving under the covers, kicking them away and freeing herself from their restraint; then he heard the click of the lamp on the bed table next to her. The light made him shut his eyes tight. He was tired and just wanted to sleep, though he knew that wouldn't happen—the night would be long.

Liz was sitting up straight, her legs crossed, Indian-style. She shook her head. "I just don't get it."

"Get what?" He rolled over and squinted his eyes open. Liz looked at him, a disgusted scowl on her face. He couldn't bring himself to try and understand her upset. *It happened, it's over, move on*, he thought.

He sat up, too.

"I couldn't care less about what you did before me, Matt. What? You thought I'd be jealous?"

"I don't know. Maybe." He whispered the words as though it was the first time he had thought of them.

"Well, I'm not, Matt. Shit. But come on, tell me the truth. Don't keep things from me. That's what's pissing me off. You can't keep things from me, especially things like that."

Matt listened to this, shaking his head and rolling his eyes at her as he did so. He could feel the upset building inside him. He wanted to scream out in frustration and anger, smash his hand down on the bed, throw something. Instead, he took a deep breath and told himself over and over to just let it go, that it wasn't worth a fight. At least not this late and especially with how tired he was.

"Whatever. You're right. I'm going to sleep." He laid down again and turned to face away from her. "It's just bullshit," he said under his breath, though she heard him clearly.

"What's bullshit? You lying to me?" Her voice rose loudly to a near yell. There was the beginning of a tremble in it.

He turned back to her. He wanted to throw the pillow across the room, smash it against the wall and knock the frames hanging there to the floor.

"You go whoring yourself around before I meet you, and then you come here and think you can get mad because of one girlfriend I had before I even knew you existed. That's what's bullshit, Liz." His voice was calm, and it surprised him as he said the words. He sat up and waited for the onslaught he knew was coming.

"What the fuck does that mean? Where the hell . . .?" She shook her head violently. "Fuck you. Fuck you." Her voice was at a near scream. She couldn't make sense of what she thought, and the confusion in her words showed this. Tears flowed in tiny streams down her cheeks; her eyes were red, and snot ran from her nose. She choked back sobs and looked away from him.

Matt could only shrug back at her. She looked so ugly when she cried, and he tried to push this thought from his mind. He wanted to focus on something good: her smile, which showed just how beautiful she was.

She continued. "What's that supposed to mean, Matt?" She choked these words out. "I never . . . not once . . . I don't even know what that even means." She grabbed her pillow and hugged it in front of her body, finally burying her face into the cushion of it and letting the cloth take her tears away. More tears came.

"I'm just saying."

She pulled her face away from the pillow. "Saying what? That I'm some slut? A whore? That's what you said. Jesus, what's that that supposed to mean?" She looked over to him; there was a pleading look in her face as if she were being chastised for something she knew she was guilty of but wanted nothing more than the words to stop and the memory to be erased. "You know me, Matt. You know me." She kept repeating those words over and over, growing quieter each time she said them until she let the sobs take over for the words.

"Bullshit," Matt snapped back. He could feel the dormant adrenaline kicking back in. He stood suddenly, pacing back and forth over the carpet. His fists were clenched tight, shaking. "Bullshit, Liz. I don't know shit about you. You don't tell me anything. I don't know who you are or what you want. It's bullshit for me. I go around trying to make you happy, trying to get you what you want, but I barely know what that is. I fucking guess half the time and hope I'm right." He was yelling now, and he could feel his own tears coming, though his tears, he knew, were from rage.

"How am I supposed to know who you are if you don't let me in, Liz? Ever." He continued. "I know you had a shitty home life. Well, guess what? Wake up and see that everyone had a shitty home life. I did. You ever think of that? My mom's dead and my dad's in prison. How's that seem to you? Is my life so perfect? Really? So much better than yours?" He leaned toward her with his arms out to his sides. His breath came in short gasps; it felt as if he had just finished from a long run—a pain had started just above his left eye, and he could feel the muscles and tendons tight on his neck.

Liz had covered her face with the pillow again and was now screaming into it.

"You never tell me what happened after you left home. I can only guess what that was, what you did. And my guesses . . ." Matt sat down on the edge of the bed; he did not look at where she sat. His voice broke more with each word. "They're all so bad, Liz. Those guesses are all so bad." After several seconds, he turned and looked at her. She still hid herself behind the pillow. When he saw this, he found himself wanting to laugh, but he couldn't. Somehow, she looked cute hiding herself in the pillow, like some innocent child, but she wasn't, and he kept reminding himself of that. He wanted to reach out and hold her, to ouch her skin, at least. Matt wanted to look at her and laugh the argument off like they used to, but he knew that wouldn't happen. That time was over. *What's left, then?* he wondered. His voice fell to a soothing tone; there was no more anger, just pain and sadness and worry. "I just want to know who you are, Liz. I just want you to let me in. Please."

Liz dropped the pillow from her hands and looked across the bed at him. He seemed so far away. She wasn't crying anymore, but her eyes and cheeks had grown bright red.

"Let me in," he whispered again. He looked at her, wanting to go over and hold her and tell her he was sorry, that he was an idiot, that it would be okay. But he didn't, and he didn't know if it would. Instead, after a while of looking at her and she at him, Matt stood up and walked out of the room. He shut the door behind him, turning the knob as it closed to make sure that it didn't slam, making sure there wasn't even a sound.

Chapter 17

Matt looks at the map. They are still in Utah, having made their way through two states in the past day. Halfway to the Pacific, almost there. Matt thinks of the places he has seen during these past thirteen hours driving a road that has threaded its way through grasslands and deserts, forests made of trees and greenery with birds and animals lost within.

Arapaho, Routt, White River. These names have passed quickly on signs turned brown from time. These signs continue every few miles, pointing the way west. They mark progress, mark destinations that appear on maps, and he wonders if he will ever know these places or whether they will remain merely signs that faded in the distance behind him as he passed them by.

Time has passed quickly, and Matt finds himself now sitting on the ground; it is still moist from the rainstorm that moved by hours before, though the ground has dried out some. It is a brown and red ground that stains his clothing, but he does not concern himself with this. Before he sat, Matt checked the covers and straps in the bed of the truck. Some of the blankets had pulled free a bit during the drive and were flapping loosely about; he shoved them back down and tied the straps off as best he could. He put his hand on the box underneath the covers for a moment, leaving it there before turning away and sitting down with his back and head propped up against the rear tire. This is how he now sits, looking out at a pair of hawks that circle high in the distance. Beneath them, their shadows play freely on the ground in the dull sunlight. He watches them circle as he sits on the earth, and he falls asleep like this.

When he wakes, it is completely dark. Above him is a new moon, and high clouds block out the stars. He doesn't know how long he has been asleep, but he thinks it cannot have been too long. Behind where he sits, Matt can still hear traffic from the interstate, and these sounds remind him that he is not dreaming anymore. He cannot see her, yet he knows she is there beside him. This gives him comfort, though he wishes that it didn't. He rubs his eyes with the calloused palms of his hands, rubbing life into his body, and he wonders if there is any warmth to her touch now.

When Matt stands, he can feel the tightness of his body. His back is cramped and sore from sitting so long; his legs hurt and his shoulders and arms ache from the night before. He has had plenty of forty-hour days without sleep or much rest, though he has never felt like this before; never in the hospital did he dig a grave and haul a casket from the earth and fit it into a truck-bed or driven for thirteen hours with the fear of being found out. His head is pounding, and he rubs his temples with his thumbs, trying to knead the pain away. Liz used to do this for him while they laid on the couch together, his body covering hers like a blanket, a protection over her legs. He continues to massage his head. If this works, he thinks, then he'll rub the rest of his body with his thumbs. But it doesn't, so he stops.

In the distance out near the low hills that he can barely see, he hears the chatter of some strange animal. It talks in a staccato cackle to the night or to him, maybe. Matt brings his knees closer to his body; from a distance, he looks like a terrified child trying to ball himself up and disappear from the world. A few minutes later, he hears the sound again, though this time it is closer. He imagines the animal's breath on his skin, and he stands quickly, not minding the pain in his body as he does so; the adrenaline begins pumping through him again.

Matt hurries over to the passenger door and throws it open. The light from the cab of the truck shines brightly in the dark, and he turns toward the sound behind him. Just barely can he make out the coyote in the night as it scampers away from him; after several steps, the coyote turns back to face Matt, and he can see the animal's eyes shining brightly in the dark like some otherworldly creature. *Or maybe I'm the one that shouldn't be here. The alien,* he thinks. Matt takes several steps out toward the coyote, toward the glossy eyes that watch his every step; the coyote seems to be studying his movement, sensing his fast heartbeat. After four or five steps, Matt stops and kneels slowly. He watches as the coyote turns in a circle, and then it quickly turns away and runs off into the wild of the place beyond while Matt watches it go.

His body shivers in the cold. There are no trees around, at least none within walking distance. If there were, Matt would gather wood and build a fire, but he has nothing to burn. From the back seat of the truck, Matt takes the two extra blankets he had packed before leaving Omaha—in case one of the covers flies off, he told himself then.

Shutting the door, he carries the two blankets over to where he had been sitting earlier and unrolls one of them. He drops the other on the ground next to the spread blanket. As he sits down, Matt takes the other blanket and wraps it tightly around his body. The fabric takes on his shape, shivering with him. It warms him. He sits this way for a while, his eyes constantly searching the black of the night out there. When he leans back against the truck, Matt feels the bump in his back pocket, the thing's form pushing into his skin uncomfortably. Reaching into the pocket, Matt pulls out the purple cigarette lighter he had gotten for Liz years before. She always kept it in her purse, but after she died, he found it there and carried it with him in his pocket—a constant reminder of Liz. He looks down at it in the darkness and then flicks the wheel, creating a small flame. Inside the cartridge, he can feel that the butane is getting low, but he waves it in front of him, fending off whatever demons are out there in the night. The swaying flame of the thing dances before his eyes. In the faint light he sees Liz; she seems to grow and then shrink in the shadows that play upon her. She is seated beside him, just a foot or two away. He wishes he could bring her close and warm her with his body, make love to her in the clouded night where all is sacred and quiet. But he cannot, and he tries to distract himself of this thought by looking back at the flame that comes steadily from the lighter. The fire that makes him remember her as she was then.

It was her birthday, and they'd been married for just over a year when they went to the concert just outside of Lincoln. The drive had taken an hour and a half, longer than he had expected but not by much, and though on the way there she kept asking excitedly what they were doing, he didn't tell her anything.

Matt had been planning this for weeks, ever since he heard from Sam Henley, one of the R.N.s in the hospital, about the local Tom Petty cover band, The Heart-Achers. "They're so good—sound just like him. You close your eyes, and you can't tell a difference," Henley said. Matt went home and looked on the internet and saw that they were playing near Lincoln the night of Liz's birthday. He quickly bought tickets, hiding the printed pages in his locker at work next to the small picture of the flower and bee.

As they neared the city limits of Lincoln, Matt told Liz to open the glove box. He had cleaned out the contents: a flashlight; the old, coffee-stained owner's manual for the Corolla; registration papers; whatnot. Only two small objects rested inside. She took them out and looked over at Matt. He looked back at the road and smiled as she unwrapped the purple paper that concealed the gifts. The first was a necklace; he had spent nearly two hours looking over the glass counters of three different jewelry stores, starting at the shop he bought the ring from the year before. Reaching above him, Matt turned on the light so she could see the necklace, a white gold heart with diamonds filling the inside of the opening. The heart bowed out wide before coming together at the bottom, and from a distance, it looked to be a thin butterfly.

Liz's eyes stayed fixed on the shining necklace in her hands; she moved her fingers over it slowly, as if testing whether it was real or not. Liz told him later that she had never been given a necklace or earrings before. The engagement ring was the only piece of jewelry she'd ever owned. Matt could only smile sadly when she told him this, thinking quietly how she should have grown up with jewelry and beautiful things. Then he told her that there were plenty more birthdays to celebrate, and before she knew it, she would have an entire collection of gold and diamond things to wear whenever she wanted. After she died, Matt would always think of that empty promise with tears in his eyes.

After hooking the clasp of the necklace and studying it in the small visor-mirror, smiling as she touched it softly as if it would disappear with too much handling, Liz tore the paper from the other gift. She let the purple wrapping drop to the floor. When she finished, she held in her hand a small, purple cigarette lighter. Matt smiled at the confused look on her face and then reached his hand over to where she sat, resting it gently just above her kneecap.

"You'll need that soon."

Ten minutes later, Matt pulled the car into the parking lot of a small club. He paid the attendant and then found a spot.

When they got out of the car, Matt noticed how the necklace glimmered in the distant lights from the club. She walked over and wrapped her arms around him, standing on tip-toes to meet him eye-to-eye.

"Thank you," she whispered, kissing him gently on his lips.

He smiled. "It's not what I was hoping, but you told me you'd never been to a concert before."

She turned quickly to the club as if it was the first time she saw where they were. Then Liz turned back to Matt.

He thought she was disappointed, and he had feared that, but the thought evaporated from his mind as she grabbed hold of his hand and began walking toward the door, tugging hard at him to follow her.

Inside the club, they found themselves ushered into a small entryway of sorts. From a distance came the sounds of house music playing from speakers, the heavy thumping bass rumbling the floors and walls even from the other room.

Matt broke off from Liz and walked over to a small folding table where a fat woman sat with an open moneybox in front of her. She had an AC/DC shirt on and ripped jean pants that showed the bulge of her skin through the frays. When he walked up, she smiled wide, showing two or three missing teeth, but she was friendly and asked what she could do for Matt. Her voice was deep, but there was a weird grandmotherly compassion to her weathered and pocked face.

Matt glanced over the merchandise quickly but immediately saw the T-shirt. It was light blue and felt soft to his touch; on the chest was a large, pressed image of dark clouds that seemed to have a strange glow from a lightning bolt breaking from them; the bolt stretched down to the navel of the shirt. Peeking just above the clouds, an image of a yellow sun could be seen. He picked the shirt up and looked at the image in better light. It seemed so appropriate to him, but he didn't understand why. There was no reason to like the shirt, really, though he found himself smiling as he looked at the image. Before paying the woman, he turned the shirt over and looked at its back: the band's name was printed there.

Liz had just walked inside the other room and was looking at the stage, the small crowd growing around her. Her body swayed rhythmically back and forth, like a gentle breeze was moving her. You would have thought she was caught in the middle of an ocean, gently bobbing this way and that to the sound of the music that came from the speakers in the ceiling and walls above the stage.

Matt walked up behind her and draped the shirt over her face. She turned quickly, pulling it off her head, and looked at it.

"Happy birthday," he said. He smiled. "I'm sorry it's not the real thing here. It's all I could do." He looked away, over to the stage and then continued. "Maybe someday we can see the real Tom for you."

She shook her head quickly and then reached up to him. With both her hands, she moved his face toward her so that she could see him clearly. There was a sad disappointment behind his eyes, and she saw this.

"It's perfect," she said. Her voice seemed far away. She stared at the shirt, studying its image. Looking up at him again, Matt could see that she had tears in her eyes. She smiled. "Everything's perfect."

Matt wakes to the sounds of cars a distance behind him. The blanket is pulled over his head, the earth hard as rock beneath him. He doesn't know what time it is or how long he has been asleep, but judging by the placement of the sun above, it's later than he expects. There's no real rush at this point, though, he thinks.

Rubbing his eyes, he sits up and looks around, trying to survey the place in daylight. The brown-yellow and red ground seems to reflect all of the sun's light, and he has to cover his eyes with his hand while he slowly adjusts to the brightness. Eventually, he is able to see without too much trouble, though he still needs to squint. The headache is still there, but it has diminished in his sleep.

Shaking his head, Matt stands and folds the blankets loosely. His arms and legs feel rested, but his lower back is now sore—the hard ground, he thinks as he stomps loudly on the floor with his shoe—and he cannot move quickly without pain. He tosses the blankets in the back of the truck and then twists his body to loosen his muscles.

Liz stands near the front of the truck, watching his movements and actions silently. Her face carries a look that seems as if she's ushering him onward, though he might be wrong. Matt smiles sadly to her, wondering if he will ever feel comfortable with this silent version of his wife; he catches himself as he thinks this and corrects himself: *This is not my wife.* Yet when he looks back at her and sees the lines of her skin, the freckles in the places Liz had freckles, the movement of her hair in the warm wind that reminds him of that first day on the beach, he cannot be sure what she is or what she is not, and he turns quickly from her.

Matt walks out a distance into the desert landscape. The hills are farther off than he'd thought the night before in the dark. There is no shade in this place. Just dirt and rock and sand and stone.

Off a distance from the truck, Matt kneels and puts his hand to the earth. The ground has dried from the storm the day before so much that you can't even tell it had rained. The sky is clear, and he doubts any more rain will come in. He stands and turns back to the truck and Liz and to the road. Matt remembers the highway patrol from the night before and feels his pulse quicken even in its memory; he wonders why no one has bothered him in the night, why no cop has come to tell him to leave. Maybe this is private land, he thinks. Though there is no such thing as private anymore.

Before heading back to the truck, Matt walks toward the hills but stops after several steps. A small, green plant has made its way through the dried earth with cracks formed around the base of it; the roots of this small thing push up from the surface. It seems out of place, Matt thinks as he looks down at it, but then he realizes that he too is out of place in this land. A short distance from the plant is a small grouping of stones, and he walks over to it. There are twelve smooth stones, none bigger than a fist, all piled on top of one another; they form a small pyramid of sorts and Matt bends down to take a closer look at them. It is not until he reaches out to grab one of the rocks that he realizes why they are here, and he stops himself quickly. He had not seen it until now, but lying just beyond the rocks, having fallen over in a windstorm, is a small cross. It is painted white. Matt pulls his hand away and looks down at the wooden pieces nailed crudely together and feels the hollowness inside of him deepen even more.

"I'm sorry," he quietly whispers and then stands. He turns to begin walking back, but then stops once more and goes back to the rocks. He stands a moment longer in front of the pile of rocks, wondering whose grave this is, how this person died, whether family members ever came to cry and pray over the grave. Who buried this body, stacked these stones, affixed this cross here? Was this person even remembered? *I'm sorry.*

Matt bends down and rights the cross so that it once again stands within the rocks, protecting and signifying the memory of its keep.

Chapter 18

It's not until after driving half an hour on the lonely interstate that Matt realizes he hasn't eaten anything in almost two days. His hands begin to shake as he thinks this; his mouth becomes dry and his stomach starts to cramp. He shakes his head, wishing he hadn't thought of food at all. Can you trick your mind, your body? Lie to it long enough so that it believes you? *How long until you die of starvation? Until you lose control of yourself?* The needle on the fuel gauge flicks just below a quarter tank, and he realizes that he hasn't gotten gas since just outside of Denver.

The clock reads ten to one when Matt sees the station and pulls the truck off the road. He looks at the shack in the middle of nowhere. It looks abandoned sitting in the middle of a red sea of sand and rock and dirt. Next to the pumps is a small building, seeming to be falling apart before Matt's eyes. The attendant waits inside for customers. He is an old man, fat with rolls bunched up under his sweat-soaked collared shirt; his hair is combed over from the right side of his large head, and he sits propped on a highchair. A portable fan is aimed at his sweating face, a magazine in his hands. He whistles a strange tune from some long-ago time.

When Matt walks in to pay for the fill-up, the attendant smiles and thanks Matt, plugging the numbers into the register;

the tray pings loudly open. The old man goes back to the magazine after handing the strip of receipt to Matt, goes back to whistling his nameless tune.

Matt looks at the man, wants to ask where he lives, why he stays in a place so far removed from anything—*What is there to do?* he wonders—but he doesn't say anything. Instead, Matt scans the picked-over shelves of the place; even though he is starving, none of the sweets offered sound satisfying. He'll stop someplace up the road for an actual meal. From the refrigerated case, Matt takes out a water bottle and brings it to the counter, handing over a five-dollar bill.

"I'll get this, too."

The attendant sets the magazine down. "Nothin fer the missus?"

Matt feels his heart drop heavy in his chest. His stomach tightens. "What?"

The attendant glances out the small, dirty window to where the truck is parked. "Oh, never you mind." He smiles, embarrassed. "Jus you, heh? Solo road trip. I see."

Matt looks out to the truck. Liz sits in the front seat, her eyes fixed peacefully on him inside the shack. He looks back to the attendant. "Why'd you think I was here with my wife?"

"Jus saw that," he says, motioning to Matt's ring. "Sumed you was ridin with yer wife is all. And I thought I mighta seen someone else out there with you, but I reckon not. Old age, I s'pose." The man laughs quietly, handing Matt the water bottle.

Matt takes the sweating bottle and turns and walks to the door. He stops when the attendant calls out to him.

"Man can learn a great deal bout hisself on a trip across. You remember that."

Matt nods to the old man.

"You have a good trip, son," the attendant says and then smiles and turns back to his magazine, beginning to whistle the tune again. The air from the fan feels good in the hot day.

Matt drinks the water quickly and then drops the empty bottle on the truck-floor behind him; he looks over to Liz. She stares out the window, watching the road signs pass by in streaks of color. Matt reaches out slowly to touch Liz's arm but stops and pulls it back when he sees Liz turn her head. He keeps his eyes on the road in front of him. From his periphery, he sees Liz turn her head to look at him. He wants to laugh at this child's game he's playing, but he doesn't; when he was younger, he would stare at Travis in the car seat next to him, holding his focus there until Travis turned his head to look at Matt. When Travis did, Matt would turn quickly away from his brother. He would continue doing this until Travis grew angry and told their mother that Matt was bothering him.

They pass a sign that shows a crude image of a plate and fork and spoon. A few miles ahead, Matt exits the freeway and drives over to where he sees a small building; it is still a short distance away.

As soon as he parks the truck, Matt feels his hunger completely set in; he nearly doubles over when he tries to stand, and he hears the low grumbles of his stomach. It takes him a second to catch his breath before he heads inside. On the windows of the place is painted in large flowing script "Stanley's Café," though when he sees the inside, he realizes that it is simply a small, run-down diner.

The air conditioning feels good, though. An older woman in her mid sixties comes out from the back and smiles to him.

"Sit anywhere you want," she calls to him as she grabs a laminated menu and walks his way.

Matt finds a table by the front window and sits. The woman comes over and hands him the menu and a rolled napkin and fork.

"Jus you here, hun?"

Matt nods and orders a glass of water and a soda. He watches the woman walk away. She is thin and seems younger than she looks; Matt wonders if maybe she is younger and just has a weathered look about her face. She has a high perm that bounces from side to side as she walks away to fill his drinks.

When she comes back, she sets the glasses on the table and hands him two straws. He orders a burger and fries and a piece of banana cream pie. She nods and smiles, writing the order down on her pad. When she walks away, he unwraps the straws and begins to drink, first from the water, then from the soda. From across the diner, he studies the waitress as she puts his order in. *Who are you?* he wonders. *What stories do you tell?*

From a back room, a man walks out and makes his way into the kitchen area. Matt wonders if he is Stanley or if Stanley is just some name that an owner came up with years ago. This man is tall and thinner than any man Matt has seen in a long time; what hair he has left is combed back, and there are noticeable streaks of gray in it. His skin looks red and blotchy with age, though Matt cannot tell how old he is.

The waitress walks over to the man and hands him the order. The thin cook takes it and reads it over. Matt watches as the cook makes the food, taking out the hamburger patty and putting it on the grill. The sizzle of the meat sounds from across the old diner, and Matt watches as the cook takes a small basket of frozen fries and sets them in the deep-fry oil. It isn't until the cook turns from the fryer back to the grill that Matt sees that the man has only one hand. The right hand is missing; in its place is a metal hook, though the thin man does not seem to use it for anything in the kitchen.

When Matt turns his attention from the cook, he nearly jumps back in his seat when he sees Liz sitting across from him. She smiles sadly at him, and he turns away, not wanting to see what pain there is written on her face; there is a melancholy that Matt sees only in these quick glances of her.

Matt catches his breath—his heart still beats quickly—and looks around the diner some more, studying his surroundings.

The room is painted a pale yellow that seems darker in the dim light of the place. There are pictures of cars and airplanes framed on the walls throughout the room; many of these frames are tilted crooked, either by accident or by choice: it is too hard to decide, and Matt does not think more on it.

Matt scans the room again and stops when he looks to the far corner. There, in a small, lonely booth, sits a woman, the diner's only other patron. She looks to be in her late fifties or early sixties, he would guess. She wears a gray sweatsuit that looks old and used with thinning material in the knees and underarms. Something had once been written across the chest of the sweatshirt, but it is now faded and flaked, leaving only a light impression that cannot be read; Matt remembers a pharmacy in Corvin Valley that went out of business long before Matt was born—the building stood vacant, though the letters spelling out "Pharmacy" lingered still on the light wood like a tattoo, a ghost impression, an elegy.

The woman wears small glasses on her nose, and she looks over them carefully as she eats her sandwich, dipping the food into a pile of sauce on the plate in front of her before taking each bite. Her hair is short and gray with some white buried within. She looks as if she is a librarian, or once was, and maybe that is so, though where a library could be in a place like this baffles Matt. He turns away and looks at Liz, wondering if she would one day have looked like this woman.

It is not until he looks over at the woman once more that Matt sees that she is wearing large, black headphones. She stares blankly at the empty seat across from her, and her body rocks gently with the music playing through the headphones as if she is covering the sounds of the present with something recorded in the past, escaping the now for a time she can only remember having once existed long ago.

Matt does not know why, but he feels a sadness for this woman, and he turns from her. He wonders if he is not looking at what Liz could have been some day but is instead looking at who he himself could be, or even still, who he is. And this terrifies him.

When the waitress brings his order out, Matt finds that he is no longer thinking of the other woman across the diner but instead on the food.

The first bite seems to relax his muscles. Matt offers Liz a fry, though she only shakes her head. Matt had done this out of habit several times, not realizing until after he offers that she will not eat. *Ghosts don't eat, do they?* He takes another bite and then thinks about the cook and the waitress, wondering who they really are in a deserted place like this. He always took for granted the fact that those people he meets, even if for the briefest of times, live their own lives. They don't just exist in his story, but rather, for them, he is merely a small aspect in theirs.

Matt will not know this, but the waitress's name is Dee. She has known Stanley for years, though she only started working for him seven months ago, when the other waitress moved away and left Stanley with just himself and the young boy Kevin to help out. Kevin was still in school, only working to save for college, so most of the time it was Stanley working alone. That wasn't bad, since few people came to eat at the café. But there were the few regulars who came in for coffee every morning, driving the ten or so miles from the small town southwest of the diner to eat in the comfort of the known.

When Dee came in and asked Stanley if he had any openings for work, Stanley practically jumped at the woman, telling her she was hired before she could finish asking him. She worked most of the shifts with Stanley, who slept on a cot in the back of the diner. He had known she was married, had attended the wedding years before, though when he thinks back to that summer afternoon, he wonders if it was really him there or some other person he's carried the memory of.

It wasn't until she had been working there a few months that Dee told him that her husband Greg had Alzheimer's and that she needed money to pay for his medical bills. They'd sold the house and moved into a double-wide—she still kept a garden out front, but it wasn't the same as the house they came home to after the wedding. Whenever she talked of Greg or the house, Dee smiled and looked straight ahead, no matter who she was talking to or where they were sitting in relation to her. Stanley knew right away the pain that lived just beneath that smile, knowing that each evening she drove home she would cry in memory of the life she once lived, the life she always thought she would continue to live. The realization of a dream destroyed is the hardest of things to forget or forgive, for that matter.

At the beginning, when Greg was just starting to lose his memory of her and of random things in the house—memories she would ask him to recall in what seemed to be a continuous test—Dee would become angry, storming out of the house like an unhappy teen. She'd kneel in her garden until the anger subsided and she was able to make her way back inside to face the man she knew and loved. The man, though, could not remember her.

The double-wide was bare; most of their belongings, photos and decorations were still in boxes from the move. Dee and Greg had three kids—all were grown and with families, all living their own lives, all visiting only once or twice a year.

On good days, Greg would know who Dee was; she would take advantage of these days. The two would sit on the musty smelling couch together, his hand on her leg, and they would talk of the past, for there was no true future to speak of between them, and she knew that the next day she would become a stranger to Greg again.

Their plans of retiring and traveling the country, driving up into Canada, up to the Alaskan wilderness and into the Arctic—where all was white and perfect and untouched—all these plans had been erased when he started forgetting. On the worst of days, she would cover the mirrors for fear that he'd startle himself with his own reflection, though she never knew if that was true.

But in Stanley, Dee found a strange comfort. Most days were slow at the diner, and the two would pass the time talking. He had a habit of telling the same stories over and over again to her, but with each telling, she reacted surprised and interested as if it was the first time hearing them. She couldn't understand what it was about Stanley that attracted her to him: he was completely different from her husband. Where Greg was compassionate and tender, kind to everyone around him, Stanley was abrasive and gruff, saying whatever was on his mind at a passing moment. She did find his comments funny, though he always said them seriously, and he would watch her laugh as if she were speaking a different language, one he was totally disconnected from.

Their relationship matured quickly: by the time they each realized they had one, they had already slept together and were looking forward to the next time it might happen.

It was Dee who first came to Stanley and kissed him. It was just after closing on a Thursday night. He thought she'd already left and had shut himself in his back room at the diner when he heard the soft knock at his door. He opened it to her tearstained face. Stanley took her in his arms gently. When she kissed him on the cheek, he was caught off guard—it was the first time he'd felt a woman's lips on him in nearly ten years—but he pulled her close and kissed her hard on the mouth. A feeling of lightheadedness came over him quickly, and he felt a strange, empty feeling in his stomach, but he continued kissing her.

Afterwards, they lay on his small cot and stared at each other under the harsh light from the naked bulb above. Both felt guilty, though neither admitted it to the other; Dee offered a form of justification by telling of when Greg had almost blown the microwave up when he put the tray of silverware inside and started it. "Thought it was the dishwasher or somethin like that," she said. "But we don't even have a dishwasher in the trailer." She kept the rest of the story from Stanley: since the incident with the silverware and the microwave, Dee disconnected the power in the trailer while she was away at work.

Stanley listened quietly to the tales of her life and then held up both his arms, stretching them into the air above them. He asked if his stump bothered her, and she looked at his arm, the missing hand—he had taken the hook off and left it on the small table across the room—as if for the first time. She shook her head slowly and told him that everyone had something special about them and that this was his special quality.

He nodded. Then he told her how he had been engaged to a girl long ago, before he had ever known Greg or Dee. Her name was Betsy Miller, the girl he loved. They were living in Boston, where they both grew up, and had planned to marry in the fall. But he received his draft card that summer. He asked Betsy to go to the courthouse and marry him before he was deployed, but she shook her head and said she'd wait for him. "Wanted the perfect weddin, she said."

He was away only three months before he was sent back to the states. He carried home with him nightmares of the sounds, the bombs and gunfire, and then the stillness in the air. He carried with him scars all over his body and in his mind and was left with a missing hand. When he came home, he felt incomplete and ruined. Dee asked how, and Stanley turned toward her and frowned. He had not told this story in years and had hoped that in the absence of telling it that it would be made void, cleaned from his past. But the stump of a right hand always served as his reminder that he could not fully erase what had been done. The past has a persistent way of staying around.

"Was a mine," he said. "We were walkin, thinkin we were safe an all. It was quiet, I remember that. Guy next to me dropped somethin from his belt—can't quite member what it was, but it rolled off to the edge of the grass. When he went over to pick it up, he stepped on the mine. I can't hardly remember it. They told me later I was knocked clean over, that I still had a hand when they sent me to the medic, but there was too much metal and stuff in there to save it. They took it from me there, with me layin on that table. Only thing I can remember from that whole thing was the bright lights an the dizziness. They gave me medicine for the pain, but I had to watch them take that saw an slice it off. It still hurts some days, an I still go to hold it or scratch it sometimes but only scratch at the air."

"I'm sorry," she said. "I wouldn't have asked."

"It's life. Got me shrapnel all up into my leg and side, but they were able to take that out pretty much clean, an I got used to livin with it. But my hand, I see it in my dreams, all torn to pieces, an then there they are with that saw again, an I have to live through it all again."

She reached over and put her hand on his stomach, feeling the concave of it.

"When I came home," he continued, "Betsy stayed with me for a while. I wanted to marry her the second I got off that plane, but she kept puttin it off. After a while, I knew what was happenin, knew it was wrong, but I never said a thing about it. Wasn't much of a surprise when I woke up one mornin an she was gone. No note or nothin." He was quiet for several seconds before he broke the silence. "Maybe it's best that way."

He reached over and kissed Dee gently on her cheek and then turned away from her to fall asleep.

Dee let herself out of the diner that night, quietly shutting the door and turning off the lights behind her.

Chapter 19

People live and die. That is the reality of life, and Matt understood this well. In the hospital, he often stopped and looked around him, smelling the congested air and feeling the buzzing excitement of the place. Life was balanced on the edge there: one move and it would fall one way or the other.

For the children Matt worked with in pediatrics, it was not about giving them extra time—he knew the reality of it—it was about giving them time at all. And it was this thought that kept him awake at night. He would wonder what lie it was he lived: doctors didn't cure anything—he understood this more and more with each passing day—instead, it was a doctor's duty to simply postpone the eventual end, though that end was always just a few more breaths away, a couple days in the future, really. It would come, no matter what he did or didn't do. On those sleepless nights, Matt would think back to the beginning—there was a strange comfort in that, and he found it easier to fall sleep after remembering how it all started.

It was the first day of med school. The tiered seating in the auditorium spread up and back from the black lectern—from the bottom, it looked as if the back seats and desks joined with the ceiling.

Matt found a seat and pulled the laptop from his bag. A nervous tightness had invaded his stomach a half hour earlier and had not gone away. He took a drink from the water bottle he brought in to help wash away the feeling, but it didn't work. Sweat from his palms made dark stains on the desk in front of him, and he watched as the ghost handprints evaporated and disappeared. Matt swallowed hard, tasting the bile lodged in his throat, and tried to act like this was just another class, just another first day of school. Around him, the other students were doing the same.

The instructor walked in three minutes late; he was short and had gray hair that just covered the tops of his ears. The moustache above his lips seemed too white to be natural, and Matt found himself staring at it. Until the man's arrival, the auditorium was abuzz with conversation. Matt had made small talk with some of the students around him; they were all first-year students, and they talked about the nervous energy in the room, so real that they could feel on their skin. He looked around at his peers, sizing up the competition. Matt knew he was only there because of the scholarship; only a select group of students received any help, and he knew he couldn't afford jeopardizing the opportunity—no weed in the apartment, nothing like what happened in undergrad that could interfere with school. There were no excuses for him now, no Jeff there to take the blame.

Matt's seat was near the front of the classroom, and he watched as the small instructor with the white moustache walked quietly from the door to the lectern in the front of the classroom. The man's head was bowed as if he was lost deeply in some thought; a bald spot in the center of his head reflected the light from above him. When he reached the podium, the man looked up at the class. A white lab coat covered his whole body, stretching nearly to the ground; only a pair of black shoes poked out from beneath the white gown of the coat.

"Ahh," he said. He smiled, glancing quickly over the rows of students. "There you all are, and here I am. And if you aren't here, then where the hell are you?" He waited for the laughter, which came—the man knew that the laughter only came from nerves and not from any true humor in what he said. "My name is Dr. Brennard. And welcome to Creighton Medical."

A chorus of applause began behind and around Matt; he didn't join in. Instead, he looked down at his hands resting on the keys of the laptop; he could feel the sweat on his palms. He looked up again to the small man in front of him.

Brennard leaned forward on the podium and continued: "I want to tell you a little story. A parable. Jesus was the finest teacher in history, and he taught in parables, so why not learn from the best? Right?" Brennard smiled slyly to the class. He went on, moving away from the podium, walking slowly as he spoke; his hands moved gracefully in front of him as if he was conducting an invisible orchestra that only he could see. "A very nervous man went to a fortune teller and asked the woman there how he would die. The fortune teller looked at the man's palm, consulted her magic ball, glanced at her cards there, and nodded. She looked up at the man and said simply, 'You will be shot.' The man paid the fortune teller, thanking her profusely for this information, and then he left. From that day on, the man avoided any place there might be a gun, whether it was a family member or a friend's house, the man kept away. His eyes searched everywhere he went, looking for someone who might be carrying a gun. One day, several months after the man went to the fortune teller, he got sick. It was a simple bacterial infection, nothing more. The man went to the doctor and was prescribed a dose of antibiotics. The nurse filled the syringe, stuck it in the man's arm, and sent him on his way. But, you see, the needle hadn't been cleaned properly—it was dirty and infected. The man died three mornings later, the whole while cursing the fortune teller for lying. Little did he realize that it indeed was a shot that killed him."

Brennard was silent, letting the story settle upon his audience. Several students chuckled under their breaths at the tale, unsure what the correct response was.

The small instructor smiled. "So," he said. "What does this mean? What does this parable teach you?"

There were no answers from the students.

Brennard stopped walking; his face grew stern. "It means simply that things are not always what you think they are. Now, let's get started."

The early afternoon sun is hot through the windshield, and a glare has formed on the glass, making Matt squint his eyes. Sweat has begun to gather on his forehead, and his eyebrows catch the rolling beads momentarily before letting the sweat fall down his face and gather at the gentle crease of his chin. He wipes the moisture away, though he can do nothing for the wetness of his shirt or the sweat that coats his chest and back.

The air is turned on full blast, but he does not feel it at all; it isn't until he has driven for an hour or so that he decides to save gas and the engine and turn the air down. It's hot either way, he figures, and there's no point risking a breakdown out here.

Ahead on the road is a large truck pulled to the side of the road. Matt slows a little when he sees this and moves into the other lane, away from the shoulder where the parked truck sits. As he passes, he looks over and reads the words on the side of the truck: "Correctional Facility." It isn't until he has passed the truck that he sees the men out in the distance of the valley. They are all dressed alike save for the several men who wear wide-brimmed hats and walk around shouting orders to the workers. These workers each carry a large plastic trash bag and they walk around slowly, shuffling themselves forward in the heat. Every few steps, one or more of the men bend down to pick up trash from the earth and put the garbage in a bag before moving on.

Matt counts these men as he passes. There are fourteen of them; there may be more out there even farther, but he isn't sure. He watches their dark images in the rearview mirror. Then he puts his foot down hard on the gas and feels the engine move into a higher gear. There's hurt in this world, he knows—he's seen it all too well and in all of its different forms. Eventually, though, he will need to face it, but it doesn't feel like the right time now. Behind him, the truck and the workers fade into the past.

They often went down to the Missouri River, Matt and Liz; they'd lay on a blanket under the trees that stretched along the shore and watch fishermen casting out to the middle of the river or kayaks and canoes floating on the water, drifting, it seemed, without any purpose. The two of them would lay cradled within each other's bodies, her body spooned into his. Matt would run his hand up and down her leg, feeling the taut muscles beneath the skin. His hands would creep slowly up to her hips, hard bone there, the softer portions of her middle. Pull her into him to feel her warmth, to transfer her heat. Their heartbeats combined to one sound. *Yours, mine, one, ours.* He breathed the scent that came from her hair—how he'd always loved the smell of her shampoo—and kissed her bare shoulder blade.

Summer evenings there on the banks of the river with bats flying erratically in the skies above them. There would be dozens of them, all moving without sense of direction, though somehow, they knew exactly where they were and where they were going. They would swoop low over the water and maneuver easily around the branches of trees. When Matt and Liz went to the river, she would fall asleep within his hold, and

Matt would marvel at these creatures of the sky, noting how the bats fell like umbrellas caught up in a windstorm, diving quickly only to be returned.

Liz would wake on these nights, the sky dark with night, and they would fold up their blanket and make their way to the car.

One afternoon, Liz woke from her nap while the sun was still setting behind them.

"What was your dad like?" she asked. Her voice sounded low; at first, Matt thought it was only the sound of the water next to them. She repeated the question, this time moving her head toward him as she spoke.

Matt took a deep breath. He hadn't told her of his father, hadn't thought of the man in months, possibly even years.

She turned her upper body fully now so that she could clearly see Matt. He smiled down at her.

"When I was really young, maybe four or five, I can still remember it so clear, my parents would send me to bed. I'd wash up, usually just splash water on my face, and I'd brush my teeth and then get in bed. I'd lay awake there, though. I was always so scared at night—not of monsters or anything like that. Just scared of being in there alone. I wanted that feeling of having someone there next to me. My dad knew it too—this was all before he got sent away—anyways, my dad knew I was scared, even though I never told him. I don't know how he knew, but he did."

Matt looked out at the river, watching it closely and forgetting himself, if only for that moment in time when everything seemed right, like it was meant to be. The water moved slowly that day, and Matt could see the places in the water where bugs had landed or were landing. These skittering things on the surface formed rivulets and rings on the calm surface: tiny wakes formed by some skipping stone thrown by God. He closed his eyes to this thought and continued:

"After a few minutes of me laying awake, listening close to the sounds of my parents in the other room, my dad would come in and lay down next to me in my little bed. My bed was pushed up against the wall, and he would be on the outside so that I was sandwiched in-between him and the wall, protected on all sides in the middle there. He would just lay there quietly, thinking whatever thoughts were in his head. And I felt safe with him there. So safe." He said this quietly to himself.

Liz reached down and placed her hand over his to where he was running his fingers absently over her leg. She smiled sadly for Matt.

"I knew my dad would leave as soon as he thought I was asleep; he'd wait there with me, listening for my breathing to change. But I never wanted him to leave, so I'd wait for a few minutes, the whole room dark and quiet, and then I would ask a question—can't remember now what kinds of questions, but he would do his best to answer whatever I asked. His voice was always so soft, like a whisper. I didn't care what he said, though. I didn't really ever listen to it. I just wanted to hear him talk to me and know that he'd stay longer. I knew that his time in bed next to me would start over when he finished his answer, and he would wait until he knew for sure that I was asleep before he'd leave me there."

Matt hadn't noticed until then that he was crying. The tears fell onto Liz's shirt, soaking into the fabric. He brought his hand up and wiped his eyes.

"Goddamn it," he said.

"It's okay," Liz said, turning. She reached her arm up and circled it around his head, bringing his face to her shoulder. "It's okay. You can cry whenever you need to," she whispered.

He wiped his wet face on the back of her shirt and then lifted his head. Clouds had begun to form in the late sky. He looked up at them and then closed his eyes.

"I think that's what was so hard about what he did. It was just him and me and my brother after my mom died. He left us, and I hated him for it. We needed him so much when she was gone. He'd always been that person laying next to me when I was scared, the one that made sure I was asleep and okay before he left me alone."

Mornings were always the loneliest time of day for Wilson Blaire. He would wake early, usually before his alarm sounded. The room would still be dark with nothing but the sound of insects speaking and night animals moving around outside the window. Wilson would roll over on the small bed he shared with his wife and kiss her on the forehead before getting up for work. At the beginning of their marriage, Linda would wake with him, make him coffee and breakfast, sit with him as he ate, though he told her time and again not to, saying that he'd rather she sleep in for the both of them; after a year or so of this routine, she obliged. Now, she hardly moved when he kissed her good morning and goodbye for the day. Some mornings, she turned away in the opposite direction.

His shift started at six, but he usually got to the elevators by a quarter to the hour.

Wilson would walk up with his thermos full of coffee, which he usually never drank—it had just become a habit to make a pot and keep it warming until Linda woke. In his other hand he carried a piece of dry toast and a small bag; in the bag was his lunch, a turkey sandwich on wheat bread, an apple, and a piece of candy—the lunch never changed, and he never complained about it. In his back pocket were two photos: one of Linda sitting on a rock next to the river and the second was of his two sons, Matthew and Travis.

In Corvin Valley, unless you were one of the special ones to go off to college, you ended up working the mines or, if you were a woman, you found a mineworker and married him, settled down with a small house, picket fence and maybe a dog to run around the yard barking at the lightning bugs at dusk. You found happiness in the small things—you had to. Though he had offers from colleges after high school, Wilson turned them all down his senior year, deciding to stay with Linda and do the work his father and grandfather before him had done. It wasn't anything to be ashamed of, working in the mines.

After long days down there, when he came up the elevator with the other workers of the dayshift and looked into the amber twilight sky, Wilson felt a sense of peace with himself. He loved the feeling of coal, all grimy on his calloused hands. There was something strange and beautiful, looking in the mirror and seeing your face turned a different race down there. Wilson would smile at this new person and wonder at how his teeth turned a more brilliant white from the black face.

He'd come home and say his quick hellos to everyone on his way to the shower, where he would scrub his skin raw with brushes and washcloths he kept in a small caddy inside the shower. The tan of the towels would turn black—Linda would clean them in the morning, hang them outside to dry in the humid air. In the shower, the water beneath him would circle at his feet in a tar-black color that had long since stained the tub. Now a cauldron. The man emerging from the shower was different from the one that entered—he loved this transformation, too. It was said by many people who knew him that Wilson was someone who simply enjoyed being alive; they envied this about him, hated the way he looked at his world, though they loved this about him at the same time.

Down there in the winding cavities of the earth, Wilson could be another person, one different from the caring man he was around his family. In the mines, Wilson would laugh at the jokes the others made, come up with his own, tell stories of pussies and tits he'd seen, tales of nights spent binging on alcohol and the stupid things he'd done while he was drunk.

The others would laugh as they picked the earth apart below its surface; though he didn't know it, they laughed mainly because they knew it all to be fiction—it was a well-known fact that Wilson Blaire had loved only one woman and that he'd never taken a drink in his life. It was something they all admired in him, even the young ones who came in fresh out of high school. Wilson was a friend to everyone down in the mines, even if he gave the others an earful of shit when they didn't pull their weight.

We live by rituals because they give order to a chaotic world, peace to a convoluted life; and the Blaire household was no different. After he showered, Wilson would walk down the stairs and find his family waiting for him. They'd be sitting on the couch, as they were every evening; the television would be off, and Wilson would walk over to them and sit on the other chair that faced the couch. In this way, they would talk of the day. No matter what mood he was in, no matter the soreness of his arms or the pain in his hands, the bruises on his stained fingers, he would smile and listen as each told their day's stories.

When Matthew and Travis were younger, their father would make up tales of dragons and gnomes that lived within the mines. The two boys would come crawling over to where their father sat, moving as close as they could on the carpet floor near his feet. The boys' mouths would be open in awe; behind them, Linda would smile and hold back the sound of laughter. As he told his stories, Wilson would look up at his wife occasionally return Linda's smile, and in those fleeting moments he would think, *If life could just be like this for all time . . .* He could never finish the thought because there was never anything that could compete with those moments.

At night, after he put the boys to sleep, Wilson would crawl into bed with Linda, and they would talk. There was comfort in the other's voice, and they would each listen closely in the dark room for even in the silences there were spoken words of love. When they made love, Linda would pull Wilson tightly to her body, believing if she brought him just a little closer that he would join her flesh completely and they would be the same. After they finished, Linda and Wilson would lay awake and laugh, dreaming up the world that awaited them after the boys were off to college—the things they would do, places they would visit, memories they would make.

But plans only exist to be changed.

Wilson was told by messenger in the shaft one afternoon. It was only an hour or so before his shift was over, but a young guy—one of the new hires—came up to him and tapped him gently on the shoulder. Wilson had to squint to see him and had to bend his head down close so as to hear what was to be told. All the young man said was that Wilson needed to go up, orders from the top.

Wilson nodded and took the elevator up alone, something he'd never done before. When he reached the top, he saw the sun high above him; it was something he wasn't used to seeing during workdays—they took their lunches out there, sure, but other than lunch hour and days off, Wilson didn't know what a sunny afternoon looked like; instead, his days were kept in the darkness of the tunnels, the black of earth and coal surrounding him. That dark was home to him, and he felt comfort in the solitude of it.

Mr. Norrington saw Wilson walk out of the tunnel elevator and headed toward it. Norrington was dressed in a navy suit, and when he came close, Wilson could see the sweat running down the man's face in the humid afternoon. Norrington could barely finish telling him what happened before Wilson took off running over to his truck, throwing the door open hard and driving out of the dirt lot with squealing tires and a revved engine.

He made it to the hospital in time to see her die. Her face had been cleaned of the blood that had been splattered like a Pollock painting, but there were cuts on her face and blood in her hair. Linda held his hand, the black coal staining her newly cleaned, white skin—it was something he would always remember and regret, never forgiving himself for not cleaning up first. Wilson's face was dark except for the streaks of clean on his cheeks from the running tears. He held her hand while the nurses waited outside; there was nothing left to do except make her comfortable and wait for her to go, they said. She smiled at him one last time before she breathed one last time, and then she was gone, her body slowly becoming cold on the table beneath the sheet that no longer served any purpose.

He was told later that night that Linda had been walking across the street to the market, shopping for dinner that night. She had waited for the walk signal, starting across only when she saw the white hieroglyph telling her to cross the road. The car ran the light completely, never once hitting the brakes, they said. He drove off, as if he had simply run through a swarm of flies hovering over the highway. She was nothing more to the driver than that, and it was this thought that devastated Wilson.

On his way home, Wilson drove past the intersection. He slowed briefly and looked over the black asphalt. There were no marks on the road to indicate the man had made any attempt to avoid Linda. Wilson put his foot down on the pedal and drove away from the intersection, wondering how he would tell the boys what had happened; there could be no right way to do it, and Wilson wondered if he should even tell them at all.

The police later told Wilson that the driver had been coming home from a binge at Roy's when he hit her. Wilson shook his head when they told him this; he couldn't understand why she had been walking to the store. Why hadn't she driven? But then he remembered that the battery of her car died the night before—the interior lights were left on overnight, and though he said he would replace the battery, he hadn't had time yet. He never said it aloud, but Wilson always blamed himself for Linda's death. He could never bring himself to remember that it had actually been one of the boys who'd left the light on in the car; an accident he never blamed them for—how could he when they were all he had left?

Corvin Coal gave him two weeks paid time off. It was not until the last day of those two weeks that he went to the jail to see the man who had hit Linda. His name was Johnson. The police arrested the man an hour after the crash parked on the side where he had pulled over and fallen asleep.

When he saw Johnson, who was walked slowly over by two officers to where he sat on a picnic table in the jail yard, Wilson couldn't help but notice how the man moved perfectly fine. He had no injuries; there was no limp to his step, no broken bone. Johnson came up to him, his chin buried in his chest; if Wilson had been looking for it, he would have seen regret and pain in the man's face, but Wilson was not looking. He saw what he wanted, and he knew what needed to be done. There was nothing else to it. The two officers stayed back several feet, letting the two men have their conversation in peace. Both men tried to put themselves in Wilson's place, though the idea of it was simply too much, and they cleared the thought from their minds, thanking God silently for their own lives and luck.

Out there in the open air, the man tried to apologize to Wilson for what had happened; his eyes wandered all around him, from ground to sky, never once looking at Wilson. His words of apology were cut short when Wilson pulled from under his shirt a kitchen knife he had tucked into his pants. Wilson quickly stabbed the knife into the man's neck and then tore it forward in a quick movement. Johnson let out a low gurgling sound as he fell heavily to the ground. The two officers froze momentarily at what had just happened before they ran over to Johnson. As soon as they looked down at the man, they realized he was too far gone. Johnson lay on the ground, the knife sticking strangely from his neck; blood ran onto his hair and down to the dust beneath him where it collected in a warm, shining pool.

Wilson sat down on the ground, his hands clasped over his head. He knew it was over; he had nothing more to give. If there was a heaven, he thought, Linda would be watching him in horror, disgust, sadness. But he had not stopped thinking of doing it since he watched her die in the hospital. As he sat there in the jail yard, rocking his body back and forth, barely feeling the handcuffs being put onto his wrists, Wilson kept waiting for the sense of relief to wash over him. Surely it would come, he thought, but it did not come. And as time passed, he hoped that one day in the future he would find relief—maybe someday.

The boys were taken to their grandmother's house that night. Wilson was tried and found guilty, given life in prison for first degree murder. Despite what Wilson thought, neither Matt nor Travis came to visit him. It wasn't until nearly ten years later that Travis finally came; the two talked and tried to smile, but it was hard to do; they both came to the sad realization that neither man really knew the other and that they never would be given that chance now.

When Wilson asked about Matt, Travis told his father how he was. Then Travis said quietly that Matt wasn't coming to visit and that he doubted Matt ever would.

Chapter 20

Fifteen miles or so southeast of downtown Omaha, the Missouri meets up with the Platte River. From there, these waters snake together in a downward direction, coiling and unspooling along their way until they turn east and become lost in the countryside, hidden among the plains and hills of the place, the valleys of the land—all parts once cut by prehistoric rivers' flowing.

He remembers it all; though years have passed, the memories are clear in his mind. It was springtime then, almost a year since they'd been married. Matt would graduate from Creighton a few weeks later and it was one of the few days he had off at the end of the program. Liz packed sandwiches in a paper bag with fruit and drinks in a small cooler. She and Matt set off, driving south until they reached the Platte and could go no further on the road they took.

After they stopped, Matt and Liz climbed out of the Corolla and into the warm air. It was just past noon, and the sun was high above them with their shadows directly beneath their feet. Liz set the lunch on the hood of the car and then looked down at the water. Though there were trees and other greens lining the riverbank farther down from where they stood, what lay before them now was a nearly barren riverbed. What water there was looked dark and dirty and seemed to move slower than normal, seeping carelessly over brown, sandy earth. Muck floated stagnantly over the water and gathered in small areas so that from a distance these things looked like islands. It all seemed to sit there, awaiting some demon beast to trudge through it.

Matt first heard the sound from where they were, and they followed the noise for a long while, hiking the dusty path, stepping carefully over tree roots that had punched through the earth. Finally, they looked down at where the river was, but instead of water, the area was covered by small moving forms. It wasn't until Liz said it aloud that Matt realized the riverbed was covered by birds: pelicans stopped in their flight north from Mexico and other places south.

Matt and Liz watched from a distance as the birds pecked at the ground, foraging for corn seed, worms, and other food to fatten themselves up on before continuing their journey.

Matt knelt down, never letting his eyes stray from the birds below him; he watched these things intently. Liz sat down on the ground, and a few seconds later he sat next to her. Far off from where they were, a group of the birds set off in flight, lifting high into the noon sky. Matt and Liz watched them pass overhead, turning quickly away from the brightness of the sun; they looked at the ground only to see bright spots in the dark—all remnants of a past vision.

Matt stood, and Liz rested her head steadily on his leg. She smiled, though he did not see this. Instead, he was focused on the birds and their chatter-speech.

"If I die before you, I want you to move on with your life." She said this seemingly from out of the blue.

Matt looked down at her, unsure he had heard her.

Liz continued, not looking up at Matt. "Don't focus on me not being there."

"What?"

She looked up at him. "I'm just saying."

"Why would you say that, though?"

"I don't know," she said, lifting her head from Matt's leg and shrugging. "I'm just watching those birds, and there's so many of them. If one of them dies out there, I can't really see the whole group stopping and worrying about that one. I see them flying off, moving on with themselves." She paused, rolling the words around in her mouth, trying to decide on the right ones. "That's what I want for you."

He shook his head. "No," he said. "And anyways, I'll die before you." He smiled, though there was sadness in it—there could be no happy ending along those lines of thought, and he knew it.

"I hope not."

"Huh?"

"I don't want to think of life without you."

"Even with the tough times?" He smiled. He reached down and ran his fingers through her hair.

She smiled back. "Even with the tough times."

Nodding his head slightly and looking back out to the birds on the river, he spoke. "I don't thank you enough. You know that?" His voice sounded hoarse and tired, but there was something more genuine that came with it, and she could sense this. Liz knew that if ever there were truth in his words, it was now.

"For what?"

He looked down at Liz sitting next to her. Her legs were pulled tight to her body, her knees brought up near her face.

"For who you are," he said. "And for letting me love you."

"You don't have to thank me. I know." She smiled. "Don't worry."

Matt wanted to tell her that he did worry—he worried all the time—but he kept the words to himself. Instead of saying anything, he knelt again so that their heads were nearly level. Then he put his hand on her knee, steadying himself on her.

His legs felt tight from kneeling, but that wasn't the reason he held her leg.

"Forever and always."

He sat down now, moving his body so that his hip rested gently against Liz's. She rested her head on his shoulder, and Matt could feel her hot breath through his shirt sleeve.

"That's how long I'll love you," he said

He remembers this moment often, especially since Liz died. He remembers the sound of the birds out there on the beach below them, the smell of the place, even. Her warmth next to him. Her smile and light, her beauty and love. Her love. Her love for him. The love.

They have reached Arizona now, though the scenery has not changed much from Utah. The occasional gas station and small town made entirely of abandoned, rotting wooden shacks with rusted metal roofing pass quickly in the side windows. These things are snapshots of life in blurred colors, so indistinct that they seem to have never existed at all. Out there, the sky is cloudy, but it does not look as if there will be anymore rain. The window is rolled down half-way, and when he passes semis on the interstate, Matt can smell the exhaust heavy in the air; the smell stings his nose.

As the truck makes its way to the California border, Matt sees oil derricks scattered haphazardly about the desert. He wonders if there is any true organization to it all, any rhyme to their placement, or did some old man in a Western cowboy hat drunkenly point to a spot of baking land and say, "Right there"? Most of these giant metal beasts sit unmoving, though some continue their cyclical rise and fall looking to Matt as if they are otherworldly birds dipping their beaks into the water of the land for drink.

Looking down quickly, he finds the map in the cup-holder and spreads it open on his lap. He traces their route, moving his finger from where they were to where they are now. It is as if they are Dorothy on their way to Oz, following this yellow brick road marked in highlighter lines on the paper. He has checked the mile markers and signs on the road periodically, comparing them to the map. It's not until he drags his finger along the remaining road that he notes how short a distance it is until the end or how far it is that they've already traveled.

He looks up from the map, settling himself into driving the road again. Every now and then, he glances to his left and sees the scenery that runs parallel to the interstate. The mountains and hills have long since passed, though there are at times in this place small plateaus and mesas, and they drive past these parts of the desert quickly and without much notice. The red earth seems to stretch on in each direction here, like an endless sea from which there is no escape. *Why is the earth stained so red? Blood? Burned that way by the sun? Tribal fires?* Matt thinks silently of what the original explorers had thought of this place as they crossed it on foot and on horse. A barren wasteland with nothing to it except the sharp pointed cacti and Joshua trees to provide shade. They must have been terrified then, wondered if they had actually died on their journey and now were in purgatory, or worse.

Matt rolls the window down completely, letting the air rush inside the truck cab. He sticks his arm out into the afternoon and lets the rushing air propel his spread hand up and down like the tail of a plane. The air outside is hot.

A while back when he got out of the truck at a gas station and walked to the small shack building, Matt found himself sweating through the heavy fabric of his T-shirt. It was a different type of hot than Omaha's. This heat seemed to bake your skin from the outside rather than the humid heat he was used to, which roasted you from the inside out. Even though most of it has dried in the air-conditioned truck, he still feels some sweat on his shirt and pants.

Signs for the Grand Canyon pass by on ramshackle signs along the sides of the road. The only parts of these signs he notices, though, are the mileage postings to Los Angeles, the numbers growing lesser with each passing sign.

Just ahead, where the interstate curves gently to the south, Matt can see a small bump in the road. It is not until he gets closer that he can tell what it is: the frame of what had once been a car. Matt slows the truck and pulls to a stop just behind it. The thing is now nothing but a shell of metal, now just an indefinite shape, rotted and rusted from the sand and wind and sun. It is too hard to tell how long it has been out here, how long it has taken to transform from a car into this. Matt can tell from where he sits that it had once been a station wagon, long in the front with a hatchback in the rear.

Matt opens the door slowly and steps out onto the road. He walks up to the frame of the car and places his hands on its top. It had once been a green color, he can now see, but it has since faded to an earthy brownish red. Under his palms, he can feel the parts where paint has scraped off and left only the silver skeleton.

As he runs his hand gently over the frame, Matt looks inside through the shattered windows; glass is strewn across the ground, scattered in a dazzling spray on the torn seat cushions. Inside, there is nothing left. What had been there has either been taken by the owners or stolen by those who came later. Matt wonders why the car is still here, why no one has towed it. How long will it take for the road to claim it completely? Will animals live inside and make it their home, stealing its purpose away in doing so? The tires are nearly gone, the rubber shredded, barely hanging on in the shade of the car's belly, and the metal rims are rusted over and dented.

Matt kneels near the front of the car when a semi-truck flies by behind him; it isn't until the semi is a distance ahead on the road before he feels the warm breeze from its passing, sweeping air upon him, up and into the fading afternoon. Below him, the pavement feels like a hot skillet, even in the shade, and Matt jerks his hand back in surprise at the temperature. When he looks up from the ground, over to the truck where Liz sits waiting for him, he feels the tears running down to his chin.

Standing, Matt takes a deep breath and walks quickly over to the truck. He starts the engine and pulls out onto the road, watching the abandoned car fade into the distance behind. After a while, he can no longer see it in the mirror; it is as if the car had never been there. He tries to make himself look over to Liz—he knows she is watching him, waiting for him to do something, say something—but he cannot. It is still too fresh in his mind—*Will there be a time when it's not?* he wonders. Each thing they pass, each object on this journey, all of it serves only to be a reminder of Liz and the person he used to be.

The three or four months before Liz's death had been the roughest for the two of them. There seemed to be an unsaid disconnect between them. They both felt it, noticed it in the terse conversations that seemed to be their sole communication; Matt and Liz tried hard not to acknowledge these realities in hopes that everything would work itself out in one way or another. During these months, when they saw each other, they would argue, starting usually with some pointless thing—"You said you'd do the laundry; I don't have anything to wear to work"; "I thought you were picking food up on your way home. How'd you forget?"; "I can't stand the way the car shakes when I drive it," "Well, that's not my fault," "I never said it was." And so on.

Many nights found them facing away from each other in bed while they slept; it was as if the mere thought of having the other's sleeping face directed toward them was too much to handle.

There were plenty of good moments during these months, sure, but after she died and he thought back on these few months, Matt always found the good moments few and far between, hard to remember. He would think of her smile, her laugh and the way she made him feel. But these memories never seemed to come from this period in their relationship. That said, the one moment he could still think of with a smile on his face from these three or four months was the afternoon Liz asked to drive to California instead of fly. The road trip would do them good—they both had thought that—and they held fast to that hope, even during the following weeks when things only grew worse.

They hit their lowest point two weeks before she died. It was morning, and Matt had just come home from a long shift at the hospital. He was still in his green scrubs, the soles of his feet sore and raw from the hot shoes he wore at work. Both he and Liz sat at the kitchen table eating frenchtoast that Liz made as a surprise. He'd come home later than she expected that morning and she was running late for work—Liz had gotten the job at the bank because of Matt's constant complaints that she didn't do anything with her time; in truth, she got the job more to pacify him than for her own benefit, though she did enjoy the constant activity and the friends she had already made there, but the job seemed to only put more strain on their already fragile relationship, and though Liz tried to arrange shifts that let her have time off with him, she and Matt often did not see each other for more than an hour or two a day, and most of that time was spent preparing for bed or work.

Liz shoveled the food quickly into her mouth and got up to kiss Matt goodbye. When Matt asked her to stay longer and spend time with him—"Call in sick," he said—she frowned and tilted her head slightly to the side.

"You wanted me to get a job," she said. "And I get one, and now you complain that I shouldn't be working." She smiled and laughed as only a person frustrated to tears can. "I don't get it, Matt. There's no pleasing you. Ever." She snorted angrily, some mixture of laugh and sigh.

Matt threw his fork onto the table, letting it fall to the floor loudly. The fork cut a gouge into the wood tabletop. He often looked back on that gouge later and felt a sense of loss and desperation, wishing so desperately to take it all back. That morning was one of the few times in his life he wanted so badly to fix, if a time and situation could be fixed like a stalled watch or a broken radio.

Matt watched the fork fall to the floor after it careened off the table, but he didn't care in that moment. "I can't keep doing this shit, Liz." He pushed the plate away from him violently, covering the gouge in the table with the uneaten food. "Why should we even be doing this? We never see each other. It's like we don't even live together. I just . . . I just don't even know why we still do it. Why?" His voice had risen to a shout that seemed to soak into the walls, stay there trapped, awaiting its release at some distant time when the world was calmer.

Liz had grown angry as he spoke, and she looked away from him, feeling her hands grip tightly into a fist around the keys in her hand. When she finally turned back to him, Matt could see that there wasn't any expression to her face. It was blank, unreadable. And this scared him; he hadn't seen her like this before.

"Then we shouldn't," she said.

"What?" He hadn't expected agreement—that had never come before; she normally looked at him and begged him to take back what he said, forcefully telling him that he was wrong. But not this time; this time there was a strange power of acceptance on her face, and he didn't know what to say to her.

She shook her head. "Jesus, Matt. What the hell do you want me to say? To say your wrong? I've tried that. You want me to agree with you? Either way, it's the wrong answer." She turned away from him, grabbing her purse from where it rested on the small pass-counter by the front door.

Matt stood silently, feeling his chest tighten. The anger welled up inside him. "Then we're done, Liz. Fuck. I try to do everything for you. I try to . . ."

Liz turned sharply to face him; her heels scraped loud against the hard kitchen flooring. "Don't you do that. Don't make yourself out as Mr. In-the-Right and put all the rest of the shit on me. It's not fair, Matt. You always do that to me." She began to cry, her face now smeared with mascara and blush that ran together over the soft lines of her face like tribal warpaint.

Finally, after several silent seconds between them, Liz shrugged. Matt saw his failure in the movement, a forfeiting on her side in the rise and fall of those shoulders. "I don't know how to make you happy, Matt." She bit her lip, trying to hide back the sobs that were rising from her chest; she looked away from him, as if the sight of Matt would only bring more pain. She breathed deeply, composing herself as best she could. "I told you before that the only thing I want to do is make people happy, but I can't make you happy." She raised her arms up in a sign of defeat. "What good am I, then? You say it's over? Then let it be if that's what you want." Liz was about to turn and leave but she caught herself and stopped. She looked directly at Matt, looked at the sad and scared boy that stood awkwardly before her; she wanted to smile at this boy, to tell him she loved him so much it hurt, but she could not say these things. Not now, at least. Instead, she simply whispered. "You're still the one I think of when I sleep, the one I want to hold when I have nightmares."

Matt took a step toward her but stopped when she put her hand out.

"Just don't. You can't do that. You can't apologize and think it's all right. We're screwing up too much for it to keep going like this. You're right."

Liz hung her head low for a second, her chin almost resting on her chest. In her hands, she moved the keys around. The jangling sound of the metal was the only thing either could hear for a second. With the back of her hand, she dried her eyes and then looked at him.

"If it really is over, then why go on the trip? Why try to spend time with me or try to fix us?"

She turned and opened the door. Just before she walked out, she took a deep breath and said quietly, "Why don't we just get a divorce then, if that's what you want." She walked through the door, not bothering to close it behind her; she was afraid that if it shut then that would signal the closing of her and Matt. While she walked to her car, Liz hoped that Matt would come running behind her, stop her in the driveway and kiss her like she'd seen so many times in movies. But he didn't. When she drove off, the door was still open, and she could see Matt still standing inside. He had made his decision, Liz thought as she drove off.

They didn't say much to each other after the fight that morning. What was there they could say? It wasn't until three days later that Matt woke Liz in the middle of the night when he came home from his shift. Usually when he came back that late he would sleep on the couch, not wanting to wake her. But that night he needed to talk to her.

The previous three days had passed slowly for Matt, and he wondered if it was the same for Liz. They had hardly seen each other during those days, and when they were home together, they each found themselves secluded to opposite sides of the house from each other.

Liz woke sleepily, squinting in the bright light from the bedside lamp. She saw Matt's face close to hers, dark with shadows, and she pulled back quickly, not sure if she was dreaming or if this was real. After a second, she found her bearings and relaxed, though her heart still beat heavily in her chest.

Matt slowly brushed the tangled hair away from her eyes. "You're right," he said quietly. He was kneeling by the side of the bed, wearing a sweatshirt and shorts—what he changed into from his scrubs at the hospital. "I'm sorry. I know I say it a lot, but I am." Tears began to roll down his cheeks, but Liz didn't move. She watched him silently from the bed, not reaching out to touch him, not wanting to help him let the emotions pass—she would have done this a year earlier, but there was so much unknown now. She had gone to bed each night since the fight wondering how happiness could fade away so quickly, so unannounced. Surely there was some clear signal she missed, something to have prepared her for the feelings she now had. During the past three days, Liz found herself constantly thinking back on the times when she was happiest with Matt; she found herself now questioning those times, wondering if they had actually existed or if she'd simply remembered those moments wrong, remembered them only as she wanted those times to have been.

"I love you," he said. Matt moved his fingers through her hair, and Liz found her eyes growing heavier with the gentle massage. "I don't know why it's gotten so bad with us. I don't know. But I want to fix it. We need to fix it. I told you that I'd love you forever and always, and I will. I promise. But only if you let me." Matt wiped his eyes and then shook his head; a pained smile spread on his face. "I fucked up, Liz. I did. I let it all get to be too much: the hospital, the hours, the money, your job. I forgot us in it all. And I think we both did."

Liz nodded. She sat up and leaned the back of her head against the wood bedframe.

Matt continued. "I told them I needed to cut back on hours. I told them I wouldn't pick up any extra shifts, at least for a while."

"But we need the money."

"Screw the money. We need us." Matt set his hand on top of hers and squeezed gently. The muscles were small, the bones fragile within her skin. The feeling of her body always comforted him. Nothing had changed with that feeling, he thought as she turned her hand over and locked her fingers within his. "I forgot that," he said with the traces of a smile on his face. "But you helped me see it. Please don't let my mistake ruin something right and good. Please."

Matt stood and wiped his face with the bottom of his shirt. He had thought of bending down and kissing her forehead but thought better of it and turned to leave. He was stopped by Liz, though, who grabbed hold of his sweatshirt and tugged him toward her. She stood, still holding the fabric of his sweatshirt, and buried her face into his chest. Inside his body, she could hear the beating of his heart; it sounded loudly against her ear, as if it was trying to escape and make its way to her.

Matt wrapped Liz in his arms, and they stayed like this for a long time, swaying gently in the dark of the room. They held each other tightly, afraid to let go.

Chapter 21

When Trisha came home from work one night, she found the house abandoned. She'd planned to go out to dinner with Derek to celebrate their anniversary from the week before—Derek had been in Europe on business and told her over the phone that they'd celebrate when he got back home. She walked up the winding stairs to their bedroom and found all of Derek's clothes gone. The same went for his laptop, checkbooks, and files from the study.

Trisha thought they had been getting better since she found out about his late-night affairs at the office and told him that she knew everything; Derek had broken down in tears then and told her he'd stop, that he was sorry.

Though she'd known about the affairs for several weeks, hearing it in whispers at parties and gatherings with his coworkers, Trisha hadn't said anything to him about it. But when she walked in on Derek in the study with his phone in one hand and his pants at his ankles, she found herself in the middle of a situation that there was no getting out of—she couldn't just deny that it had happened.

After a long night of tears and apologies, Derek bought Trisha a diamond necklace. He gave it to her in a small box and told her silently, with his eyes staring sheepishly at the ground, that he had an addiction and he wanted it to stop but that he didn't know how to make it go away. He was willing, he said, to do whatever it took, and Trisha believed him.

The next morning, she scheduled Derek a session with Dr. Milner at the hospital, a psychiatrist she had gone to school with at Creighton. He was now practicing privately, but he agreed to see Derek immediately.

Derek went to Milner for a month, meeting for two sessions a week with the psychiatrist. Trisha thought things were better until she came home that afternoon and found Derek's belongings cleaned out of the house. Except for the photos left of the two of them, she would never have known Derek ever lived there. Trisha called Derek's cell. When he picked up, she could hear a scuffled sound in the background, whispered voices and music. It was hard to understand, but she was able to clearly make out what he said: "We're done, Trish. There's nothing for me with you." Then he hung up.

Trisha let the phone drop and sat on the couch and cried herself to sleep. Just before she let herself drift off, she remembered back to when she was younger, how she had fallen asleep so many times in the same way, with tears drying on her cheeks and pillow. She wondered if this was her fate, if she was simply destined to always be alone, and she closed her eyes tightly to this thought until the darkness of sleep came over her.

Matt and Liz were supposed to leave for California the next morning, their anniversary being two days away. It was as if a new leaf had been turned for them after the night they held each other in their arms and cried together. Liz didn't know how long they had stayed that way, but however long it was, it seemed to have made all the difference. That night had been nearly two weeks earlier. Since then, Matt's schedule had become lighter, and she now saw him most evenings; he went into the hospital in the middle of the night and stayed usually until three or four in the afternoon. They still had a distance to go before things would return to how they had been at the beginning, but she saw that life was headed in the right direction. Memories of the two of them flooded her mind as she drove home; she knew her news would only help strengthen them.

Liz had told Matt that she'd be working that afternoon—she wanted to keep everything as much a surprise as it could be. That morning, she told him that she wouldn't be home until after five. It was only three now, and Matt would still be at the hospital—he was working a longer shift since he would be gone on the trip for the next week and a half.

Liz pulled onto their street from the main road. She looked at the passing front lawns, the children home on summer break, all of them playing under the humid sun.

Their house was the sixth on the right, and she slowed as she neared it. Matt's Corolla was in the driveway and parked on the street in front of the house was another car, one she'd never seen before. She couldn't understand why Matt would be home already. She pulled to a stop behind the strange car and sat in the heat for a while. After several minutes of sitting there, sweat began to bead up and roll down her back; this feeling made her finally get out of the car. The warm breeze was a cool relief on her body. She walked past the other car and looked in the windows; the interior was clean, though there were several magazines scattered on the passenger seat: *Us Weekly*, *People*, a few others she couldn't see the names of. Liz assumed the car belonged to someone visiting one of the neighbors and tried not to think anything else of it. Her mind, instead, turned again to what Matt could be doing home already. He told her the night before that he wasn't supposed to be off work until six.

She thought about calling him, checking first to make sure everything was okay, but she decided to just go into the house and surprise him. As she walked up to the front door, Liz thought of the clothes she still needed to pack: beach towels, underwear, shorts and some tank tops, the new bathing suit she had just bought the week before. Liz smiled, but her smile faded quickly when she neared the front and looked through the French windows just to the side of the door. The windows looked in on a sitting room, and inside the room, she could clearly see Matt. Liz hid behind an overgrown bush in front of the window and watched as he stood and walked away from the window; she could tell by the way he moved his hands that he was talking, though she could not tell who he was talking to. She noticed from his hand movements that he wasn't talking on the phone—someone else was in the room with him. Liz stood a little higher, peeking just above the bush. Then she saw that someone was sitting on the chair past where Matt stood, but he was blocking this person from her view.

Liz crouched down again, feeling herself silly for creeping around her own house, spying on her own husband. She looked around the neighborhood with a worried smile on her face. Then she turned back to the room. A long minute or two passed as she watched the happenings inside; it wasn't until Matt began to pace back and forth across the room, his hands working even more excitedly in front of him, that Liz saw that the person in the room was Trisha. Though the woman's head was down, her face cradled in her hands, Liz could make out the long blonde hair and thin body frame from the wedding the year before. When she realized it was Trisha, Liz's heart sank in her chest. A beating began in her head, and she felt herself growing dizzy. She reached her hand down to the cement walkway to steady herself as she kept watching the two inside.

After several seconds, Matt stopped pacing and walked over to where Trisha sat. He knelt down and put his hand gently on her knee. Outside, Liz began to breath hard, feeling herself choking back the tears she knew were coming. A feeling of nausea grew in her stomach, and she wondered if she was going to throw up. But she kept watching, afraid of what she might see next. Trisha lifted her head and looked at Matt; there was a smile on her face, though Liz could not tell what type of smile it was—a guilty smile, perhaps? Then, seemingly without warning, Trisha leaned forward and kissed Matt; she reached out with her hands and held Matt's head in place, her thumb gently rubbing the soft part of his ear. Liz let out a slight cry and stood quickly. She turned and felt lightheaded as she walked quickly down the pathway and over to her car. Her headache seemed to grow more intense with a focus just above her eye. Tears fell heavily from her cheeks and landed on her arms, legs, and the ground beneath her, leaving a thin and spotted trail of her passage.

As she was about to open the door and get into the car, Liz closed her eyes, letting the dizziness pass. A breeze swept itself around her, tossing her dark hair into the sky freely. She tilted her head and listened to the wind; she needed to hear those words of comfort from all those years before: she needed to hear the wind tell her good morning, that she was dreaming and that when she woke, everything would be normal. But she could hear nothing in the wind, and when she did open her eyes, she felt as if nothing in the world would ever be right again.

Her arms and legs felt heavy and tired as she started the engine and drove away. She didn't know where she was driving to, could barely see through the wet of the tears in her eyes, but she drove.

The car moved quickly down the block past the children all at play.

Matt had told them at the hospital weeks ago that he was leaving early on Friday for his trip. They all wished him a happy vacation before he left, the kids in the rooms smiling as he told them he would see them in a week. Several of the children drew him pictures in crayon of a stick man standing in the middle of a blue ocean—he took these drawings home with him, planning to show them to Liz once they reached California.

That Friday, on his way home, Matt stopped at a flower shop and picked out two dozen roses and a dozen tulips. At the market, he bought a ready-to-cook chicken and a bottle of red wine.

Once he got home, Matt looked at the clock and saw that it was only a quarter to three—he still had over two hours before Liz would be home from work. He put the chicken in the refrigerator and set a timer so that he knew when to put the meat in the oven; then he took the flowers to the bedroom. He laid one of the dozen roses and the tulips on the bed and took the petals off the other roses and dropped them on the carpet so that the petals led from the hallway into the bedroom. He smiled when he saw the unfolded laundry laying in a heap at the bottom of the bed; he was about to fold the clothes but decided to do it later. Instead, he went into the closet and took out the large suitcase and began to fill it with clothes for the trip.

The suitcase was nearly full when he heard the doorbell. He went to the front, careful not to disturb the petals on the ground. Trisha looked up at him from the other side of the door. It was clear that she'd been crying; her eyes were wet, her cheeks flushed. He felt his body go cold when he saw her.

"I'm sorry, Matt," she said. "I didn't know where else to go."

He let her in and asked if she wanted anything to drink. She said no, and he told her to sit on the chair. Looking down at his watch, he saw that it was just after three o'clock. As he looked over at Trisha sitting on the couch, he couldn't help but wonder what he was supposed to do and say in a situation like this. He thought of calling Liz and asking her advice, but he tossed that from his mind when Trisha started talking.

She told him about everything that had happened in the past month: her and Derek's fights, what she found him doing in the study, the therapy sessions with Dr. Milner, and the phone call from Derek. It had been a week since he'd left, but she hadn't been able to get over his disappearance. Besides the call, Trisha hadn't talked to Derek at all in the past week. She didn't know what to do or where to go. Her parents were vacationing in Spain for the summer, and she told Matt that she'd gotten in the car and just driven, not fully realizing that she was driving to his house. She apologized for everything. The entire time she said this, Trisha stared at the carpet in front of her, her hands holding her hair back, hiding her face.

Matt listened closely, feeling a strange compassion for Trisha as she told him of her recent life. He paced the room, not knowing what to tell her, whether to say that he and Liz had been going through bad times, too, but that they were in the process of working things out and that the same could be true for her and Derek. He didn't believe that to be true, though. Derek sounded like an asshole and there was no excuse Matt could think of that allowed for anything Derek did to be viewed as acceptable. He ran over the scenario again with Trisha, repeating what she had said, letting her nod her head in approval with everything he listed. His hands moved violently in front of him as he spoke, and he felt himself getting angry at Derek. Instead of giving her advice, Matt stopped pacing and made his way over to where Trisha sat. He knelt down and put his hand gently on her knee and smiled, though he felt himself forcing the smile, and he hoped she wouldn't look up and see the lie in it.

"It's gonna be okay. I promise," he whispered. "I'm so sorry for everything, but you are beautiful and so damn smart.

And if Derek can't see that, then he's a fucking idiot, and you don't need him. Okay? And you know that. Right?"

Trisha lifted her head to look at him. She smiled, laughing quietly at what he said—there were still tears in the laugh, though it felt good to laugh and smile again. She always had felt comfortable with Matt; he always made her feel special, even at the end of their relationship. She leaned in then and kissed Matt, placing her hands on either side of his head. She didn't know she was going to do it until she found her lips on his, her eyes closed tightly in a kind of prayer of hope. Trisha had felt a long-dormant passion stirring within her as she looked at him, though the feeling left quickly as Matt pulled his head away from her. The kiss was momentary, fleeting like a flash of lightning in the sky of her heart. She knew it was wrong, that she shouldn't have kissed him, and Matt's reaction assured her of these feelings.

"I'm sorry. I can't," he said, standing.

"Oh, God," she whispered. "I'm sorry. Matt, I'm so sorry." She buried her face in her hands again, shaking her head and feeling the tears begin once more. "I don't know what I'm doing."

Matt looked down at her. He didn't know what to say, though in a strange way, he was happy she kissed him—he felt no excitement or joy in the kiss; his only thought the whole time was that he missed Liz and couldn't wait to hold her in his arms again.

He smiled sadly at these thoughts and then whispered quietly to Trisha: "It'll be okay. I don't know how. I know it doesn't feel like it, but I promise it will."

Chapter 22

It wasn't until after six that Matt found out what happened. From five o'clock on, he called Liz's cell phone over and over, hanging up when he heard her voicemail pick up and then trying again. Eventually, Matt dialed her work. Though the bank had been closed for nearly an hour, he figured there was no harm in trying—maybe a manager was still there, someone working late. Anyone. But no one answered, and he began calling Liz's cell again.

Trisha had left hours ago. He'd given her a heartfelt and long hug and then she left, thanking him for listening and caring. She apologized over and over for coming over, but Matt only smiled and turned away from her slightly, laughing uncomfortably and telling her to call if she needed anything else.

The timer for the chicken had gone off a half hour before he heard his cell phone ring; the cooked bird now sat on the stovetop, cold now. Matt had already played through the different possibilities in his mind, from accident to affair, though he assured himself that Liz would never be caught up in the latter—he only thought that because he still had Trisha's voice and story echoing in his mind. He and Liz were on the right track again; he continued to tell himself this over and over, at times speaking the words out loud to the empty house.

There was a sense of hope in the words, the sound they made off the tall, white walls, the soft sofa, the other memories that floated invisibly around him.

Love is strange in the fact that you can fall out of love with a person and then, for seemingly no reason, you can fall back in love with them. Since the night they held each other, Matt found himself looking forward to his time with Liz, even if it meant sitting on the couch with her legs draped over his. He hadn't felt this way about Liz in months, maybe longer, he thought. Things felt good again, like everything was how it was supposed to be. At work, Matt constantly found himself moving into the On-Call Room and dialing her number on his cell, just wanting to hear her voice and thinking of the feel of her skin.

The clock on the stove read 6:15. He thought about driving around the streets looking for her, but he didn't for fear that she'd come home just when he left and they would play a strange musical chairs game of sorts.

When the call did come, Matt flipped open his phone without looking at who was calling, assuming that it was Liz.

"Where are you?" he asked quickly. "Are you okay?"

"Matt?" The voice on the other end wasn't Liz's. His chest tightened. He knew the voice from somewhere, but he couldn't place it. "Matt? It's Mary, from the hospital."

Matt put his hand on the counter to balance himself. He didn't hear the rest of what Mary said. He knew already.

Matt ran through the hospital parking lot, stumbling over his feet as he went. His legs felt heavy and tired, his breath shallow in his chest. Though his legs kept pumping him forward, the hospital seemed so far away, and it felt as if he would never reach it. He nearly fell as he made his way to the front entrance. Passing by an ambulance, he looked inside the open back doors, fearing he would see someone—not just Liz, but anyone—he knew there, though there was no one inside. Sweat ran down his face and down his neck. He burst through the door, not waiting for the mechanical one to slide open for him.

Mary sat behind the circular desk. There was a short line of people, most of them elderly, all standing in front of where Mary sat, but when she saw Matt, she stood and came out from behind the desk, excusing herself to the people still waiting in line; her pink scrubs seemed out of place in the drab, large room, though Matt didn't think that anything made sense at that point.

"Where is she?" he asked. His voice shook.

She led Matt through the swinging doors toward the ICU, trying to fill him in with the little she knew, but her voice was rushed, and he could barely understand what she was saying. From the corner of his eye, Matt could see Mary's necklace, the large, gold cross of it, bouncing up and down as she walked.

"They said there was a fire, Matt. Her car went off the road and then it the fire started. I don't know. I don't know. My God, I'm so sorry. I'm sorry, Matt. I was taking charts back here when they brought her in. The police, they didn't even know who she was. Said her ID was in the car, but I knew it was her when I saw her face. Oh, my God." She took several deep breaths as they neared the swinging doors that led to the operating rooms. "They took her here from Emergency."

"How long ago?" he asked.

Neither slowed their pace.

"I don't know. Not much before I called you."

He nodded and quickened to a full jog as he moved through the doors. Mary stopped walking and watched Matt disappear into the cool hallways beyond the doors. She put her hands on the top of her head and turned around, looking at the area as if it was the first time she'd seen it.

When Dr. Hilston saw Matt making his way down the hall, his face red and puffy, wet from tears and mucus, he stopped Matt.

"Matt," the man said, forcefully. "Matt, stop. Stop."

Matt fought Hilston, trying to shove his way through the one-man blockade, but he felt as if he had no strength left in his arms. It felt as if there were a dozen arms holding him back, his body paralyzed and raw. Exposed. He could feel his chin quivering, a feeling of hopelessness he'd never remembered before.

Matt knew there was nothing more to be done when Hilston wrapped his arms around Matt and held him tight. Matt had seen this so many times, been part of it before—the doctor trying to calm the frantic husband while the wife lay dead in a room just yards away—though never from this side.

"Where is she, Terry? Jesus. Terry. Where is she?" The words spewed out in a frantic gibberish. Matt's voice searched for some meaning he knew didn't exist in that moment, an answer he knew he would never be given.

"Matt. You need to relax yourself. Come on." The doctor's voice was soothing. Matt had always liked Terry Hilston; he'd been one of the few doctors who smiled and welcomed Matt to the hospital when he was still in school doing rounds with his class. Hilston was a large bear of a man with a thick, gray beard that he'd cut into a box on his chin; so many of the students had made fun of it, but Matt always went out of his way to nod hello to the doctor and shake the man's hand when he could. But now Matt hated him, felt as if Hilston was the only thing keeping him from Liz.

Matt sunk slowly to his knees and found himself sitting on the cold floor of the hallway. Hilston sat down beside him. Below his breath, Matt kept repeating the same word over and over through the broken sobs, and Hilston had to lean close to

Matt to understand what he was saying. Just the word "No" repeated again and again. "No, no, no, no."

They stayed that way for a long time, two men sitting in the middle of a bright hallway. Though no one walked by, no wheeled tables or chairs moved past them, you would have gotten a sense that had there been anyone, these people and these things would have found some other route to their destination, as there is nothing more powerful than a man broken, nothing more quieting than someone giving the consolation that is so desperately needed.

Hilston rested his hand on Matt's back like a father might; the latter hung his head between his knees, letting the tears and saliva fall into a puddle beneath him. He felt cold, and he shivered. While Matt wanted to push Hilston away, he also wanted to grab hold of the other man and not let go. But he couldn't move; the only thing Matt could do was listen while Hilston spoke.

The doctor spoke softly, so much so that Matt had trouble hearing all that Hilston said. "I didn't know she was your wife until Mary told me." He sighed, not loudly. Looking around the hall, Hilston saw there was still no one there. He continued: "It's hard to tell what it was for sure. Too early yet. There was definite trauma to the head, to the chest and body—we can see that. It'll take a few days, Matt. You know how it is. It's just too early to say anything for sure. She wasn't epileptic, was she? Shown any signs?"

Matt moved his head back and forth quickly, his movements seeming to be those of a child.

Hilston nodded and then held Matt tightly, letting this man cry and scream and be angry, knowing the whole time that if it were him, he would be doing the exact same thing.

When the front door shut behind him, Matt made his way to the back of the house. He kept his eyes focused on the end of the hallway in front of him, trying not to see the things in the house that reminded him of Liz. But he was surrounded with reminders everywhere he went; Matt could sense these things, as if they were watching his every move, judging him more and more with each step: shoes she'd kicked off laying by the door, earrings on the table that she'd set down the night before, an empty cereal bowl, rose petals on the carpet.

Matt stumbled into the bedroom and shucked off his pants and underwear as he walked. He took off his shirt and left it in a bundled heap on the bathroom tile. He didn't know what he was going to do. What does a person do after something like this?

He'd stayed for hours at the hospital. After being helped up by Hilston, Mary came and walked Matt to the On-Call Room, telling him to lay down and get some rest. Though he tried to sleep on one of the small cots, closing his eyes tightly and willing them to stay shut, his shivering body and racing mind kept him awake.

After three hours in the darkness of the On-Call Room trying to hide from the rest of the world, Matt finally walked out of the room, cringing under the bright lights above. He had never realized how bright the hospital really was. Matt stumbled around different people there, beds and carts, before finding a seat in one of the blue cushion chairs in the ICU. He stared at the ground between his shoes. The hallway floors looked slick, like they were covered in a thin layer of ice. It seemed that he'd slip and fall if he were to stand up and walk on it. Like if he jumped high enough and brought his feet down hard on the floor, then he would crack the ice of it and fall through to a world below. Matt kept his eyes fixed on the floor, wondering where Liz could be right now: in some place among the stars, gone forever in the darkness? There was no lie he could tell now, nothing to make him believe. No answer that made sense.

Matt watched the doctors and nurses walking around; he caught sight of them in brief passing seconds, their shadows all about him. Shoes on the ground, running, pivoting quickly, turning and walking to exchange a chart or ask a question. As he sat there, Matt kept running the day over in his mind. He felt the excitement all over again of sprinkling the petals on the hallway carpet, the strange emptiness of the kiss from Trisha, the pain of the phone call. These events replayed themselves in his mind like a distorted cinema screening just for him, and he shut his eyes occasionally to rid himself of the empty feeling that found its way to his stomach.

He had since stopped crying, though his eyes seemed sensitive to the light and to his touch. He felt tired. Matt knew his face was bright red and would be for some time. At one point, Matt felt as if he was going to throw up; he'd stood and was about to make his way to the restroom, but the feeling passed, and he sat back down. His head was the only thing that hurt now.

The doctors and nurses moved about beyond him. They all knew what had happened, saw him sitting there, yet no one came up to him to offer any support or condolence. What words could they give him? What words could help? As each of these people walked by Matt, they turned their heads away and moved on with their own lives. *If you don't see a problem, does it still exist?* It was this thought that gave them some kind of comfort in the situation, and that was enough.

Matt remembered all this later as he turned the tap of the bath, fixing the stopper over the drain. Steam rose from the clear water, and he adjusted the temperature. It had been years since he'd taken a bath; the last time he could remember was their wedding night: they'd come back to the apartment from the courthouse—Travis and Jeff had gotten a motel room for the night—and he asked Liz what she wanted. He could still remember her smile, the sound of the giggle that seemed caught in her throat. She told him it would be sexy to take a bath with him. It wasn't until after they both found themselves in the cramped tub, half their naked bodies pushed out of the water, that she told him she meant it only as a joke. They laughed and splashed water on each other, spilling most the contents of the bath on the floor. After they got out, he carried her from the bathroom to the bed and laid her down on the soft mattress. She hadn't toweled off—he didn't give her chance to. When he pressed his body down onto hers, he felt her clammy and wet skin, but he didn't care. Matt knew as he looked down at her face that it was the only face he wanted to see. The only one that would ever matter.

Now he found himself once again in the tub. The water was hot, but he could hardly feel it. He pushed himself down, letting the bath cover his chest and move up to his chin. His knees were out of the water. After a few minutes, Matt let his head go under and he kept it there for several seconds. He hadn't planned on it, but once the water closed over his head, he screamed as loud as his throat would allow. Bubbles rose in a typhoon from his open mouth; he could feel the blood rush to his face, the skin tightening on his cheeks, his throat becoming raw. Above the water, he knew there was no sound, but he could hear his scream echoing clearly around him under the water: animal and pained. He began to feel lightheaded, but he continued screaming, wishing he had the strength to stay under, that the fear of it wouldn't keep him from lifting his head back to the surface and drinking in the air, but he finally pushed his head up and breathed in deeply. Laying there in the tub covered in water like some strange womb, he felt safe somehow, and he let himself feel this way, even if for a moment. He closed his eyes.

Matt wasn't sure how long he was asleep when he woke up, but he thought it had to be a good amount of time. The water was turned cold. His body shivered, and he brought his hands up to his face. Through the small window, he could see that it was completely dark outside, still the middle of night, still the same horrible day. He wondered if it could ever truly end, this day, this feeling, and he judged that it probably could not. Matt had to bring his fingers close to his eyes, but he could see it clearly: the skin was folded in over itself in tiny valleys and crevices where the smooth pads of his fingers had once been. The rest of his body felt the same: heavy and deformed. And as he looked at his fingers, he wondered how long he could stay in the bath before he would disappear forever, freeze and die and float off.

His penis was shriveled, and he reached down and grabbed hold of it. He massaged it slowly, closing his eyes and trying to picture anything else besides the hospital and the sounds of the day, but he could only think of those things. Matt stroked himself for several minutes, and when he saw there was no reaction, that he was still limp and cold, he gave up.

He wanted something to take his mind off what had happened, off what was and would continue to be, though he realized that this was his life now. And he thought of this as he closed his eyes again and drifted back off to sleep in the bathwater.

Matt spent the next two days inside the house, passing most of the time on the couch. There was enough food in the refrigerator and freezer to keep him fed, but he knew he would need to run out to the market soon. The drapes were pulled shut all throughout the house; he did this after he looked out the first afternoon and saw the Corolla in the driveway and thought of how they were supposed to leave for California that day.

He slept most of those two days, getting up only to eat and to use the bathroom. Matt's body had begun to stink, though he paid it no mind. He'd turned the television on only once, but when he saw the first story on the evening news—one about a deadly outbreak of bacteria in Mexico—he turned off the TV and stared at his warped reflection in the dark screen. He thought he saw something in the corner of the darkness there, a figure maybe, a movement behind him, but when he turned, Matt found himself alone. After that, he fell asleep quickly.

Matt would wake at various times during those two days, not wanting to open his eyes to the dark room. He would lay there quietly, listening for something to move within the house, a sign he was not the only one there, but no sound could be heard. During those first moments of waking, Matt would bring his hands up to his face, rubbing the skin to bring forth some kind of feeling to the numbness that invaded him. He had seen the effects of sorrow on some of the families at the hospital, had studied the psychology of denial and grief on those who lost loved ones, but this was different; this wasn't a textbook he could close the cover on, this wasn't another person he passed in the hall of the hospital—he couldn't walk away feeling sorry for the loss and then be able to just forget. This was real, and this was his life.

On the third day after, the electronic ringing of his cell phone woke him. It sounded loudly in the room, seemed to echo off the vast emptiness there. Matt felt around beneath him on the couch for the lighted thing. The screen showed only eight percent battery, but he didn't care: if it turned off in the middle of the conversation then that was fine with him.

On the other end was a familiar voice. He couldn't place it at first. The caller identified himself, but Matt didn't hear. It wasn't until a minute or so into the conversation that he recognized the caller as Terry Hilston.

Hilston spoke slowly, as if he was talking to a child. Several times, the man stopped speaking altogether, wondering if Matt had hung up, but when he heard the muffled breathing coming through the earpiece, Hilston knew that Matt was still there, and he continued with what he was saying.

Hilston began by asking Matt to come down to the hospital, but Matt told him that he wouldn't—that he couldn't—go back there. Whatever the doctor needed to say, he would have to say it over the phone.

"Okay. We ran Liz through the normal process, Matt." Hilston spoke in a direct manner, frank and to the point. There was no sense in trying to tie everything he had to say up in pretty packaging—Matt had had these conversations before with family members and friends of deceased patients; there was no right way to go about it—you just did the best you could.

Hilston continued, his voice sounding monotone now, though it could have just been the cell reception. "It looked at first like it could've been trauma from the accident that ultimately caused the death, but when we looked closer, we saw that there was something else going on."

Matt listened quietly. His eyes looked out into the darkness of the room. He didn't know what time it was, but he felt hungry; Matt could feel his stomach tightening in pain, though he pushed these feelings away so that he could focus on what Hilston told him. After a minute or so, though, Matt stood and walked slowly to the kitchen.

"We ran her through a postmortem CT."

Matt had been searching through the refrigerator for leftovers but stopped when Hilston mentioned the CT scan. Until then, he had assumed that it was the crash that killed Liz, but a CT scan meant something entirely different.

"Listen, Matt: Did she show any signs of fatigue, dizziness, nausea, anything like that during the days leading up to her death?" There was that word, *Death*—so many times, Matt had tossed this word around like balled-up paper, throwing it out into the world as if it meant nothing. Only now, when the word described something so close and personal to him, did Matt fully realize the insensitivity in the way he had acted and felt for all those years, as both a student and doctor.

Matt asked Hilston to repeat the question. The doctor did. "No," Matt answered after Hilston finished. Matt's voice was hoarse, seemed fresh to him, like it had been something he'd lost not long ago and only just now found again. "Why?"

"There was plenty of bodily trauma, but it looks like what caused both the initial accident and the eventual death was a stroke brought on by a subarachnoid hemorrhage." Over the phone, Matt could hear the shuffle of papers before Hilston spoke again. "Looks to have been a ruptured aneurysm in her brain."

Matt was silent on his end of the conversation. He sat down on the kitchen tile, the refrigerator door open so that the cool air blew out onto him. Matt closed his eyes and focused his attention on the cold, wishing the refrigerated air could sweep him off to some other place where he did not need to have this conversation. When he opened his eyes again, he felt himself growing angry, something he hadn't felt since before Liz died.

"Why didn't anyone check for that?"

Hilston spoke calmly; he could sense Matt's anger, his frustration.

"Matt, why would anyone have checked? You know that if a patient doesn't report any symptoms, then it's pointless for us to look into anything. And you tell me that she didn't complain about anything prior to the episode. Also, I spoke with Dr. Garcia, and she said Liz hadn't . . ."

"What?" Matt asked, cutting Hilston short.

"I'm sorry?"

"At the hospital Dr. Garcia?"

"Yes." There was a pause on the other end. "What's wrong?" Hilston asked after several seconds of silence.

"Why would you talk to Garcia? That doesn't make any sense, Terry." Matt's voice moved from angry to confused. He searched in his memory for an answer but found himself continually coming up short.

Matt saw Samantha Garcia nearly every day; he had even helped her the year before with a paper she was presenting. Garcia was one of the few OB/GYNs at the hospital that Matt could stand—the rest seemed to all carry a haughty, above-everyone-else attitude around with them. But Samantha Garcia was different. She cared and showed this often, following up on many of the children she'd delivered, checking in with Matt and the other pediatricians.

He closed his eyes again, willing the next words away, though he knew that they were coming regardless of what he did or said.

Hilston was silent for several seconds while he tried to find the best words to say. He couldn't come up with any and decided instead to just tell Matt as simply as possible.

"She was pregnant, Matt. You knew that, right?"—though he knew from Matt's tone that he didn't.

The phone was silent for several seconds before Hilston heard a loud crack from when Matt dropped the phone.

In the kitchen, Matt sat with his head down, his eyes closed tightly. The phone laid open on the floor between his legs. Hilston asked in a distant, far away voice from the phone if Matt was all right. But Matt had no words. What words could there be? Words are only what you say on the outside, meant for other people to see and hear and feel. But for the speaker, those words have no importance. Matt came to realize this truth at that moment. He continued to sit in front of the open refrigerator door. The light spilled out onto the floor, carving out the black shadow of his body that lingered gently within the frame of the light. This shadow rocking back and forth, this being that could not be held or comforted, nor one that would be stopped or made right again.

Chapter 23

Matt didn't tell Travis or Jeff what happened until a week after the funeral.

The service was held on a rainy day two weeks after she died, but Matt couldn't stay for the service. There was nothing for him there. What was the purpose of standing beside the body of someone you loved? It wasn't her anymore. You act strong and smile when people come up to shake your hand and tell you how sorry they are? *Sorry for what?* Matt thought after he left the cemetery, walking blankly in the direction of the park that he would end up at. The people in attendance hardly knew her. And to feel sorry about something like this made no sense—isn't a person sorry only if there is guilt? It wasn't their fault. They had nothing to feel guilty over. Except for Matt. For him, it was different.

Even when he eventually made his way back out into the world after she died—went shopping at the market, made arrangements for the funeral—Matt hadn't felt right. Something was missing. He knew it was her, but there was something else, too. It took him a week to realize what it was. He looked at himself in the mirror as he brushed his teeth one morning and saw the exact emotion he had been feeling. While he stared at the dark eyes that looked back, the dark, stubbled chin below, he thought of that day. He remembered the kiss Trisha had given him. He hadn't pulled away quick enough, he thought, over and over. Did he want to kiss Trisha? Did he enjoy it? Matt couldn't remember. But in truth, that didn't matter now—it had happened. While Trisha kissed him, Liz was dying. In her last moments, he had felt comfort in someone else's embrace, in someone else's being. There was no reconciling that fact; he simply needed to live with it.

As Matt continued to study his reflection, tracing the sleep lines on his face, the scars of defeat that ran from his eyes down past his nose and mouth, he tried to remember back to the week or so before Liz died. There were no signs he could remember—no headaches, no complaints of pain, discomfort—but there had to be something, he told himself. There needed to be some change in her he hadn't noticed. But there was nothing. *Why?* he asked himself over and over. He couldn't understand it. It was his fault, he told himself. It had to be.

Looking down at the counter around the sink, Matt saw the shaving blade. He picked it up and dragged it sideways across his arm. He saw the small openings in his skin, watched the blood come out and bubble at the top of the line. But he stopped. It didn't help what had happened, and he knew that if he continued with the blade, he would only be doing it for appearance. It wouldn't change anything. The pain from the cuts couldn't rid himself of the internal hurt and sadness. Nothing could.

Not many days before the funeral, Matt drove out to where she had crashed. He'd called Terry Hilston and asked where it happened. Hilston told him and also said that he had been planning on calling Matt later that day anyway; the hospital was giving Matt a few weeks off to collect himself before coming back to work. Though Matt didn't tell Hilston then, he wasn't planning on going back. There were too many memories, too much of Liz still there.

On his drive out of the city, Matt couldn't help but wonder why Liz had driven this direction. As far as he could remember, they had never driven to this part of the city's outskirts. He tried to find reason within it all as he watched the farmlands come into view, searched for logic when there was nothing but the illogical. Ultimately, he found himself thinking of Liz on that day a week and a half before; Matt wondered if there had been any intention in it all, this place and what had happened.

After a while, Matt stopped the Corolla. He looked down at the note he'd written quickly, rough coordinates of the crash site, and then looked back up. It was just a short distance away from where he was now. He drove on, looking out the side window, taking it all in. A giant tree covered the road in shade, and he stopped the car under this shade for a time—there was no telling how long it was. Crops stretched out a distance in either direction from the road. There were gigantic rolls of sod, tall and brown, sitting lonely out along the horizon. Matt got out from the car and smelled the manure heavy in the air: the soggy perfume of the earth. From where he stood, the rolled earth looked to be prehistoric animals, their armor dark and hard, shells to ward off the world.

A section of the wooden fence that separated the street from the crops beyond had been destroyed. There, the grass and part of the fence was black from burn, the ground flattened and dry. Matt walked over and stood in that spot, realizing completely in that moment that he was standing where Liz had last been. Kneeling down slowly, he rested his hand on the brittle, blackened grass. He left his hand there some time, standing only when a farmer, the landowner, came out from a shed not far off from where Matt knelt.

"Hey there," the farmer said. The man was dressed in jeans and a collared shirt. His clothes were stained from dirt and time and sweat, and Matt doubted these stains could ever be gotten rid of.

Matt nodded to the man. He was tall and thin; it wasn't until the farmer came closer to where Matt stood that the latter could see how young the other man was. The farmer had on a baseball cap that he took off as he approached. The man wiped the sweat from his forehead and replaced the cap.

"You here from the papers," the farmer asked.

"No." Matt shook his head as he said this.

The farmer looked off down the road. Maybe looking for someone to drive by, someone he was expecting. But no one was on the road, and the farmer looked back.

"Had some come by last week or so."

"What happened?" Matt asked.

"Nothin much I coulda done but what I did. Was out hoein the crops out there," he pointed, "when I heard the sound of a car comin by real fast. You know that sound. Don't hear it much out here, though I reckon I do some, when them kids is stupid and run their races up the street. Anyways, I look over and see this car movin up quick—couldn't see inside the car from my distance—but then, out of nowhere it seems, the car jus took a fast cut right from the street out into where yer standin. The fence, I reckon, stopped the car from goin out into the crops here." He motioned behind him with his hand. "And I came runnin over, and that's bout when the whole damn thing started to catch fire. I yelled to my wife in the house there to call fer the ambulance and then I went over and took the girl out of the car. Pretty girl, brown hair. But there was blood everywhere, I tell you. I laid her out there next to the street a ways from the car. The thing jus burnt down a long while—they came and towed it away the next day.

"But the ambulance an police, they came and took her away, asked if I'd grabbed her phone or wallet. Told em I didn't. That was that. Ain't heard anythin else bout how she is. You know if she's alright?"

Matt shook his head. His eyes had tears in them that he wiped away.

The farmer nodded and then looked off into the cropland.

Matt cleared his throat of the emotion that settled there before he spoke. "I know it sounds strange, but did it look like she did it on purpose? You know, like she meant to run off the road?"

The farmer looked at Matt. There was a strange look on his face, and he turned away again, shuffling his feet over the ground.

"Shit, I don't know. Ain't my place to say." The farmer looked up at Matt. "Didn't seem right, though. I can tell you that."

Matt nodded quietly and thanked the man. After a minute, the farmer walked off toward the small farmhouse. Matt looked at the house, at the newly painted walls, a satellite dish set high on the roof, its bowl pointed to the heavens to capture the waves that surround the sky. On the porch was an American flag that had folded over itself in the wind; it was old, ripped in parts, the tendrils of it hanging low.

When he was left completely alone again, Matt got back in his car and drove in the direction he'd come. After a short while driving down the road, Matt stopped the Corolla and turned it around. He began to drive again, going the same direction he had just come. He pressed his foot down on the gas pedal until it reached the floor and could go no further. Matt could see in the distance ahead the spot where he had just been, where the grass was black and dead, where the fence was broken in pieces.

Taking a deep breath and holding it in, Matt lifted his hands from the wheel, pushing his palms hard against the ceiling of the car, believing in fate or destiny in that moment, providence or whatever you may call it, to right the wrongs of the universe. But he passed the spot, the car's tires following the gentle curve of the road, taking him out beyond where Liz had crashed. He slowed and then turned again and sped back the other way, lifting his hands the same as before. He did this four times, twice in each direction. But each time he drove by the spot, the car stayed true to the road, never swerving or drifting to either side.

His body felt cold as he drove, replaying in his mind what had just happened. Why hadn't the car drifted? Matt couldn't shake himself of these thoughts as he made his way home. He drove slowly, cursing what god there might be for not taking him too.

Chapter 24

Since Matt last saw him, Travis had proposed to Sandra McClellan. He was still working at the high school, but Sandra now worked at an elementary school in Barrett. Travis had moved in with Sandra not long after they started dating, and a year later, on a trip to New York, in the middle of Times Square, Travis got on his knee and proposed. He called Matt and Liz that night to tell them; they congratulated Travis and said they would be at the wedding, that they couldn't wait for it.

After Travis hung up, Matt told Liz how excited he was to show her where he'd grown up. The wedding was scheduled for the following autumn, only a couple months after their road trip to California.

Though he didn't say anything when Matt called and told him about Liz, Travis doubted his brother would come to the wedding. He tried to put himself in Matt's place, to feel the complete loss and pain his brother felt, but he found it too hard; instead, Travis walked over to Sandra and held her tighter than he ever had before, deciding that he would tell her about Liz later.

Not long after Matt and Liz's wedding, Jeff and Kathy split up. She was the one to leave, telling Jeff that it was too tough with their constant fighting over everything, big and small; just before she left, she said calmly that one day things might be right, that she hoped so, but she didn't know if they ever would. Kathy went and stayed with her parents, taking Kylie, who was now three years old, with her. Jeff was left by himself. He thought briefly of going home to Connecticut, but the thought of facing his parents after all the years terrified him—their questions and comments, the looks they would give him, looks of pity or anger, he would never know the difference. These thoughts kept him from returning to the northeast. But he stayed in St. Louis for the simple fact that if he left it would mean he was giving up on his family. And he was not about to do that.

Nearly a month and a half after Kathy and Kylie left, Jeff went to her parents' house with a ladder. The night above him was dark and the two-story framed farmhouse towered over him in the night. He rested the ladder against the side of the house, aligning it perfectly so that it set just next to the bedroom window where Kathy and their daughter were sleeping. Jeff took a deep breath and climbed up. On the windowsill, he left the engagement ring for her—a quarter carat with diamonds embedded on the band: even in the dark night, the ring seemed to shimmer in sparkle. Jeff had bought the ring the night before. He looked over the sea of options at the jeweler, deciding finally on one near the top of the display case; when he pointed it out to the man on the other side, he smiled, knowing that there wasn't anything he wouldn't do to get Kathy and their daughter back. They were his world, the only things that made sense.

Every argument they ever had was about money, about the things they couldn't do; Kathy constantly compared herself to the other women she knew, the neighbor women, those at work; Kathy compared their family to other families, feeling inferior each time she did so. She watched others from a distance, saw the happiness and the carefree lives of these people; she wished in some regretful way she could feel the same way they did.

After he set the ring on the sill, Jeff knocked loudly on the window and then climbed quickly down the ladder, nearly falling in his giddy excitement. When he reached level ground, Jeff stepped back from the ladder. He stood as calmly as he could manage out on the open yard and extended his arms wide at his side. When the light went on in the room above, he felt his pulse quicken. He smiled; in the back of his mind there were worries, fears that she would let her stubborn sadness rule her emotions, that she would reject him again. But he pushed these thoughts from his mind as best he could and waited for his wife above him.

After several seconds, Kathy's face showed in the window; she looked out and saw him below. Throwing up the glass, she looked down and, in a harsh whisper, asked what the hell he was doing. She hadn't seen the ring yet, her focus being solely on Jeff standing stupidly in the night with his arms extended outward and a boyish grin on his face. He yelled loudly up to her, not caring who he might wake or who would hear him in this private moment of confession. "I love you, Kath," he said. "We've screwed up, I know it, but you're mine till the end. Marry me." He paused, feeling the wetness of his eyes grow. "Marry me again, Kath."

Just as he finished, the sprinkler heads lifted from the yard and began spraying the ground with water. Jeff thought of running for cover, but he stayed where he was, waiting for the cold sting of the water. When it came, he smiled wider, his breath catching in his chest, and watched Kathy laugh in the window above him.

"I'm staying here till you say yes."

As she continued to laugh, Kathy's eyes drifted to the windowsill. The ring shined in the light behind her. She stopped laughing and felt her body tense and her skin grow cold; the feeling moved quickly throughout her body. Behind where she stood, Kathy heard Kylie begin to make noises in a dream. Kathy looked at the sleeping girl and then turned her attention back to the ring she held in her hand. She smiled and realized that tears were trickling slowly down her face. Below was her husband, waiting stubbornly for her to say something, to answer him.

Kathy grabbed her robe from the chair, wrapped it tightly around her body, and went down the stairs. She opened the back door and walked into the night; Jeff's smile widened when he saw her, and she felt a smile spread on her own lips. Jeff's arms were still outstretched as he waited in the sprinkler rain for her. She walked over—she was shivering in cold from the water that misted around her, the sprinkler making its way in their direction and finally hitting them hard, taking away her breath in the cold wetness and making her clothes heavy—and fell into his arms, wrapping hers around his waist. It was there, with their bodies growing cold from the water, that they felt the warmest and most comfortable they'd ever felt before.

On the drive home from the spot where Liz had crashed, Matt screamed at the top of his lungs, his voice filling the small car, his echo bouncing sharply off the windows and coming back to him even louder in return. He felt as if his brain hurt, throbbing, pulsing inside his skull, though he knew this was not true.

He shook his head angrily and then thought of the conversation he'd had with Hilston on the phone; Matt wondered if the doctor's words had only been said for comfort. Had she driven herself off the road purposefully? If so, then why? And if why, then how had he not seen the signs?

It was in the process of these thoughts that he realized the other reality: he would have been a father. It hadn't sunk in yet;

he hadn't even given it thought—not until that moment, at least. He could have easily seen the two of them—Liz and himself—in the backyard, the baby crawling around the grass, growing into a toddler, running around under the cool shade of the trees outside; Liz would have a video camera while Matt grilled hot dogs on the barbeque. When the toddler grew, they would go to Little League games or dance recitals, soccer games, first days of school, the tantrums that came before all this, the conversations and advice that came after. But none of this would be. And in that moment, as he pulled into the driveway and turned off the engine, he hated the child he would never meet.

Matt was struck with a sick, nauseous feeling, and he wanted to throw up everything in his world, rid himself of all the bile and pain. The baby had killed her, taken Liz from his life and left him alone. What he needed was for Liz to hold him tight and tell him everything would be fine. But this would never happen. He sat in the dark of the car for several minutes, feeling himself swirl with loss and sadness, anger and want.

Later, inside the house, Matt sat on the couch and looked blankly around him at the aftermath of his world, at what his life had become—what it was and would be. His eyes hurt, though he could not cry. There was a heaviness to his chest that strained his body when he breathed in deeply, so he kept his breaths short and shallow.

He hung his head so that it rested just between his knees, and then he slumped his entire body forward so that he knelt on the carpet, his forehead on the floor. Darkness blanketed him. The only light in the room came from the small digits illuminated on the cable box below the TV.

With his eyes still closed, he whispered quietly into the room. "God. I don't think you're there. And if you are, then I want you to know that I hate you. I hate you. I fucking hate you." His voice trailed off slightly the more times he repeated the words. He was about to lift his head, but he stopped and kept it resting against the ground. From the back of his throat, he let out a short laugh that came from humiliation in praying, something he had not done since he was a young boy with his mother in church. When the feeling passed, he continued. "I can't believe I'm doing this. But if you exist, then you owe me that I'll see her again. You owe me that." His voice grew stronger, and he could feel the rage beginning to settle within his mind again. "I've done everything to be a good person. She was the best person."

He lifted his head finally, staring upward, his eyes now open, tears falling down his cheeks, somehow now running the length of his arms, down to his fingertips and onto the carpet.

"Please let me see her again. I can't lose her. I promised forever, I promised always. I can't lose her. I can't lose her. I need her back."

Matt looks out now at the dark shadows of the late afternoon landscape. California surrounds him; a place he hadn't thought he'd see again—not after she died.

He turns his head and watches the numbers of the gas pump flash by quickly. Under his hand on the nozzle, he feels the rush of gasoline inside the curling black hose. Ten minutes earlier, he decided to get off the interstate and fill the truck up with the last bit of fuel needed before reaching the beach. Beyond the lonely gas station, the road stretches out in the distance like a midnight river. The trucks and cars with their lights shining brightly drive quickly in different directions like insects treading the waters beneath them carelessly. Matt turns his head to follow these passing cars, wondering where they are headed.

The air is hot and dry. He can smell the fresh-laid road not far off from where he stands. The black tar sits in the sinking sun now, finally cooling after a long day of baking. Soft to solid.

Inside the truck, Liz watches Matt closely. He turns back to the new street pavement and sees where the orange cones have been set up around the tar, keeping drivers aware of the fresh ground.

And his mind fills with thoughts. *Years from now, what things will scientists find of us? What fossils will be trapped in the earth to tell our stories? The tars and concretes and petrified things that store our ways like hieroglyphs to the world.*

But we are like all people of the past and those who come after. How will we show them who we are now? And what is to come once the rains pass and the thunders quiet, in the time after we're gone? What stories will there be left? How will I tell mine, and who will believe it to be true? He wonders this as he sees Liz looking back at him, a smile beginning on her lips.

PART 3:
AFTER

Time seemed to pass more slowly during the days after Liz died, though Matt did not notice it much. His days revolved around waking late, dressing and eating breakfast or lunch—whatever time it was dictated what he ate—and leaving the house. He would drive the streets that were darkened at times by passing storms, lit brightly at other times by the sun. He had no set destination on these drives, though he constantly found himself passing the farmlands, eventually arriving at that lonely and sad stretch of country road where she had crashed.

Matt would park the Corolla under the tree that hung over the road; its shade spread over the earth in patches of dark, the dips and valley patterns of sunlight scattered within. He would sit there and watch the spot from a distance, playing the events from before over and again in his head, constructing and then reconstructing them, though never knowing if he was right or not. Days that the farmer was out in the field, Matt would drive past the spot or, if he was already parked there and the farmer came out of the house, Matt would start the car and turn it around, watching in the mirror how that sad place disappeared behind him. He wanted to believe that he was leaving it in the past, moving on, but he carried it all with him wherever he went, knowing that it was forever there waiting for him.

He wondered if the farmer ever watched him drive away, if the man he'd spoken with weeks before would remember him; Matt figured that the man would, and that he had always known who Matt was, even at their meeting.

Nearly a month after she died, Matt drove up to the spot, pulling the car along the side of the road under the tree. Thunder sounded loudly around him, though he could not tell from which direction the storm was coming. The field was empty, everyone inside. The air was warm and dry. Raindrops, large and heavy, began falling onto the car's hood, falling from the sky and dropping from the branches above; the water thumped loudly and sounded like war drums. In the distance, lightning bolts appeared, rapidly stretching across the darkening sky before disappearing into the earth, or so it seemed to be. It was hard to see the spot of grass and broken fence through the stained and foggy windshield, and it was not until Matt opened the window and moved his head out into the storm that he saw it: a blurry shape of something sitting on the ground where she had crashed.

Matt opened the door and ran quickly over the wet gravel. Beneath him, his steps sounded of crushed leaves and scuffed rocks. It was hot out and the rain evaporated in a sizzling sound when it hit the ground; the smell was rank, sour and strong, though he did not notice it, did not feel the rain anymore. He stooped down as he approached the spot—the black scars on the grass were still there, even in the darkness of the storm—and lifted the stuffed bear that seemed to be awaiting him. The thing had once been white but now, in the rain, it was turned a dirty brown. The bear's sunken face looked as if it was crying, and Matt tightened his grip on the wet sponge of a toy, looking around for whoever it was that left it, as if that person was still there watching keenly from a distance.

He took the bear with him back to the car and then started the engine. When he got home, Matt put the thing in the fireplace and was about to set fire to it, but his hands began to shake as he tried to light the match, and he found himself only able to rock back and forth in front of the dirty bear. From afar, he looked a penitent man praying before a shrine.

Over time, weeks turning into months, Matt watched from his shaded spot as grass grew tall and covered the black burned patches of the earth. First the beginnings of green grass, then yellow as summer bled into autumn, fall. Winter was still a distance off, but it would fast approach with its frozen mornings of white snow newly blanketing the fields. The broken fence was repaired, though Matt never saw the farmer out there working on it. After a while, the place held no outward acknowledgment of what had happened; no more memories existed except those that Matt continually reminded himself of. These were the things of life, happening when his eyes seemed to be closed to it all.

The darkness of the Pacific seems to stretch out into the farthest reaches of the night and bleed blackly into the sky. The water moves up onto the sand and then recedes back into the voided darkness.

From where he has stopped in the small parking lot, Matt can see only about fifty feet of the beach; what he can see of the area is lit from the small parking lot lamps that glow a fuzzy yellow. There is one other car parked in the lot, but it looks old and beat up and Matt wonders if it has simply been abandoned here. He and Liz are alone, and the wasteland of the night surrounds them.

Matt had smelled the water several miles away and had turned to tell this to Liz, though when he saw her, he felt his voice catch, and he turned back to the road and said nothing.

Still now, as he sits in the parking lot, Matt is angry for this, for not having been able to say anything to her: whatever she may be, she is there with him, and there is nothing more to do or think about.

The night sky is darker than he would have imagined it to be. There is no moon above, but there are several stars that shine brightly, and the white reflections of these seem to set parts of the ocean on fire as if he was looking down from a giant mountain at the dotted campfires of lone settlers stretched out across the plains.

Out there, the blackness of the sky is forgetful. *I wish I could drift slowly up into it. Pass through the mists and clouds, into the cold and quiet of the sky, the dark of it all. I wish I could find you once again out there and hold you, taste your breath, cry your tears, feel your heart's beat. It's there. I know.* He thinks this as he listens to the movement of the waves.

It wasn't until almost eleven months after Liz died that Matt began to see her. At first, she came to him only at distances too great for him ever to be sure it was actually her; she showed herself only in snatches of time, stolen moments, it seemed, from whatever place she was now part of.

The first time he saw her was at the corner of the street. Matt had pulled the car out of the garage and was backing it slowly down the driveway when he looked over to his left and saw a thin woman in a blue shirt and jeans standing there. He squinted at her, noticing the brown hair that stretched down her back, and then he brought his foot down hard on the brake pedal when he heard the horn behind him. He looked back quickly and saw his neighbor, Michelle Wellington, driving home from soccer practice with her son. He smiled a fake smile at her and waved an apology, which Michelle returned. But when Matt turned back to the corner where he'd seen the woman, she was gone.

These incidents happened more frequently as time progressed: at the market and gas station, along his morning and afternoon drives. The woman he saw—always dressed the same, always too far away for him to distinguish for sure—seemed to watch him quietly. And each time, when he turned away, she would disappear and leave him questioning whether he was making himself see things.

Not long after the funeral, Matt pulled down all the photos of Liz in the house: he removed the framed ones from off the walls, leaving only the small nail hole to remind him that her face had once belonged there; then he took down the small frames and polaroids from off the tables and dressers. These things he kept in the back room, which he could never bring himself to enter—the blue-painted study with small drops of paint still clinging to parts of the ceiling and carpet. Each time he walked by the room with its closed door, he remembered that afternoon he spied her dancing alone and free.

As the months passed after she died, Matt found himself forgetting the aspects he'd always loved about Liz: the smooth lines that ran from her eyes downward when she smiled and the groupings of freckles that dotted her shoulder and neck, so fine that he could only see them when he rested his face against her shoulder blade and moved his face down her arm's length, smelling in her body's perfume. During these moments, he would trace his finger along her soft, white skin and connect the dots of muted color.

During those months since she died, her face became blurred. Even when he closed his eyes and called up the image of her, he couldn't decipher if it was really her face he saw or just some version of it in his mind.

Several months after she died, Matt drove the Corolla to a junk dealer and got a few hundred dollars in exchange for it. He didn't care what he got; he just wanted the car gone. It reminded him too much of his past life and who he'd been; he always thought of Liz when he climbed inside, of the nights they drove down to the Missouri River, the love they'd made in the cramped back seat and the hours they'd spent under a blanket or their clothes, laughing with each other after.

He walked from the junk dealer to a used car lot and picked out the first truck he saw. He didn't care what type of truck it was, just as long as it was a truck—something completely different from the cars both he and Liz drove. The truck was a late nineties Chevy with a long bed; it was blue, Liz's favorite color. An hour later, Matt drove out of the dealership and back to the house.

The next day, Matt drove the truck out to one of the farms on the outer portion of the city and asked if there was any work. It wasn't until the fifth farm he went to that the man who owned the land said he needed some help tending the fields. The farmer asked what experience Matt had with corn and other crops; Matt said casually that he had none but that he was a quick learner.

"Why you wanna work out here, son?" the farmer asked.

Matt shrugged his shoulders. "I need to."

"Need to what?"

"Get away from everything. Feel sweat, let my muscles work."

The farmer looked him up and down and nodded before hocking a wad of dip spit from his throat onto the ground. He smiled. "Yer thin, but I reckon we'll find yeh some way to build on that."

Matt worked six days a week, constantly asking the farmer, a man named Wiggs, what other jobs needed to be done. When Wiggs told him to go home, Matt said he didn't want to, that he'd rather keep working. Though Wiggs wanted to ask Matt what he was running from, what he was afraid to go home to, he never did ask and instead gave his new worker more and more chores.

Though he'd been hired on seasonally, Wiggs kept Matt on a permanent basis, but the schedule only allowed for Matt to come and work four days a week. On his days off, Matt stayed inside the house, still sleeping much of the day away on the couch, watching reruns of sitcoms and eating microwavable meals.

Matt found a strange sense of peace when he worked the fields, though this vanished the moment he left the surrounds of the crops. Out there, he found himself forgetting about Liz and the pain that was there waiting for him; in the field, it seemed as if he had never been a doctor but that he had always been a farmhand. Matt smiled when he found himself alone in the crops with the sun sinking into the western valley. He often thought of Jeff and college, remembering the nights his friend went around telling everyone that they were Lennie and George—he had become George, though this thought also made him sad as he realized that he was without a partner, without a friend or anyone else to talk with. All that was left of this George was a sad man alone in the world with no one to go home to.

After working in the fields, when he did drive home, he found himself in the darkness of the house thinking only of Liz. Matt constantly ran that day over and over in his mind, thinking of his excitement with the rose petals and then the pain that followed. Many nights he became angry and slammed his fists into the couch, screaming out loudly into the empty house. But he didn't cry—he didn't think he could anymore.

Matt couldn't imagine that she'd drive her car off the road, but the farmer's voice kept echoing in his mind, telling him that the car swerved out of the road like it was on purpose, like something was wrong. *What could I have done? There was something I missed*, he would think. *I should have caught it. Should have seen it.*

The rose petals were still in the hallway and on the bed, though they had shriveled up into flaky pieces of flesh now.

Whenever he went to the back bathroom to take a shower, Matt would step carefully over the fallen petals, careful not to disturb where they lay, and he would turn his head away from the bed and the pile of laundry there.

He thought that he would be able to forget his sadness with work, but the house only served as a constant reminder that her death would always be there, a scar upon his life, a black mark on his world.

He takes his shoes off now, leaving them inside the cab and climbs slowly out of the truck and walks out onto the beach. Beneath his bare feet, the sand feels cold, and he stops and digs his toes into the loose earth. A heavy, fast wind whips about him, spraying his face with mist from the ocean. He walks on, slower now than before, making his way to the water's edge. The black ether stretches out far beyond him.

What world is out there? What would we see if we could look into that other world? He turns back to where Liz walks beside him; her head is hung low, and she watches her feet as they move over the sand. Matt wonders if her feet make any impression in the ground, but he cannot tell in the darkness. He can only make out the side of her face, lit gently from the light off the pier in the far distance down the beach. Even in the darkness of the night, seagulls fly overhead and call out to one another in loud squawks.

Eventually, his feet feel the cold sting of the water and he stops walking. He had not known where he was on the beach until the water laps up his legs. He stands here a moment, letting the skin of his ankle and shin adapt to the cold of it all.

After several minutes of standing in the ocean, Matt turns around and walks back up the beach several steps and stops to sit on the cold sand. Not far off to his left is where he had first seen Liz all those years ago. The memory of it seems so real, like he can close his eyes and live that moment again, ask that brown-haired girl what her name is, spend a lost night of happiness on the beach with someone he knows nothing about. A bonfire roared to life that night, but on this night, there is no one around. It is dark and quiet now, and he wonders how long it will stay like this.

Beside him sits Liz—he hadn't noticed her there until just now. Her continued silence has scared him all this time. If only she would speak and let him know she was real, that she was there. Just to know.

And for the first time since she first appeared to him, Matt slides his hand out toward her, moving it slowly to where her hand rests lightly on the earth. He stops just before he reaches her skin. Looking up at her, he sees that she is looking quietly at him. In the dark, he thinks he sees a smile, small and hidden, on her face, though he is not sure if this is only the shadows or his imagination, or both. It is the first time since she appeared to him in the kitchen that he has not looked away from her gaze, that he has not flinched his hand back in fear that she would see him or touch him.

In her face now, he can only see the remnants of the life he wanted her to live and the memories he always hoped to have someday.

The dream had come to Matt several times before, though only in bits and parts, never in full. It was not until the morning he woke and found Liz standing in the kitchen, waiting quietly for him, that the dream played out completely.

Some nights, he would only see the beginning of the dream that he'd come to know by heart; at other times, after he settled himself for sleep and closed his eyes, he would be given a preview of the rest of the dream—all in small glimpses—yet he could never understand its meaning. It seemed broken down into too many different pieces, a narrative he could not put together—some strange puzzle he didn't know the answer to. But there was something important to the dream, he knew that much.

It had started the night of her funeral, after he came home from the park, his suit heavy with rain. Matt hadn't been asleep for more than an hour when he woke up breathing heavily, his arms thrashing above him. His throat burned then—he could remember it clearly—and he thought it was from holding his breath in his sleep, but he didn't know for sure.

Months later, when the dream played out for him in its entirety and he awoke crying out for Liz loudly, reaching his hands up toward the ceiling, he had not expected to open his eyes to the sunlight that came through the window. He also had not expected to walk into the kitchen and find her standing there, waiting for him with sad eyes, Liz dressed in the blue concert shirt and jean pants. That happened just over a month ago now.

Inside the dream, he was always sleeping; he would wake from his dream sleep by the sound of glass breaking in another room. When he opened his eyes in the dream, Matt found himself in his bed, though Liz would never be next to him. Each time, he would reach over and try to grab hold of her but there would only be an empty bed and the slight impression of where her body had once been.

He would next sit up in the dream and see that the house was on fire: smoke would be coming from under the doors and collect above him, hovering there like some judging entity that was watching his every move and knowing his every thought. Further off in the house, Matt would hear more glass breaking as well as the cutting sound of flames. The bedroom door would begin to glow red and then black as the fire burned through the wood and made its way toward him. No matter how many times he had this dream, he always found himself shaking, crying out to whatever god might hear him; he called out for Liz also, but there would never be a reply.

Then, as if by some miracle, the room would begin to fill completely with water; it always seemed to him after he woke and thought back on the dream, that it was like some giant had lifted the house with him inside and submerged it completely in the ocean. His body would be thrown to the ceiling, and he would need to take a deep breath as the water rose to the very top of the house. He would look around and see that all the fire was extinguished by the water, and with his breath held, Matt would swim down to the floor and squeeze his way through the burned bedroom door.

Most nights when he had the dream, Matt would wake at this point, holding his breath and wondering what else there was in the sunken dream house. It didn't matter if he fell back asleep immediately or if he kept himself up for another hour and then drifted off again, the dream would never come twice in the same night—usually not twice in the same week. Other times when he had the dream, he would see a fleeting image of the living room as he woke, the water high to the ceiling, the sun shining through the closed windows.

However, the last time he had this dream, just before he woke and found Liz waiting for him, Matt saw the end.

His eyes began to grow tired as he swam his way down the hallway in the dream, his body floating peacefully and free, his lungs burning without oxygen. He felt as if he was about to give up and let himself float away, but he continued on, making his way into the living room. There, below him, Matt saw Liz laying perfectly still on the couch; cradled on her chest was a baby girl, its small form wrinkled and still, wrapped in a white blanket that seemed to float toward him in the water. Above them, Matt began to cry, the tears adding to the water that consumed the house; the pain in his chest left him at this moment, and he felt as if he could breathe under the water. It was the first time he'd seen her face since she died.

Then in the dream, both Liz and the child turned their heads up at him; Liz smiled a strange smile of joy, as if she too was surprised to be seeing him there in that strange place. Liz reached her hand up slowly, trying to usher him toward her through the water, keeping it there so that Matt could grab hold. He began to swim down to her. Just as Matt was about to touch her outstretched fingers, he heard Liz's voice from somewhere else entirely: "Wake up. Wake up. Forever and always. Now, wake up."

He opened his eyes at that moment and found himself laying on the couch in the middle of the living room. His arms were stretched above him, still reaching out for Liz. He stood quickly, looking around for Liz and the baby, though neither was there. When he took a step, he felt dizzy and then sat back down on the cushions. The world underneath him seemed to shift, and he felt as if he would fall down from the couch and be thrown back and forth across the room until he eventually rolled off the earth entirely.

Behind him, the morning sun filtered into the room. It was hot in there, and he pulled the bottom of his shirt up to wipe the sweat from his face. He took several deep breaths and then stood again, this time making sure to hold onto the couch in case he felt dizzy again.

Shaking his head, he walked into the bathroom and studied his reflection in the mirror, shifting his weight back and forth on his legs, feeling the pricking pins of the blood returning to his limbs from the dream. Behind him, he could see the framed photo of the bee and flower, the one picture he kept hanging on the wall. He turned on the faucet and bent over the sink, mechanically collecting a puddle of water in his hands and bringing it up to his face. He dropped his hands, dripping the remnants of water down into the sink basin. His face was cold and felt puffy from sleep. Though he couldn't explain it, nor could he know for certain, there seemed to be a warmth that passed over his chest in that moment, and he gathered more water from the tap and brought it up to his face, rubbing his hands through his hair and onto the nape of his neck.

After he dried his face and hands, Matt walked slowly into the kitchen and turned on the air conditioner as he passed it. In that short walk from the bathroom to the kitchen, there was an unexplained change in the air, a giddiness of Christmas morning, an anxiousness he could not fully describe. His feet dragged over the carpet and onto the tile flooring of the kitchen, and he watched his feet carry him forward. It wasn't until he looked up and saw Liz standing next to the kitchen table that he felt his head grow light. The world beneath him seemed to move again, and the air became hot and heavy in that moment, feeling like it does when you walk through a length of spider web—try and shake it from you but you can't.

Liz smiled sadly at him, and he stared back at her, waiting to wake up from this dream, waiting for it to end. But it never happened. He was awake, and she was there in front of him.

In the distance, a mile or so down the beach in the other direction from the pier, there is the small haze of lights: a truck patrolling the beach, searching for squatters and bums who shouldn't be here at this time of night. When Matt sees these lights, he swallows hard and watches their movement through the fog that has begun to settle in. Then, after a few seconds, the patrol truck turns away from Matt's direction and makes its way back up to the road behind the beach.

Looking over at Liz, Matt sees her face, now completely hidden in the darkness—his shadow spreads over where she sits. He shakes his head, wondering what he is doing here, wondering if this is the right thing. If any of this makes sense at all. Beside him, his hand still rests close to hers; he looks out at the black waves. It is not until this moment that he realizes how afraid he is of looking over and not seeing her there.

Though he hasn't been able to bring himself to speak to Liz, he knows that there is a sense of peace that's come with her constant presence this last month, and he fears the day when she is no longer with him, if that day should ever come.

So many times, he has spoken to this Liz in his mind and heard the words returned to him from this quiet version of her. They are always words of comfort and love. It is only in these imagined conversations that he feels any sense of completion and happiness, yet this is a façade of his true self, and he knows it. These words, these captured moments, they don't exist. Rather, they are merely created in his mind, and they stay there. Whatever this woman is beside him, she is silent. To have true words with her again is merely a dream that Matt can only wait patiently for.

His feet are still wet, still cold from before, but he doesn't mind the feeling. There is a strange comfort in the wet and the cold of it.

His eyes close gently. The morning is still hours away and he knows, though the reasons for it escape him, that he must wait until the morning to do what he has come here for. With a weary body, tired legs and arms, muscles rotted with fatigue, he begins to stand—he will wait out the night in the safety of the truck. There are less memories in there than there are to be found on this beach with its faded images of the past and ashes of a bonfire from a time long ago. Within his closed eyes, he remembers that night again; he keeps the darkness around him, afraid of what he might find otherwise.

What happens with the memories we have? With the times that pass during our lives? Are they gone completely, never to be found again, only to be brought back to us in some incomplete form by our minds? There has to be a way to relive those moments. Nothing simply fades away and disappears. He thinks of these things, though he is not sure of anything anymore.

Matt stands and turns to head back to the truck, but he stops when he hears her voice and sits back down heavily on the sand. He closes his eyes tightly again. The words have frozen him, taken his heart and skin and wrapped it in a feeling of loss, one cold and terrifying though familiar at the same time. "Wait," the voice said. It is the voice he has loved since that first day on this beach years ago, the voice that has invaded both his sleeping and waking dreams.

Matt fights with his body; he wants to open his eyes and look over at her, he wants to watch her speak the words he's wanted so desperately to hear, but he forces his eyes to remain closed, to simply listen to her voice. *Is this a dream?* he wonders. He hopes it is not, though if it is, he hopes it is one he will not wake from.

There were plenty days of sun after Liz died, but these days seem to escape his memory, coming to him like unfulfilled promises. Matt can only clearly remember the short mornings and long afternoons of overcast skies, of rain that lasted throughout the night knocking like fingers on the windows and roof of the house. The rain seemed a constant reminder of all that had passed. It was hard for him at first, but as time passed, Matt let the sound of it all be a lullaby for him, one that would take him to dreams where he could hear Liz's voice and imagine what their future would hold.

Many times throughout that year, Matt woke in the middle of the night and reached over for Liz. It would always take him several disoriented seconds to realize where he was and know that she would not be next to him and that she would not be coming back. Even the ghost that stayed awake through the nights watching over his sleeping body could not be held. The ghost Liz had no beating heart within her chest for Matt to rest his head upon and listen to; she couldn't tell him softly that he was only having a bad dream and that things would be okay in the morning. She couldn't tell him that she would be there for him forever.

After she died, Matt avoided the places that most reminded him of her. Certain places remained a necessity for him to drive by: restaurants scattered around town that they had once eaten at, shops she had taken him into. He would drive by these places only because there was no other way around them on his drive to work. When he drove past one of these places, he would turn his head away, burying deep the quick image from his mind and forcing them away as if the place and its memories were plagued with a virus.

He drove an extra six miles just to go to a different market, knowing that if he were to walk into the one down the street from the house that he would remember the Wednesday afternoons spent there with her.

Wednesday had become their unassigned date night—it began one week and continued on until the end. After several weeks of this, he began coming home from the hospital early in the afternoon on Wednesdays, rearranging his schedule with different doctors who could cover his shift. When he came home, the two of them would each shower and dress themselves in their fanciest clothes, feeling a sense of giddiness in their outward appearances like they were traveling back to a time where glitz and glam still reigned—Liz would spend an hour in front of the mirror putting on mascara and blush, curling her hair the way Matt always loved it, the brown locks seeming messy in a purposeful way, and when she smiled, he felt a sense of ease and peace with his world, no matter the trouble he might have been experiencing. It was in these brief moments that he lived his life to the fullest. In these afternoons, he realized just how much she had saved his world; she gave him someone to trust and love, someone to whisper his dreams to.

After they left the house on Wednesdays, Matt would drive the Corolla to the ice cream parlor just down the street. The place had a fifties theme, a jukebox playing old records in the corner of the parlor, a working soda fountain. The workers there wore paper hats and glasses, looking like they'd stepped out of some old, cheap movie. All this only added to the fun of their date night, making the two feel as if they were kids together, like they were sharing their first crush with one another. Like they hadn't missed the better parts of their lives in love.

Matt and Liz would walk in, smiles and laughter accompanying them as they moved to the counter to order. Rarely was there anyone else in the place at that time in the afternoon. At first, the high school workers were unsure about this couple—the man in a suit and tie, a coat either pulled snuggly around him or draped over his arm, and the woman in a long dress and heels—but after several weeks of this, the workers smiled friendly to the couple and served the two their ice cream desserts, not needing to wait for the order, as it never changed.

On these Wednesday afternoons, Matt and Liz would walk out into the late sun and watch their shadows in front of them, stepping quickly to try and catch up to their dark doubles, though they would always fall just short with each extra step. Liz would hold his hand, and the two of them would walk slowly into the supermarket just two stores down from the ice cream shop.

Matt would take a hand basket, and they would walk the aisles slowly, each carrying a cone in their hand, licking up the dripping ice cream as it rolled down their fingers.

It was a game they played, one without rules. Liz would grab random boxes, new foods they had never eaten before, new flavors to foods they had once eaten long ago. She would sneak candy and sweets into the basket hoping Matt wouldn't notice, and though he always did, he never let on to that fact.

When they returned home from the store, Matt would place all the strange and exotic items she had picked out on the kitchen counter: escargot and spices, pig's snout and tongue, chilies that had no name, sardines. He would study them like he was looking at a police lineup, looking for the right person, though ultimately feeling lost at the whole process. Liz's job was to shop while Matt was tasked with creating something edible out of the potpourri of ingredients.

After a few minutes of thinking, Matt would cook—sometimes grilling if there was indeed something to grill, other times baking in the oven. Matt remained in his suit and tie as he made the dinner, feeling himself sweat under the thick material of the clothing in the hot kitchen. Liz would always sit in the same position; she would pull one of the kitchen chairs over to the far edge of the room, near where he cooked the meal. She'd sit with her right leg crossed tightly over her left knee, her foot dangling free; her foot would keep timed bounce with some song that played in her head. In her hand would always be a can of soda, a straw stretching forth from the metal top. He never saw her drink from the can on these moments, and after several weeks of it, he decided that the soda was only a taunt for him: he was hot in the kitchen while she had the freedom to relax in the cool air and watch as he worked at it.

The smell that came from the foods was usually awful, and Matt would often need to open the windows that surrounded the kitchen and turn the fan on high in hopes of ridding the house of the smell. It never worked; the smell would linger within the house until the following week when the challenge began again, and a new smell invaded the place.

These date nights ended with the two of them sitting down at the kitchen table, all the lamps off in the house. The only light came from two candles between them on the table. The glow of the flames showed their shadows tall and graceful on the surrounding walls. Their faces would be a soft yellow-orange; black spaces hid around the corners of their cheeks and necks, keeping them just beyond each other's knowing in those moments. They each became a mystery in those dinners. They would each take a bite of the food, always together and at the same time. The food was often chewy and smooth in texture, and they would sit there working at the bite, looking at each other, trying not to be the first to smile or laugh at the awful taste. It was a blinking contest, though the loser was the first to break character—the winner usually followed just after, laughing at the other. These nights usually ended in Liz scraping the food from the plates into the sink, pushing the uneaten things down the garbage disposal. Matt would then take the plates and put them in the dishwasher.

They would then make their way to the bedroom, taking their clothes off as they walked, leaving them casually here and there in bundles along the hallway. They would make love, looking into each other's eyes as they did so; they wouldn't kiss, they wouldn't speak. There was something more serious with their relationships on these nights.

Liz would usually fall fast asleep after, her head on his bare chest, and Matt would run his fingers slowly through her hair, looking up at the ceiling, watching the steady movement of the fan above them and feeling its soft blowing breath. Matt would fall asleep like this, replaying the same image again and again in his mind. He would be back in the kitchen, making whatever the food had been for that night, though he would be looking in at himself from a distance, watching the night and its events from a spectator's view. The other Matt would always look back to where Liz sat holding her soda can, watching him prepare the dinner. He would always catch himself looking an extra second or two longer than intended, noticing the soft skin of her legs just below the dress's length. In those dreamed moments, Matt would see her smile and hear her laugh, high over the sizzling sounds of the cooking food. And, as he thought back on those nights, he would think that if he could just live in that one moment there for the rest of his days, then he would be happy. That if heaven were indeed a real place, then he was able to return there every Wednesday night. Then he would fall asleep.

Since seeing her at the street corner months before she appeared in the kitchen, Matt saw her several other times standing a distance off from where he was; he'd squint his eyes to clear his sight, though it would never be enough for him to know for sure if it was Liz or not. She would show herself and then disappear, and Matt would only be able to shake his head, rub his eyes, and then move on with whatever he was doing at the time.

He saw her in the fields of the farm two weeks before the morning in the kitchen. Matt was all alone out there; Wiggs was in the shed off near the thick oak tree next to the house. Matt had been using a knife to cut off sagging stalks and leaves from the crop, bending down low to the earth and hacking at the brown pieces, throwing the cut parts into a small bucket he carried with him. He needed to stop every few steps to push the dead foliage deeper into the bucket, making it a tightly packed maze of sharp leaf and grass.

As he moved on to the next row of crops, Matt saw in the far distance of the field a woman standing alone. She was too far away to tell for sure, but he believed it to be Liz. He dropped the bucket at his feet, making it fall onto its side with the collected pieces of stalk and leaf spilling out onto the black soil. Matt lifted his hand slowly in greeting or parting, he did not know which, and waited this way until he saw the ghost woman do the same. Behind him came a quick snapping sound and he looked back to see a small rabbit chase its way through the short crops. When he looked back to her, she was gone, and he knew that the wave had indeed been one of parting.

He would not see Liz again until that morning two weeks later.

Matt reaches over further to where she sits, moving his hands around like a blind man, his eyes still closed tightly; tears begin their course down his face and onto his shirt and pants. Her voice still seems to surround him.

He takes a breath and tries to say her name out loud, but he cannot give the words voice. Instead, he makes the sound of an infant, a guttural choked sound that bleeds itself quickly into a loud sob. This continues for several seconds, and he moves his body side to side slowly, as if he is being propelled, tugged gently by the waves at his toes. He hopes he will feel the quiet resting of her hand on his shoulder, her face brushing up against him to steady his body and quiet his tears, though this does not come, and he finally stops himself.

With the palms of his hands, he dries his eyes, pushing his palms hard into his sockets; bright stars form in that dark world that he keeps himself in. He wonders if he were to keep his eyes shut to the world long enough would he eventually see her face, would these stars connect themselves with one another and show him the truth of what he has been searching for—what he has always been and what is still to come?

Instead, it is her voice that breaks the new silence. "I'm here," she says quietly. "I've always been here."

He nods, opening his eyes to the world again. His eyes look like slits in his dark face, the white part of them barely perceptible. He can only see his hands on his knees, his legs pulled up close to him, feet tucked near his seat. Everything looks blurry through the remaining tears and white dots that swim around the world in front of him, making their way eventually up past his line of vision. He is afraid to look over and see her there, so he instead closes his eyes again and lays his body back onto the cold sand of the beach. The ocean still races its way up toward him before receding back, but he cannot hear it anymore. When he opens his eyes, he sees only the stars spread out above him, a cold blanket there, wrapping itself around his shivering body. He whispers quietly to the night sky. "I love you," he says. "I miss you so much."

Matt knows that next to him Liz is nodding her head gently, knowing exactly what he means; she, too, is searching for the right words. But sometimes there are no words to say, sometimes silence is the only comfort, but he hopes the silence does not last long.

One night a few days after Liz appeared in the house, Wiggs offered dinner to Matt, though Matt turned down the offer with a wave and a half smile, saying that he had to get home before the storm came in. Though Matt was always quiet, making sure never to talk of Liz or his life as a doctor, his family or anything else from before he asked the farmer for a job, Wiggs knew Matt had nothing at home and no one to get back to. Wiggs had come to know Matt as well as any man could know another, but the farmer never let Matt know this. Wiggs simply smiled and nodded his head and said he'd see Matt in the morning to finish up what they'd started that afternoon.

The day had been a long one spent under the sun and passing clouds above, and Matt pulled the blue truck up the drive slowly before he cut off the engine. The thin radio panel was the only light inside the cab of the truck, and, in its light, Matt looked like an alien from some distant blue planet. The sound of howling guitars surrounded the cab where he sat; pounding drums came loudly from the speakers and rattled the side doors of the truck, making an audible thump every time the bass drum sounded. Static from the poor signal hid most of the lyrics, making the song sound foreign, hidden away underwater, removed by a distance of place and time. It seemed to Matt as if these moments he spent alone were meant to be someone else's, as if he were not meant for such times and trials but had been given the wrong paperwork by whomever it was that assigned lives.

The first song ended and was followed by another. Matt knew this song well, and he sang along with the lyrics under his breath, filling in as singer during those short seconds when the static usurped the music. He knew Liz sat next to him, watching his movements, but he tried to pretend, act like she wasn't actually there, like she was just part of his sad mind.

Outside the truck, the evening sky—orange and yellow with dark clouds to the west—had now turned a deep black-navy. The clouds still held their place above and in the distance. Far off from where he was, Matt heard the roll of thunder, heavy and consuming in the sky. A few seconds later, there came a quick show of light from somewhere in the west. In that instant, Matt saw the truck's image singed onto the yard a distance away. Then it was gone; the sky was dark once again, the ground beside him cast back into shadows. Another roll of thunder echoed loudly. It was in an instant that quick, he thought—the speed of lightning—that his life was changed. He wondered if there was any way of predicting such an instant; while he knew the answer, he still felt it necessary to ask.

There was another spark of lightning and then more thunder. The storm was coming quick, he knew, but Matt remained in the truck, listening to the music. His hands rested in his lap. Looking down at them in the darkness of the cab, he saw how they were twisted closed from swinging a pickaxe all day, plotting deep holes in the earth and setting stakes inside the holes for a new fence around the different crops. His palms, though calloused, were cut open and oozing a clear liquid; they hurt when he tried to stretch them open wide, so he kept them closed in a claw.

His head itched, and he took off his baseball cap and then his tight fingers over his scalp, listening to the rough sandpaper sound that his fingernails made on his dirty and tangled hair, his dried skin. He had stopped shaving his face and cutting his hair months before, and he now rubbed at his chin, feeling the scratch of his beard on the palm of his hand.

Rolling down the window, Matt stretched his arm out and waited in this position until the rain began, and he felt the heavy drops on his upturned palm. It took only a few seconds from when he first felt the rain for it to begin pouring heavily, turning the pavement an even darker color and making the windshield in front of him blurry and wet. He rolled the window up and then rested his head against the cold glass. The drops of water banging softly against the window. He nodded off peacefully.

When he woke, he did not know what time it was; it took him several seconds to even remember that he was still in the truck. He wiped some drool from off his chin and then opened the door quickly and walked to the front door with his head bowed down, buried into his chest as if that would allow him to avoid the rain that continued to fall. He didn't turn to look at Liz—he knew she would follow him inside, invited or not.

Once under the cover of the porch, Matt shook his arms wildly, stomping his feet to rid himself of the rainwater. He brushed his long hair back with his hands and then searched the key ring for the right one. But he stopped looking for the key and let his arms fall limply at his sides when he saw the small envelope and stuffed bear sitting on the welcome mat of the front door. These small gifts had been waiting for him, though he could only guess at how long they'd been there. He looked back to where Liz stood and then looked away. His face was sad and pained; Liz saw this clearly, but she made no show of it in her expressions.

Quickly collecting these small tokens, Matt unlocked the front door and walked inside. He turned on the overhead light and sat heavily on the chair in the front sitting room. The bear was the same kind that he had found months earlier on the side of the farm road where Liz had crashed the car. That bear still hid in the fireplace, now covered in soot and forgotten with time.

Matt's pulse quickened; he could hear its steady percussion in his head; his temples swelled and then receded with the oncoming migraine. Turning the bear over in his hands, he looked into the sad black eyes that shined in the light above. The small-stitched nose looked as if it was made of a rough material, and he rubbed his thumb gently over it. The bear's smile was hidden under its long, white fuzz, but he found it and traced its curve with his index finger, studying the smile in search of his own.

Matt set the bear down next to him and then looked at the white envelope. No name was printed on the front or back; it was sealed tightly. His hands shook as he slowly removed the card from the envelope. Sound seemed amplified in that moment—the rain outside, the thunder in the distance, the scrape of paper in his hands. It was a simple card: the outline of a heart on the front. Inside were a few words written in long, flowing script. He knew this writing, knew the person who wrote the words. She had sat in this very chair the afternoon Liz died. She was the last woman he had touched since.

The words were simple and true; he knew that. "I'm so sorry. I can't begin to know what to say." Below that was a telephone number, and below the number was another short sentence. "If you need someone to talk to."

He studied the number, knowing exactly who he would reach when he called it. He stood and turned out the lights, leaving the card and bear behind. In the morning, he would call her. But for now, he headed to the back for a shower. After he finished, he would go to sleep on the couch.

His feet moved quickly over the carpet; he passed Liz without looking at her. He was tired and wanted to make sure the rain was still falling when he closed his eyes. So it would sing him off to sleep.

He had not thought of Trisha in weeks, not until the card and bear showed up on his doorstep. Thinking of other women seemed wrong; Matt felt guilty whenever he found himself glancing at a woman's legs, her butt, her chest. Even smiling back at the bagging girl at the market seemed insensitive and wrong on his part. He often wondered during that year whether he would ever know the feeling of a woman again, and he doubted this.

Trisha had always been there for him, even after they split up; though they never spoke much after, their lives going in different directions, he always felt as if Trisha would always care; she was one of the few reliable people he knew in the world. But still, there was constantly the memory of the day Liz died, the memory of kissing Trisha while Liz was in pain. Regrets of that day. So many nights, he fell asleep with a sincere hatred of himself—for Trisha, he didn't know how he felt. But it wasn't her fault—none of it was—and Matt reminded himself of this the night he found the card and bear.

In the morning, on his way to the farm, Matt dialed the number that Trisha had written in the card. He spoke with the receptionist, told her who he was and what he wanted, and she scheduled him an appointment for the next morning at 10:30.

When Matt walked into the office at 10:15, the receptionist who he'd spoken with the day before smiled and had him sign in, saying that Dr. Milner would be able to see Matt right away, something about a mutual friend.

When Milner saw Matt, he had difficulty believing him to be the same man from school. Matt seemed older now, more worn out and jaded, but Milner greeted Matt with a smile and a firm handshake, saying that Trisha had called him not long before.

Matt sat in the leather chair that faced Milner's desk. Behind him were certificates and degrees, many of which Matt had also—now hidden away—though the difference was that the word *Psychology* was written under Milner's name.

Milner saw Matt looking at the credentials and smiled. "It's crazy how much money a couple pieces of paper cost. Isn't it?"

Matt nodded but remained quiet.

"You got yours up still?"

Matt shrugged, then said quietly, "In a box somewhere."

"Why aren't they out? They're something to be proud of."

Matt sighed and then rubbed his hands together. "Yeah," he said, drawing out the end of the word so it sounded more like the end of a long breath. "I can't look at them anymore, I guess."

"Why's that?"

Matt smiled, realizing how every television show and movie he had ever seen with a psychiatrist pegged them correctly—question addicts who offered no sense of answer. What was the point of paying someone to only have you yourself figure your own problems out? It didn't seem right. Matt thought briefly of leaving, but he looked over to the window on the left side of the room and saw Liz standing there, studying the world outside. He looked away from her.

"Look," Matt began, "I know you're gonna ask all about why I quit my job at the hospital, how I've been feeling, all that. I know. Really. I don't mean to be an asshole about this, but if you could just not ask, then it would save us all some time and breath."

Milner smiled. "Matt, I'm only here to listen and help. Tell you what," the doctor said, leaning back in his chair, trying to look more like a concerned friend than a doctor whose job it was to judge the people who came in and talked with him, "Why don't you just tell me whatever you want to? No notes, no questions from me, except for one. That okay?"

Matt shrugged and then nodded. "Okay."

"Have you talked about any of the things you feel since your wife's death?"

Matt dropped his eyes to the corners of the desk. It was dusty, and he wondered if it would be too much of an insult to drag his finger across the edge and collect some of the dust. He thought better of it but kept his focus on the table.

"No." His voice was flat, monotone.

"All right. Well, I'm here. That's all I can say. I've talked to plenty of people in similar situations."

But you haven't, Matt thought, looking over at Liz. *No one else feels like this. No one else has her here with them.* He wanted to stand over the seated man and scream this at Milner. Matt wished there was some way to show Liz to Milner, to ask him if he saw her standing there in the room with them. But he didn't, he couldn't. Matt was terrified of being crazy. The mere thought of it sent a wave of nausea through him, a tightening of his stomach that made him taste bile in his throat.

Matt felt sweat bead up on his forehead, and he wiped it away quickly, hoping Milner did not see the sweat, but then he wondered if he had been too quick with his movements, too quick in wiping his forehead—quick movements and reactions were things insane people did, weren't they? *Am I?* he wondered.

He gathered himself, looking quickly at Liz and then back over to Milner. The man smiled a sad, comforting smile that Matt wanted to believe was genuine. And maybe it was. Matt cleared his throat.

"I know this might sound crazy, but has anyone who's . . ." Matt didn't know how to say it. "Has anyone who's been in this situation before ever seen the . . . dead person?"

Milner leaned forward in his chair and set his hands on the desk in front of him, ceremoniously pushing the pad of paper away from him. Milner's face looked less surprised than Matt would have guessed.

"Are you seeing your wife?"

Matt looked down at his hands—they were clammy and hot—and then at Milner. "I have."

"How often?" Milner's voice sounded assuring and calm.

Matt didn't know what to say. From the corner of his eyes, he could see Liz next to the window. She had turned and was now looking at him, watching his movements, waiting for his answer.

"Just from a distance, I guess. It's not her, I know, but it looks like her."

"Other people do?"

"I guess. Or not. I don't know."

Milner smiled softly. "That's not uncommon, Matt. It's part of the grieving process. Okay? You shouldn't be concerned with it. It'll eventually go away as you learn to cope with the loss." Milner paused, waiting for Matt to say something, and when he did not, Milner continued. "It's not like you're seeing her everywhere. It's not like she's in the room with you right now, right?" He smiled.

Matt felt his skin grow cold, his breath leave him slightly. He knew he couldn't look over to Liz—Milner would know—but Matt had to. He smiled and glanced casually over toward the window, pretending to look outside. But he couldn't see the parking lot or the birds and clouds in the sky—Liz was blocking his view. It was the first and last time that Liz had ever given him the chills.

When Matt looked back at Milner, he tried to smile. He didn't know how to answer, but he had to try. "Yeah," Matt said, after several seconds. "You're right." The words sounded wrong and foreign from his mouth, the lies sour. But there was nothing else he could do. The strange things that fear makes us do.

This happened just a few days before he set off for California:

Matt had grown tired of the quiet shadow beside him. There was something strange and disturbing in her being there. Matt had hardly looked in her direction; when she wasn't looking at him he would stare in silent wonder at the alien being, a specter from another place, an angel perhaps, though he did not believe in such things.

When she turned to look at him, he would quickly look away, and they played that strange child's game of chicken. He often felt an anger with her presence, wishing he knew what she wanted. All Matt needed to do was ask her and maybe she would tell him, but whenever he tried to speak to her, his throat seemed to tighten, and he found himself unable to usher out any sound except the dry whisperings of the wind. This silence had become their conversations, if you could call it that, and he often wondered how long this would continue before she would disappear or he would completely lose his mind, though he constantly thought he had already lost his bearing on reality—Milner could say what he wanted.

Wiggs had given him the day off from the crops, despite Matt's pleadings. Wiggs said that he and his family were headed out of state to Oklahoma to visit relatives. "It's a paid vacation, then," Wiggs said the night before. The farmer smiled at Matt from a distance and gave a quick wave of his hand before retiring inside to finish packing for the trip. Matt looked quickly over at where Liz stood next to him and thought he saw a smile form on her lips, but he couldn't tell and looked away.

The next morning, Matt woke early, well before the sun's rise. Across the room from the couch, sitting on the edge of the chair, was Liz; still, there was no impression of her body on the cushion. He pulled on his pants and shirt on and brushed his teeth before he headed out the door, not waiting for Liz. It still always startled him when he climbed into the truck and saw her from the corner of his eye already sitting there in the passenger seat, quietly staring forward or watching him; the only movement from her on these trips was the blinking of her eyelids.

He hadn't known where he was headed that morning, having started the engine and backed down the drive. All he knew was that he wanted to get away from everything.

A short time later, Matt found himself parked along the Missouri River. It was the place they had gone to so many times, though he had not visited the spot since before she died. Matt didn't look over at her as he opened the door and stepped out into the cold and still dark morning. She was there beside him, and she would continue to be. He knew that. He didn't need any reminding.

Standing on the sandy shore, he felt himself grow angry at Liz, angrier than he had been in almost a year. It all seemed to build up to this. He looked over at the spot under the tree where they laid out a blanket so many times before and fallen asleep under the blue skies as afternoon turned slowly into evening and then to night. This was their spot, just as California would always be their spot. But the joy he'd once felt when he remembered the days spent there were gone.

Matt took several short steps until his toes were on the edge of the river water; he could see his boots growing wet with small splashes from scattered rocks along the edge. He looked back quickly, saw her standing there; he opened his mouth to say something to her, though he did not know to say and so, once again, he remained quiet. He had become a mute with her—a feeling he often felt: silent to a noisy world that passed all around him.

Small fish coasted along the steady, slow current, making sharp darting movements under the water, and he followed them with his eyes as they swam. It was too early still for fishermen. He took a step forward and stopped abruptly as the freezing cold water surrounded his foot and ankle up to his shin. Another two steps, and the water was up to his knees. The river looked shallow, and it was, though parts of it in the middle were deeper than he expected.

After several steps, Matt bent himself down, fully submerging his body in the flowing water. He felt the air knocked out of him as he forced his chest under the cold water. Dunking his head under and opening his eyes, it seemed as if he was in another world entirely. With eyes closed still, he lifted his head out of the water and deeply. From a distance, you would have thought that he was performing some kind of baptism on himself, and maybe he was, though he would not have known it nor have admitted to it.

Matt found his feet on the slippery river floor and stood, opening his eyes as he did so. Far in the distance east, the beginning of the coming day showed, and he turned around, taking it all in as if seeing the world for the first time. Though it was early summer, it was a cold morning, and when he breathed out, Matt saw the fog rise in front of his eyes and disappear into the morning. He thought briefly of where the fog went, deciding that it didn't go anywhere, that it simply still existed, but you couldn't see it. He shivered.

Back behind him, past where Liz stood silently watching him, running parallel to the road he had driven off not long before, he could see the black bodies of birds sitting quietly on a telephone cable. These things were gathered together and seemed to form one solid mass. He watched these birds, watched their black forms in the blue morning light, waiting for one to move and take the rest with it, but they did not move, and they did not fly. Instead, they stayed there, each one comforting and warming the one beside it.

The rushing water surrounded his body, and he bent down again. At first, the water had been cold, but now it seemed warmer than the air outside. The river now spread itself all around Matt, enveloping him like some birthing fluid.

Slowly, Matt leaned back and felt himself give his body over to the moving water. His back seemed cushioned by the river's top, and his feet and legs were swept out from under him. All was black now that he had closed his eyes again, and he felt himself drift down the current, being carried away by the water's steady movement.

Time felt as if it stopped in that moment for Matt—

His body spun gently, and he did not know how far he drifted. He took one final deep breath and flipped his body over so that his face was underwater. He wanted to open his eyes, but he couldn't and so he forced them to stay closed so that he would not see what came next. He felt himself crying, the tears becoming part of the river. *This is life*, he thought. His breath grew short and he fought himself to stay under, willing himself to not lift his head up and gasp for air; he violently pushed his head further down into the water, the blackness of his closed eyes growing deeper until white stars appeared in the distance of that dark void that he found himself staring into. His head hurt, and he breathed in, choking on water, coughing under its hold. Tears. More tears. River water. He drifted, though he didn't know how far he had moved. *Is this it?* he wondered. He may have only been under for a second, a minute, an eternity, he didn't know. Time no longer existed for him. But there was nothing left; he did know that. There was only her standing on the shore watching him. Just before he thought he was about to black out completely, he felt something tugging at his shirt. *It can't be her*, he thought. *But what if it is?* It was the final moment, he realized: one that would change everything. The tugging at his shirt grew more frantic. It moved to his pant leg so that his shirt and pants were being pulled at together. He could hear nothing in the wet darkness. His head hurt, throbbed at his temples while water lapped at his skin and his face and head. His ears were full of water. Whatever it is that had a hold of his shirt and leg seemed to grow stronger. And then he heard her voice. It was so far away that he couldn't tell if it was real at all. *Just some strange memory that comes before the end*. But he heard her words clearly. He remembered the words, could feel that emotion he felt when she first told him on the beach so many years ago—it felt as if no time had passed since. *I'd love to just fall into the water there and float. Float away, float on forever. Become part of the water. Become part of something bigger than me, or you, or anything else. I think that's what I really want some day.* When he came up for air finally, his lungs and throat burning, he coughed out water he had swallowed and choked on. He tried to open his eyes, but when he did, he could only see black. Tears continued to stream from his swollen eyes down his cheeks. After several seconds, the black began to fade away, and he started to make out shapes and colors, smears of light within the darkness. He splashed his hands and legs quickly, still feeling the tug on his shirt and legs. It was not until a minute or two had passed that Matt saw what it is that had been pulling at him and bring him back to the world—it was simply what was left of a felled tree: its long, hollow body covering nearly half the width of the river, funneling the water under and around its thick truck. Dangling branches, strange stick arms and fingers, had wrapped themselves around his body, tangling him in their hold, and it took Matt several attempts to break himself free. He stood and braced himself against the tree, walking its length back to the shore where the upheaved roots towered over the bank and over him. His head throbbed, and he wanted to lay down on the dirt, but he forced himself back to where the truck was parked. The dripping water from his arms and legs, his back and face, soaked shoes and hair, fell behind him and left a trail that disappeared in the earth and dried in the morning air. The sun was up in the sky, and he wondered how long he had floated down the river. Up ahead, he saw Liz waiting for him. When he saw her there, he stopped walking and remembered those words again. *Float away, float on forever—*

It was in that single moment that everything seemed to make sense for the first time, and he knew what he needed to do for Liz.

What strange magic hides within our world? He wonders this silently as he waits for her to speak again. Though he dares not look over to her, afraid to come face to face with his dead wife, his hand reaches out to where she is, stretching farther and farther over the earth's floor, but he only feels the cold sand that runs through his fingers.

He sighs, and this sigh turns into a yawn. His body aches, and he realizes just how good it feels to stretch his legs and arms. His hands cradle the back of his head. Below him, the ground seems to move as if he is on a turntable that is being spun slowly and slowly around—the shifting of the world that surrounds him, archaic though not extinct. There is no control for him, and he knows it; there is only his choice to give over to whatever is to come, whatever was, and whatever remains.

His eyes flutter gently, and he begins to fall into a sleep but is called back moments later by the soft sound of her voice. When he hears her whisper, his eyes open wide. Above him are constellations. He knows the names of them all, and he whispers their names under his breath, and it becomes like a chant or prayer that he does not even realize he's performing.

"I've loved you forever," she says.

Matt strains his body tight, moving his head toward where the voice comes from. This voice that is soft and like the wind itself. He waits for it to continue, but it does not. His mouth is still now, his eyes open, becoming dry in the breeze that passes over and around him.

"I need to ask you," he whispers finally, breaking off before he can finish. These are the first words he has spoken to her since she died. His body shakes at this, his teeth chattering loudly with his trembling jaw; his shirt flaps in the night air, making him feel like some strange new creature birthed of the world.

There is no response from Liz.

Matt's chest feels as if something is stuck inside it, and he clears his throat loudly to rid himself of the emotion. He shakes his head quickly. Nothing helps, but he continues: "I don't want to hear it, but I need to know. I need to know the truth at the end of it." He still looks to the sky, silently pleading with the stars there to give him strength as he feels the tears begin their movement down his face and onto the sand beneath his head.

"What . . ." He breaks off and chokes down his raw tears, swallows the phlegm and saliva, pushing it down and away. "What happened? I need to know. Why . . ." He trails off and takes a breath. "Was it on purpose?"

His whole body shakes now, and he sits up, drawing his legs under him like a child. The sea extends out there somewhere, though he cannot see it—his entire world is contained in this one instant, this one answer, and he waits for it. His arms feel like they are not his own, the trembling legs not his either. He runs his hands frantically through his hair.

Finally, after several seconds, she whispers quietly, so softly that he can hardly understand it under the sound of the waves and the night, yet he hears the answer clearly. "No," she says. And then she is quiet again.

When Matt hears this, he buries his face into his waiting hands and rocks himself violently. His tears become a torrent now and he hushes himself from his sobs. There is peace for him in this moment. A release he has not expected to ever feel again. Contentment, maybe.

"Thank you," he whispers several times, but it is too quiet for anyone else but himself to hear.

His body stops moving, and he sits still as his mind is flooded by thoughts and memories and fears alleviated. He hasn't believed what Hilston said about the aneurysm until this moment. They stay like this for a half hour, statues cast of flesh and whatever substance she is made of. Though neither can see it, the lights of the parking lot turn off behind them, casting a complete darkness over the truck, where Liz's body rests peacefully.

After a while, Matt's voice breaks the silence between them. His eyes hurt, and he closes and rubs at them, creating white star spots again like heat lightning in the darkness of his mind. "Why'd you come back?"

"I've always been here," she says.

He shakes his head in quiet protest. "You left me. You left. Why did you have to leave?" He slowly turns to her but stops before she comes into view; then he looks back out at the ocean and at the night. A fish jumps in the distance of the water making a muted splash out there in the dark.

"I didn't. I've been here." Her voice is steady, stagnant; there is no emotion to it. It is a sound that calms him.

He sighs heavily, more for effect than necessity, yet what effect will this have on a phantom?

"I don't understand any of it." Matt scratches at his head with both hands, trying to push away the thoughts and the pain of the past year as if it has all built up and fallen on him and he has finally had enough of it. He wants this feeling to be gone, but he does not know how to make that happen.

"It's life, Matt." Her voice sounds amused; in this moment, he has become a child, and she comforts him with the single thing that there is left to give. She continues on: "You can't understand life. You can't predict it. You can't try to. It happens, it moves on, not caring about you or me or anyone. All we have is each other, and the hope that we don't miss out on most of the things we do have."

He nods and then smiles. It is as if he knows the words she will say before she speaks them. His hands run over each other in front of him, scratching distractedly at the skin. Then his face grows serious. "I miss you. I miss you so much, Liz. I can't do it without you." His voice chokes up again, but he forces the words out, pushing the sadness aside. He has cried these tears too many times before; he does not want to cry them anymore. "Everyday, I don't know what to do."

Far out over the water shines the lights of a tanker slowly passing by. Matt studies the crawling lights, the object itself black against the night, black and without texture. "What am I supposed to do?" he says. "What am I supposed to do without you? We were supposed to have a family and grow old, argue and fight and then make up and laugh at each other like we used to. I was supposed to fall in love with you more every day." He pauses for a moment, then says quietly, "I can't now. I can't."

He is silent for several seconds more, wondering if she will speak. When she does not, he continues. "You saved me. You gave me love and a reason. A family I didn't have."

Matt lays back down, resting his head on the sand, finding the indent left from before. The stars still shine above, Liz still sits beside him.

He can only guess at what she's doing right now. He imagines her looking at her wedding ring, watching it light up in sparkles even in the low light. Imagines her brushing her hair away from her face and tucking loose strands behind her ear. In this moment, he feels as if he has been swept off to a different place entirely. To another world where all things are possible, where there is indeed magic. Matt wonders, as he closes his eyes sleepily, if earth had ever been a place like that, and he guesses that it must have been but that the magic has since all dried up, disappeared with the dinosaurs and creatures of the sea.

She speaks again, but her voice sounds distant, different now. He does not realize until later that he is crying while she speaks. Liz's voice sounds like the wind swirling about him and then leaving just as quickly.

"One morning, you'll wake up and look over at the woman next to you. You'll smile knowing that she has your heart, and you have hers. And she'll love you for all that you've given her, all the love, the things you give without even knowing it. She'll love you for all that you are.

"On that morning, you'll lean over and kiss her on her temple, that soft place to the side of her eye just like you used to with me, and she'll wake and smile, and you'll think how beautiful she is. You'll cover each other in kisses and warmth. And you'll walk out into the kitchen and make breakfast together, smiling and laughing. Pancakes made into different shapes, cartoon animals.

"Your son will walk in, dragging his feet and rubbing the sleep from his eyes. He'll look just like you. He'll tell you he smelled the food in his dreams, and you'll lift him up and hold him tight.

"The three of you will sit at the table there and eat breakfast, tease each other and laugh. Sometime during this, you'll remember all that happened before. You might sit quietly but only for a second. Your son's laugh will break you from your thoughts, and you'll smile knowing that your life is exactly what it's supposed to be. Exactly what you're meant for. And it will be perfect, Matt. It will be perfect."

Liz is quiet, as if she's collecting her thoughts or maybe wiping a tear from her eye, though she cannot cry. *Can she?* Matt wonders this silently, feeling his closed eyes grow more and more tired.

She continues: "That woman won't be me, though. It was once, but not anymore, Matt. She's out there, that girl for you. You'll find her someday. You'll see her face and know, just like I saw your face here on this beach and knew. You'll find her, and you'll find your happiness in her and find your smile again. And I'll be there with you, smiling and loving you the entire time. Remember, Matt, I'll love you forever."

Matt does not hear this, though. He is asleep on the sand. The night stars propel his dreams, and in those dreams, Liz is there, holding him closely, holding him always.

They went to the bedroom early their first night in the house. Outside, the wind swept loudly around the place and the small yard that the previous owners had put in place. Inside, the house was littered with moving boxes; they'd marveled at the number of boxes that lay scattered like landmines throughout the rooms and hallways. The apartment had only been a studio, but it seemed like they owned enough to fill two houses. They had no clue where to begin and decided to leave the boxes for the next day.

They ordered pizza after they finished unloading the moving van and their cars, sitting on the carpet in the front room and looking over the place. It was barren except for the boxes, which formed their "cardboard jungle," as Liz called it. They finished their slices of pizza and drank the last drops of warm soda from the cans and then headed into the back bedroom, turning off all the lights and putting the place to rest.

The bedroom was empty except for the mattress and the parts of the bed frame stacked in a corner—Matt said he would put the pieces together in the morning. They undressed and laid down on the mattress, spooning each other: her back cradled against him tightly. He heard her breath and saw its movement from the rise and fall of the light sheet that she pulled over herself. Her bare legs felt smooth and cold against his, and her stomach felt soft and warm under his hand. Pulling her closer to him, Matt could smell her hair, a now familiar scent.

As her breaths grew deeper, her fingers twitching in a dream, Matt leaned his head closer to her and kissed her ear. She stirred a little, letting out a scratchy word of protest, but she did not wake. He smiled at her. She seemed like a child, a kitten even, who he was worthy enough to protect. There was no reason to it, he knew, but he felt as if he had become part of her and she of him. They were connected in some deeper way, one beyond simple affection and sex. He knew that no matter what happened in his life, she would continue to be there, guiding him, helping him as she had said she wanted most in life. She succeeded in this, he thought, as he closed his eyes that night.

Just before he fell asleep, he whispered in a voice barely audible, "I love you, Liz. Forever and always."

He couldn't see it from where he lay against her, but a thin smile passed across Liz's lips that night as she pushed herself even closer into his warmth, into his protection. She was finally home. With Matt, she knew she always would be.

He wakes now to the sound of the waves. They had invaded his dreams. He cannot remember when he actually fell asleep under the black sky, when the real ocean waves at his feet became dream waves. And he does not know if there is a difference between these two waves, nor if he wants there to be.

Above him, there is darkness, though there is indeed a paling to it. Matt does not know what time it is, and he quickly sits up and checks the time, pinching the small side button of his watch to illuminate the glowing green digits in the dark. 5:26. Cursing himself quietly for having almost slept past sunrise, he begins to get up but stops. Next to him, Liz lays on her side, her head propped gently on her open palm. She stares at him, the traces of a smile lingering still from the night before. He has not seen her lay down since she was alive. There is a sense of peace to the way she lays, like this is meant to be. All of it.

He wishes he could run his hand through her hair, move close to her body and share her warmth in the cool morning made colder by the salty air. Matt wonders if he can reach over and feel her once again. The night before had marked a change: she had spoken—at least that's how he remembers the previous night. It wasn't a dream. He hadn't fallen asleep on the sand until after she'd spoken to him. He believes this, remembering her words as if he himself had spoken them, though he had not. He contents himself quietly with this thought. As he looks at her, listening to the steady roll of water beyond where he sits, he wonders if that is the purpose of this trip, the reason she sent him on this errand—her knight, his grail. *You knew this*, he thinks. *All of this is meant to bring you back again.*

With a trembling hand, fingers turned blue in the night, Matt reaches over to where she lays, still watching him and smiling slyly like she knows something he has yet to learn. His fingers search for her skin, for those small ears and the strands of brown hair that cover them. Her neck, small and smooth, rushing blood beneath, memories held fast within. But his hand falls through her; the only thing he feels is cold air, like fog or dew. Her expression does not change much—she knew that would happen, he realizes. There's nothing for her to have done but wait and let him see for himself. She is not there, at least not in any body he can ever touch. This hard truth hits him in his stomach like a cramp, but he knows that it is so and that it is meant to be as such.

A crab walks its way to the water, finally becoming swept over by the sea. The water takes the crab out in its grip and the small creature is gone forever from sight, though it continues on under the current and waves. Seagulls and pelicans fly above and cry out beyond his sight; he can only hear them—where they are and where they are headed remains a mystery of nature. It is these birds that rouses him from his trance, calling him awake fully, lifting him up to his feet.

In the eastern darkness, the sun will rise, and with it, other people will be brought to the beach. There is still much to be done, and he thinks of these things as he makes his way to the parking lot, to the truck that waits there. His toes sink into the sand and he focuses on how cold the sand is.

The truck bounces heavily as Matt drives it over the curb of the parking lot, making his way down the beach. The tires turn quickly in the loose sand, making drive toward the water a slow one. The sky is a pale blue now, still dark but lightening quickly; he knows the sun will rise soon.

After backing the truck so that the tide splashes high onto the back tires, Matt gets out and makes his way to the tailgate. The rushing water seems to grab at his ankles and pull him out into the ocean; he resists and steadies himself on the truck. Climbing his way up into the bed, Matt throws off the bungees and blankets, pushing them aside before making his way to the top of the wooden box and pushing it with all his strength. It takes several tries before he feels the casket begin to slide toward the back of the truck, out to the waiting ocean water.

As the box nears the edge, Matt stops and then climbs down. He pulls at the casket's handles, shimmying the box out. He's careful not to move the box too much, afraid it might fall off the back of the truck, splash heavily down, and break apart.

After several minutes of this, Matt presses down on the box, guiding it with his body, pressing his shoulder into the heavy wood so that the casket now stands on end. He turns the box slightly and then moves quickly to the other side, doing his best to catch the solid wood of it. The box comes down heavily with a splash, and he cuts his arms on the corner, though he does not know it. At his feet, the water rushes over the box. He begins to feel his chest tighten and he looks over at Liz, back to where she stands on the beach watching him.

Liz begins walking toward him, and Matt watches as she moves with a flowing movement that doesn't seem real. When she gets closer, he sees that her eyes are closed; her head is tilted gently up to the sky. In this moment, as he watches her body, looks at her face, remembering the memories he has of her, he sees the infinite abyss of life. All of it is there, spreading before him like a blank map. There is no reason for any of it, no simple explanation for the dotted bursts of light that shine down on us every night—these things that peer their way through the blanketing clouds of the sky. Yet there is some kind of hope in these things of life, and he comes to realize this now. Looking at her, he's able to see into the future and into the past at the same time. He's able to hold on to the memory that fades with time.

Are you real? He has wondered this all these months. He has that answer now while Liz stands next to him quietly. *Does it even matter if you're real anymore? You're here with me, and that's all I could ever want.*

The sun waits just below the horizon behind them, and Matt circles around the casket and begins to pull with all his strength at the clumsy thing. It hardly moves, and he tries again and again, looking up and down the coast for someone there who might see him, but he can see no one. He takes a deep breath and then pulls again; this time, he's helped by the undercurrent that seems to sweep beneath the box and lift it gently, allowing him to pull more freely. He continues in this way for several feet until the ocean grows deeper, and the casket moves on at its own pace to the dark sea beyond.

Turning back to where Liz stands next to the truck, Matt sees her smile. It is a smile of acceptance. *You're home now.*

The edge of the world awaits, and he thinks of how Liz is finally out there. She is part of the ocean, part of something bigger than he or she could ever be. The water is to his waist and the current keeps pulling at him, urging him to follow the wooden box on its journey, but he resists it, planting his feet firmly in the ground. He wonders where the box will end. Where will it travel to? What places will it see? These things do not matter, though, and Matt knows this now.

She is floating away, floating away forever. Part of the water, part of the world. In the horizon, he can see the point where there is no distinction between earth and sky, and he knows that this is where she is and will forever be.

He watches as the box disappears from sight. Behind him, the sun begins its rise over the edge of the earth and into a clear, cloudless morning. Out there in the shining field of memory, he feels a peace settle within him. He stays like this for several minutes, letting the water rush past him to the shore and then move back out to the ocean. The box has grown smaller and smaller, becoming just a faint speckle on the horizon before it is lost entirely in the ocean and the sky.

A smile forms slowly across his face as he hears the seagulls above him calling to each other as they fly out over the Pacific; he knows they will watch over her and guide her to wherever she's headed.

After a while, Matt turns back to where Liz stands next to the truck, but she is gone. He stops moving; he feels his skin grow cold and his breath catches in his throat. She's gone now, and though he feels empty, emptier than ever before, he knows that she will forever be there with him, and that he will forever love her.

The shadow of the truck stretches out over the lapping water to where he stands. He turns and looks at the beach. In the parking lot, a car with surfboards tied to the top pulls quickly into a spot and a man and young boy climb out—a father and son. The man takes the surfboards down and the two make their way to the water. Matt smiles at this. He thinks of his own father and wonders how he is. Matt nods his head slowly as he walks through the steady waves toward the truck, thinking how he'll stop on the way back and get a postcard to send to his father. Maybe someday he will find his way back to Corvin Valley and visit the man, tell him of his daughter-in-law; he will tell his father how Liz would have reminded him of Matt's mother. Maybe someday.

He comes to the truck and opens the door. The father and son have now set their surfboards on the sand and are beginning to rub wax on them. Matt turns back once more to the ocean; Liz is not there, and neither is the wooden box.

He wipes several tears from his eyes and then smiles again. Just as he is about to climb into the truck, he stops. A breeze passes over the water. Waves are created in it, and he turns to face the ocean and the breeze head-on.

A seagull dives down in the distance, hunting fish below the water. The breeze blows more fiercely now. Now it is a wind. And in the wind, he thinks he hears her voice, though he cannot make out what she is saying. He stands quiet, stretching his arms wide at his sides, trying to decipher this phantom voice, trying to make out the whispered words that come in the wind. The words are faint, quiet and from a distance. *Good morning*, the voice says—at least that's what it sounds like. He shakes his head at this. Eventually, the wind dies down and he is left once more in silence. Matt drops his arms and smiles sadly as he climbs into the truck and starts the engine.

He knows there are many miles to drive still before he's home.

EPILOGUE

Somewhere out along the stretch of highway that leads east across the dusty heartland of the country is a stone-frame house—what's left of a structure from a time long since passed. Only a partial concrete wall of it stands erect still; the hard flooring is now covered over with dirt and time, the bones of animals buried beneath the powdered earth. Roots of plants have dug themselves deep within this topsoil.

Surrounding this ruined structure some twenty feet off in all directions is a chain link fence that seems out of place, from some different time, some different world. The fence looks new, though if you were to walk up and touch it, you would feel the rust that now covers the once smooth metal. Tall weeds and grass have grown at the base of this fence, twisting in and then out of the bottom links. Near the far back of it, the part furthest from the interstate, the fence is beginning to fall down; various sections are peeled back so that it hangs down, scraping the earth.

During different parts of the day, black birds—some small and quick, others tall and lanky—come and take pause on this fence. At times, the small black birds nestle tightly within the open links, creating portions of fence that are completely black: parts where there is nothing more than a wall of metal and skin and feathers that rustle in the breeze that sweeps across the earth. It becomes a black shadow on the ground that stretches into the far distance of the land.

Drivers slow when they pass this place; they take note of both structure and fence. They look over and see it from out the corner of their eye and wonder what this structure was once; they think of how the remnants look now, how the skeleton remains strong for the world to see, though the flesh of it is all but gone. But it's the fence that most drivers study for those several seconds it takes them to pass by—the fence, though weak and old and weathered over time, remains strong. It still stands guard, protecting what once was there and what will remain there always.

Brandon Daily is the author of two novels, *A Murder Country,* and *The Valley*, as well as a collection of fiction, *Darkening*. His fiction, nonfiction, plays, and poetry have appeared in numerous journals and magazines. He lives in New England with his wife and two children.

Made in USA - North Chelmsford, MA
32281_9781957034188
11.15.2023 0529